SILENCE

a novel

Other fiction books by Islandport Press

Blue Summer
by Jim Nichols

Closer All the Time
by Jim Nichols

This Time Might Be Different
by Elaine Ford

Contentment Cove
by Miriam Colwell

Random Act
by Gerry Boyle

Strangers on the Beach
by Josh Pahigian

The Contest
by James Hurley

These and other books are available at:
www.islandportpress.com

SILENCE

a novel

WILLIAM CARPENTER

ISLANDPORT PRESS

ISLANDPORT PRESS

Islandport Press
P.O. Box 10
Yarmouth, Maine 04096
www.islandportpress.com
info@islandportpress.com

First Islandport Edition / June 2021

ISBN: 978-1-944762-88-9
LCCN: 2021932274

Dean L. Lunt, Publisher
Teresa Lagrange, Book designer
Printed in the USA

For Colonel Peter H. Liotta (1957-2012)

Those that I fight I do not hate,
Those that I guard I do not love

Who is left among you that saw this house in its first glory?
And how do you see it now?
—Haggai 2:3

Hell makes no distinction in its rites and honors.
—*Antigone*

Morning, Samarra, 2006

Fucking desert blowtorch sun lifts off the horizon, eye of Allah, 106 degrees: onward Christian soldiers, this day's designed to personally suck for you. Specialist Nick Colonna draws 'round his face and mouth the new green shawl smelling of dyed sheep's wool, walks toward his Humvee against the *shamal* wind of sand.

Choked at the breather, the diesel won't start so he holds the glow plug, it kicks, hacks, and finally goes, then they're through the B-M checkpoint and traveling the ten clicks to Samarra concealed by a cloud of dust. Ramos has some kind of salsa on so loud flames are shooting from around his earphones, then he pulls Nick's helmet off and slips the phones around his ears: Gotta hear my man El Indio, straight from Havana. Dupuy Williams is up in the turret on the Deuce .50 but the town's quiet today so it's just a pleasure cruise: sip some Red Bull while Williams looks around from the gun mount with his sack of mini Mr. Goodbars, in case he sees any kids.

From up in the gun turret Dupuy says, "I be done this shit, I'm going to the Texas hills. I ain't bringing nothing but a shovel." Dupuy's six-four, two hundred and eighty pounds, takes three jars of Vaseline to get him through the hatch opening. It was Evans the college guy that called him Moby 'cause he was the size of a whale, and the name stuck.

"You gonna need two shovels, all your bullshit," Ramos says.

The go pills they dealt out in the FOB this morning smooth out the potholed Arab pavement like a driveway. Hadjis crowd the street and a few taxis and a number of mopeds and three figures in blue burqas that could be anyone. He drives slow and easy down the centerline past figures ducking into side alleys and doorways when they hear the Humvee's authoritative exhaust note, tuned to incite fear in the non-Western ear. After nineteen street days his eyes probe anything that could hide an IED, any window where a sniper could have his eyes.

He swings wide left for a tire casing, crowding a donkey cart against the curb, guy screaming something in Arabic which sounds like "Grow some, Mohamed Atta!" These dudes hijacked the 747s, they flew them into towers of glass and steel. *Shahid*, they call it, every one of them loves death more than his right arm; and there goes Williams up there throwing a handful of Mr. Goodbars at two tall guys, doubtless insurgents, AK-47s under their white robes with their free hands reaching out like shortstops to snatch the sweets.

Ramos calls Nick "Mo," for Mohamed 'cause he's from Maine and the hijackers boarded in Portland on 9/11, which is why Nick's here: reprisal and justice for that day of infamy, plus a little responsibility for living in a state numb enough to let them through.

An old woman with a cane brings the Humvee to a complete stop by slowly limping right into the road in front of them. Then this gaunt bone-white Arab street dog limps from an alley; something's really wrong with it: one eye gone, pink rabid-looking saliva from its mouth, long bloody stomach scar as if it's had some kind of operation. Nick idles the engine as the dog stops to chew through the wrapper of a Mr. Goodbar. Another handful of mini-bars comes over the windshield. Dupuy's throwing them right at the dog but Ramos takes off his headphones and yells on the intercom, "Fuck that. Dog's leg is broke, some evil motherfucker gashed his eye out, should be waxed for his own good."

Ramos is right, he thinks. Poor dog's whining in pain, half blind, no animal deserves to suffer in that way. As vehicle commander it's

Nick's call. Williams throws another Mr. Goodbar and the dog strains for it but it's too weak to move. Nick raises his right hand from the wheel, answered by one *thunk* of Dupuy's M4 and the street dog explodes like a thousand suns and the screen goes dark.

1

He can't remember. The hospital room is no clue. White walls, blood pressure instrument, all the other off-white machines tubed and wired to his arm, their purposes unknown; his visible heartbeat on the scope and above that a soap opera with subtitles like a foreign movie, but Nick has to read them because he cannot hear a word. The TV doctor is saying to a young woman *He can't last much longer* and the woman's eyes tear up with a big drop rolling down one cheek. How do they fucking do that, cry tears when it's just an act? He's seen a lot of guys cry and he himself cried when Baker came in with his foot gone but he could never fake it like that actress, or maybe she isn't faking, maybe she truly believes she's the character she's playing and that the man dying in the hospital is really her husband, son, brother; nobody alive knows if they're acting or if this is what they are.

The guy in the bed next to his is propped up to watch the set but he's asleep, or at least his eyes are closed. The Venetian blinds are half-open and out the window there's a low brick wall and beyond that a stand of white pines in transparent air, actual Maine air you can see through, not the unbreathable blinding dust and dried-up cedars of Iraq. His arm tattoo above the IV entrance says DERELIX, his unit's nickname; the three of them got the same tattoo one afternoon in the street bazaar. Ramos and Williams, he doesn't know where the fuck they are. He looks again to see if it's Ramos beside him but it's not. It wouldn't be Dupuy because his black skin sucks all light from the air and it's brighter than a Wal-Mart restroom in here. But if they're not here beside him in the hospital room, where are they?

His bracelet says N COLONNA and his number and CHAMBERLAIN VA. He knows where Chamberlain is; it's a Maine VA hospital maybe thirty miles inland from Ledgeport where he lives, or where someone he half-remembers being once lived, and if he goes back there maybe he can find again. There was another bracelet in another hospital room before this, in Ramstein, Germany, where his roommate was Singleton and they had to exchange their names in writing because between them they couldn't have heard a nuclear weapon if it blew up in the room. At Ramstein he made a written inquiry about Juan Ramos and Dupuy Williams but they shook their heads, indicating they didn't know. If they have also reached their own home-state VA centers, Ramos will be someplace outside of Denver and Dupuy will be in Houston, Texas, which he claims is hotter than Iraq. That's what Dupuy used to say when spit sizzled on the Samarra sidewalks, It don't hold a candle to Harris County. They used a special ink for his tattoo, darker than indigo, but you can still barely read it against his skin.

The door opens and in comes a male nurse he doesn't know, along with Dr. Borque, who has been communicating in writing, though the pills they've given him have blurred the dialogue to a single phrase flashing in his head like a neon warning sign: *Better get out now or they'll keep you in here forever.* Dr. Borque looks at his roommate first and they lip something to each other but he can no more hear them than the characters on TV. The nurse pokes at the bed controls and he's pushed to a sitting position without having to move a muscle. Dr. Borque gives Nick this wide counterfeit smile, then opens the door and in comes his old man with the same fake smile as if covering something up and Nick cries *Dad!* and feels the word rasp through his throat like a sandstorm but he can't hear it.

His father pauses and his eyes water like the actress on TV but his mouth doesn't open, then he comes over and half-kneels to give Nick a hug that pins him to the hospital mattress with love and some kind of sadness that is so strange and distant, he wonders if maybe he didn't make it and this is the afterlife. The hadj heaven gives you a hundred virgins but in the American one you get your parents. They started you out and here they are to greet you; besides, what do they expect you to do with virgins if you're dead?

Behind him, his mother Martha's holding a large bouquet from their garden, though it's almost September and she must have brought him every remaining blossom. He reaches up toward her. The IV restrains him and he opens his mouth to say *Mom* but checks himself, not wanting her to hear the weird utterances of his throat that feel more like Arabic than human speech. He further thinks he is dead because beyond his mother is his sister Angela who ran off to Albuquerque and hasn't been home for a decade.

Angela looks like she's concealing a watermelon bomb under her dress so he twists his head around looking for another exit, then realizes she's expecting; but if they wire it right even a fetus can be triggered to explode. They're pro-death, Moby says, they blew up a pregnant woman with a remote detonator that wasted a 113 and everyone inside. He pulls away from her to the limit of his connections. It's okay if his mom hugs him, she's so slight there'd be no place to conceal anything; but it's halfhearted 'cause she's afraid of the tubes and wires, or of him, the guy that left as her son Nicolas but has returned as someone else. Only eight months since he leaned down and kissed her on the forehead then boarded the plane: three months in Kuwait, two more in Basra, eighty-two days in forward operating base, Brassfield-Mora, twenty-nine Humvee missions, when the thing that he has no memory of happened and shipped him home.

His father steps forward with a clipboard holding a piece of paper. It's not a printout but lettered in his dad's own hand, the crisp and commanding typeface from his work as a stonecarver for Coastal Monuments. It's in a big font as if he's not only deaf but blind. *WELCOME HOME, NICOLAS*, it reads,

OUR WARRIOR.
BEHIND YOU 100%.

Like anything his dad writes, it looks like a headstone, increasing the sense that he's crossed over and this is death: this white room, white faces, the doctor the same color as the heartbeat machine, dreams of a white dog floating above the surface with white eyes expanding till they ignite the world. His father can't help it; it's his vocation. That's what he does. Everyplace else has switched to laser-machine carving but they still let Peter Colonna work by hand.

Beneath it, in his mom's sharp, confident, ex–bank worker's script, *WE HAVE SO MANY OPTIONS. DR. BORQUE WILL TELL YOU. THEY HAVE COCHLEAR IMPLANTS NOW. WE LOVE YOU. WE CAN'T IMAGINE WHAT YOU'VE EXPERIENCED AND WE ARE SO BLESSED TO HAVE YOU BACK.*

Experienced.

He blurts out, "Where's Dupuy Williams? Where's Ramos?" which he can't hear himself say but must get through, because Dr. Borque takes his dad out in the corridor and his dad comes back alone with the yellow pad. He knows from the look on his dad's face that he doesn't have to read the words. They didn't make it and he did. His father hugs him and puts his mouth very near his ear, almost touching, and says something he can't make out except for a distant gritty rush like a desert sand whirlwind inside his ear. They claim to have some kind of bionic eardrums but if Dupuy and Ramos are gone, what fucking good would it be to hear?

❖

His sister Angela looks like another person from the one who left for New Mexico, skin tanned dark as an Arab, gleaming white teeth and a V-neck shirt with the tops of her big expectant breasts showing the same color, like desert hills. The last women he saw in life were disguised by burqas on the cobblestones of the Samarra street. If Angela had walked forth in that outfit, pregnant or not, she would have set the paving stones on fire. She's smiling at him now and apparently saying something but she may be just mouthing words to him without sound, he has no idea. She should wear subtitles if she wants to be heard.

The doctor and nurse have left. His mother scrawls on the clipboard: *YOU'RE GOING HOME WITH US! LATER, THEY WILL EVALUATE. DON'T WORRY, THEY HAVE MIRACLES NOW.*

The guy in the next bunk's come awake, death-pale like everyone in the room but Angela, gaping over at the family gathering, then up at the subtitled TV. Now it's the evening news: scuba divers, an overturned boat, guy trapped underwater, the one thing that can't get you in the desert. A filthy waterway ran through Samarra and the Arabs were always throwing bodies in there that would float past the riverbanks at dawn. Evans once said the Tigris was the river in Paradise where the original humans lived, but its water quality has seriously declined.

He can remember every Humvee mission and every one of them ended safe inside the wire with Ramos and Williams, some salsa thing on Ramos's iPod speaker, food-stained Formica mess table, three cans of Red Bull. Not one of them went bad but here he is staring and breathing and they're dead. He wants to be with them. They shared a language then and they do now.

And Brenda. Angela's here; why is it that Brenda didn't come?

2

His dad's driving the old silver Caravan, his mom in back with Angela whose stomach is maxing out her seat belt. Nick rides shotgun, where Ramos sat lip-syncing to El Indio. His mom leans forward as far as the seatback allows, her two arms on his shoulders, and he's glad for the bucket seat's armor protection because she'd be burying her face in his neck and there would be more tears, which he can feel as a hot damp cloud right through the headrest. Why should she cry for him? He's alive on earth. It's Ramos and Dupuy whose moms are on the front steps gazing at empty envelopes.

His father's intent on the highway as he should be and can be because of Nick's unblinking vigilance. Route 13 is a country back road with mostly long stretches of trees, then a cleared field and a farmhouse or a convenience store, then trees again, but IEDs could be anywhere and the Caravan's going too fast to anticipate them even though he strains his vision to look ahead. The RFD mailboxes are where they plant them, then they hang back in the driveways to set them off by radio or the clever bastards rig them to pick up the vehicle noise or the magnetic field. Every one of the mailboxes chills his spinal cord, then they pass it and there's another, there's no end to them, one shaped like a covered wagon, one like a greenhead mallard, one black-and-white-belted like a Galloway cow. When they plant an explosive in an RFD box, its thin steel becomes spiraling death shards that slash the face open even through safety glass. He's rolled his window up tight but his father's is wide open and his bare arm must be drumming on the rooftop the way he does, though now silent, just the motion of his exposed wrist with the stainless watch band that would be sliced in two along with the arm that's inside it. The roof gunner could be up there totally unprotected, you don't know, there's no communication, no headsets, no helmets, thin fabric seat belt that could snap in an instant, and now his dad's in the slow lane and a truck's passing them whose camper shell could hold nine fucking hadjis, six feet at most between vehicles, his dad letting it happen with his whole family in the car, though he's been in the service and should have learned.

This is their house, 37 Bell Street, yellow ribbons in the door window and among the foliage of their maple tree; then sunlight strikes the brass of musical instruments and here's the whole neighborhood with half the high school band in their driveway, three kids with trombones, two bass drums, couple of girls with cornets and his old bandleader Mr. Grindle with his baton striking up something, everyone's cheeks puffed out like they're blowing to break the windows. Maybe if they play loud enough for the deaf hero his hearing will return. All he feels is the bass drums' subsonic percussions through his boot soles and as he tries to adjust his stride to them and loses his balance and his dad steadies him he can see them put down their instruments to cheer.

The next thing that spots him is Flicka, the Harrises' little Shetland sheepdog that licked his whole face in the raw cold of December when they said good-bye. It breaks from the neighbor crowd and runs straight for its old bud Nick with its tongue out but something's wrong, it's coming too fast and too close and he drops his duffel and there's a *shamal* roar in his ears that must be his own voice but the dog's going for his family so he kicks it full force in the rib cage with his combat boot. As it sprawls flailing on the driveway the band stops and the neighbors draw back in a pantomime of fear. Flicka limps home through the Harrises' hedge and Marg Harris is kneeling down to it, but with an injury like that it looks like a lost cause. Any dog kicked that hard should be put down.

The musicians quickly disperse and it's just his mom and dad and Angela in a tight knot leading him toward the white two-story house where he was born. He teeters a little on his feet and looks for a railing as if there'd be one in the middle of the driveway; his dad notices and takes his arm. They didn't tell him he wouldn't be walking right, but that's in the ear too, it's like the personal gyroscope, and he can feel it sticking and tipping him to the left, or it may be the meds or the concussion. If something's wrong with your brain, how would it know?

Taking his dad's arm feels all right, he probably taught him to walk up this same driveway a quarter-century ago; but it also makes him aware that someone's missing, someone who didn't show up at the hospital and wasn't among the driveway crowd and who should have been the one holding his arm for these first steps: his girlfriend Brenda Campion, along with her parents, who were kind of a second family to him in his last weeks home. She'd been e-mailing almost every day before the event that reset time from the beginning; but then at Ramstein he got nothing, nor in the VA either, when he could have used it. It's just as well she didn't see him kick Flicka but he's surprised—not that surprised, though, because everything else is fucked up so why not this?

One year and one month ago, summer of 2005, they'd driven her dad's boat the four miles to Amber Island and set up a tent on an old wooden platform on a hillside facing across the ship channel to the town. With a camp stove and cooler for the beer and steaks it was almost like having a home together, and although they hadn't mentioned marriage out loud, she'd said *I could get used to this*, which he took as an acceptance to an unstated proposal, and he said *I already am*. After the carbonized marshmallows and Jim Beam the mosquitoes drove them back into the tent and even though he'd used up his protection after the first two, they couldn't stop doing it till they were extinguished by the light of dawn.

All during boot camp he sweated in his bunk thinking she might be knocked up and though they'd never discussed it she must have known. When she wrote YOU CAN STOP WORRYING he had a moment of indirect sadness, as when someone's pet dies that is not your own. He looks at his mom half-wanting to know where Brenda is or why she's not there. She knows what his question is and in response tries to reach up and put her arms around him but she's teary-eyed again and the contact is too close. The world has changed. It's another century; even your own mother could have an explosive device inside.

He crowds into the knotty-pine breakfast nook with his father and Angela, who can barely squeeze in between the table and the upright bench. Nobody speaks, of course, and they just sit there with both his mom and his sister teary-eyed until he stands up and Angela has to let him past. Once they were schoolkids waiting for breakfast; now one of them's pregnant, the other's a walking ghost who may not even be alive.

He drags himself upstairs by the railing and crashes on the twin bed he slept in for twenty years. The low sky-blue slanted ceiling brings back the blue tent again on the island and the sounds of night: the owl-hoots when they kept waking, the drawn-out dawn muezzin calls of seagulls mixed with her own throat's bird-cries from on top of him or underneath. That's the only thing he'd get the cochlear implants for, to hear a girl say his name in bed, or if he had kids, to listen for emergencies in the dark. But she's not here and it's not going to happen, so fuck the implants and the lip reading. The language Ramos and Dupuy speak is silence, which he's already fluent in.

The door opens suddenly and he wonders why they didn't knock beforehand as they always did even in middle school, but of course. He just didn't hear. He'll wire a motion sensor with a flashing light, if anyone nears the door. His dad's brought him an IBM ThinkPad, which they must have sacrificed for, since his mom's out of work now and Coastal Monuments is a minimum-wage employer despite Peter Colonna's three decades of inhaling granite dust along with the atmosphere of death. The thank-you he says as his father leaves scrapes out through his throat more like a fart or a goat bleat than a word, and from the way his dad's smile drops he knows he no longer sounds like a human being, which he is not sure he is now that he's lost the gift of speech that's supposed to separate us from the apes.

His room's stripped of sound like the inside of his skull. They've fixed it up for his arrival but took out everything that ever made a noise. Radiohead posters, keyboard and Behringer amp and his stereo and CDs, his turntable and vinyl, so many kinds of music, such a diversity of pitch and voice, while the absence of music has only one single tone: meaningless white noise of the brain's channel that suffocates all memory of sound.

He checks his e-mail but there's nothing from Brenda since before the Ramstein days. It's like she learned of his accident and instead of increased caring and devotion she went the other way. Why should she have been loyal when he himself failed Ramos and Dupuy?

The most recent one's from his mom, SOMEONE COMING TO VISIT YOU AT 4.

His small dormer window is the only one in the house high enough to glimpse the sea. Beyond the Harrises' garage and the lower houses marching down Bell Street and the two-story brick buildings along the waterfront, there is this fragment of blue that does not seem to be part of earth or sky but on its own plane between them, undimensional and suspended, free as a kid's kite over the Arab skyline. *Why did he kick Flicka?* She's an old companion who could distinguish his familiar scent through the layers of unwashable Sandbox dust that have become a second skin. He used to lie with Flicka in the Harrises' red hammock and sleep off a Sunday afternoon. The kick came from someplace outside his control zone and overrode three or four years of affection since the Harrises had brought her home from the SPCA. He was protecting his family and beyond them, way back in the murk of sand and wind, his vehicle crew, though there's nothing left of them but coffins smuggled in the dark of night. It must be the meds tubed into him at the VA; his first decision as a free man is never to set foot in that place again. If rehab is going to happen, it will happen on his own terms, in this absence of all sound that is becoming his native tongue.

The internet has a billion sites but no answers and he closes the laptop lid. The sudden smell of chocolate-chip cookies draws him out of his room by the nostrils like an animal. Another smell mixes with it on the stairs: the Shalimar perfume he gave Brenda before he left. It's not quite four yet but she must be the surprise appointment, and there she is, on the couch fraternizing with his pregnant sister like a women's talk show on mute. Thirty-six weeks ago they kissed good-bye in a flood of hope and sadness; now she's a female from another culture with a dyed coppery hair streak and silver hoop earrings he has never seen.

Her smile is the same one that always met him no matter how long the journey but her small pursed eyes have not only different makeup but a different shape and seem to fill with tears from another source. She holds a hand out formally, as if to shake for an interview, but he's remembering two bodies zipped together out on the island in a double-wide mummy bag. He wraps his arms around her as if she could erase both past and future as she had in the blue tent. He hasn't had a hard-on since the explosion and he was beginning to think they got that as well as the eardrums but now with her chest pressing against his and his hands on the low-slung curve of her tail, even despite his sister five feet away and his mother bringing snacks from the kitchen, it's all coming back to him and she backs away, embarrassed, to help his mother clear a place on the crowded table for the pretzel bowl.

Later they go up to his room alone and sit on the side of the bed together, but not to touch. His fingers attempt to brush her wrist but she pulls away; she wants nothing to do with a hand that has killed human beings and will never again be clean. Out of her purse she takes her iPod and the India.Arie album, which they played on their last night together. They used to listen for hours with two pairs of earbuds, but this time there's only one and she puts them into her own ears. She switches the iPod on, then bends down toward him till their foreheads touch, as if she could transmit the music directly through his skull. He remembers her favorite from that album, *I am not my hair, I am not this skin*, and it's true, he can feel light rhythmic vibrations, he reads the lyrics on the backs of his closed eyelids, then she pulls away and throws her head back to lip-sync when India sings *bad hair makes you look like a slave*; but the only sound reaching his brain is an itch as if a tick or sand fly is gnawing the empty hole.

Suddenly she puts the iPod away as if abandoning the idea like a failed experiment. She looks at her cell and then scrawls MY RIDE on a lime-green Post-it, then sticks it on his nose and gets up, straightening her clothes and fluffing her hair as if they'd done something, which they had not. They hold hands on the way down to the living room where Brenda kisses his sister and parents on the cheeks, but her step seems to lighten as his dad opens the front door and he can see it's a guy behind the wheel, though he doesn't recognize him or the truck he drives.

His mother, who has begun crying again, pulls him back from the open doorway, closes the door, then pushes it extra tight against the frame the way she does in the dead of winter when it's ten below zero outside.

3

He's been home a week without laying another eye on Brenda Campion. Memories of the blue tent sting like the little pricks of a Ka-Bar when the guys are fooling around in camp, but she's not dead in the same way as Dupuy and Ramos, so the pains twitch when her image comes to mind but go away when he thinks of something else. His sister Angela's gone back to engage with the incoming baby in New Mexico. The VA has e-mailed to set up a rehab schedule and take advantage of Uncle Sam's latest in surgery and technology but he deletes it. There's nothing in this valley of death and betrayal that he wants to hear. His old boss at Davis Stonecraft would welcome his return, and even his dad's boss Virge Russell made an offer, but the only headstone he can imagine carving would be his own.

His father's convinced you can replace hearing with reading, so the walls of his room which were once all CDs and vinyl are starting to look like the high-school library. He doesn't protest this because the sad barren shelves only reminded him of the lost music, but he has no desire to read either, or, more accurately, he can't choose what to read because all the stories and histories seem equal and he'd rather look out the window than make a choice.

He crushes a dex with his back molars so it will work faster, then leans back in his recliner like a cosmonaut waiting for the lift. He's focused on the single small squarish shape of ocean—*trapezoid*, that's what his old math teacher would say—barely visible from his room over rooftops and trees and steeples, its color every day and hour a different tonality of blue: black blue, green blue, and when the sun's at a certain angle, dazzling diamond blue. After twelve weeks in the dehydrated khaki desert he could stare out at it all day long. If there's any escape it won't come from close-captioned TV or his mother's parade of childhood dinners or even the evenings of stonecutters' poker with the guys from work, betting with their fingers and trying to lure him back. It won't come from artificial eardrums because if this has happened, it was intended for him, and it's in this silence that he has to stake his life. The guy who would have come home and walked the aisle with Brenda to one of her Avril Lavigne songs disappeared into the black hole with the two soldiers that went before. This is someone new living in someone else's room in a vacant world. All three of them are dead and their deaths occurred on a cloudless September morning in 2001. The planes the towelheads flew into the Twin Towers keep exploding like a chain reaction till eventually they'll get every fucking human on earth in their own way.

He rarely opens the internet because he wants no scenes of combat or distractions from the present time and place. But one morning the sky darkens ominously as an eclipse and he opens the Weather Channel: serious waves break over the pier at Old Orchard as the subtitles read REMNANTS OF HURRICANE ERNESTO. He closes his window and heads downstairs to help his mom lower the storm windows; then they stand together on the small sheltered porch as the first drops crater the pavement and become a flood sluicing down Bell Street toward the sea. Without a sound the roof gutters pour over the lawn and the surviving elms bend to the northwest with their leaves and whole branches tearing off as if it were mid-October.

Wearing nothing but his T-shirt and camo shorts he hops down the porch steps into the full torrent and lets it pour over him, not cold but bearing the warmth of its tropical origins. His mom reaches in and grabs a yellow slicker from the hall closet, but he shakes his head no. It's just what he needs to rinse off a desert coating that a hundred hot showers haven't been able to erase. God had the right strategy for the Middle East: a six-week downpour, then bring in a shipload of animals and start over. It would have been better than Tomahawk missiles for shock and awe.

❖

Labor Day's come and gone. The sun reemerges, but he's still inhabiting his room like a vegetable, exhaling smoke out the open window with its view of the sloping rooftops and the blue trapezoid beyond. This is the first week of school; kids laugh and skip down the sidewalk with new clothes and backpacks, mouths opening in visible yells and shrieks but no sound coming out. The distant patch of ocean momentarily flashes the exact color of the blue tent on Amber Island and he drops as through a trapdoor into the double sleeping bag, the two of them so woven or zipped together they couldn't tell who was which.

He's got six thousand dollars left from his signing bonus. He'll drive to the Ledgeport Marina and buy a boat. He'll take it out to the island and sleep in the same place even on the bare ground till the ghost cries of that night go quiet like everything else. He drops his week-old camo into the laundry chute, hits the shower without shaving, and comes out of his room disguised as a civilian in cargo pants and an LHS hoodie from his baseball days. His balance is picking up. He can move the length of the upstairs hall without lurching.

His mom smiles at his confident staircase descent like it's all been a misunderstanding and his hearing will soon return. The air's thick with chocolate and she taps his mouth with an oven-fresh cookie which he swallows like a piranha in a single bite. She forgets herself and says something, her lips moving for a moment, then stopping as she remembers. She stands on tiptoe so he can kiss her cheek, then she hands him the car keys. They burn his palm like spent shell casings and he drops them on the welcome mat. They left the FOB on a routine street patrol and he woke up in Ramstein, Germany, then he was in Chamberlain afraid even to read his dad's lettering that said *Marcel Dupuy Williams, Juan Jesus Ramos, KIA.*

In the VA they wrote that he'd be able to drive okay—just be vigilant with your remaining senses and watch the mirror for blue flashing lights. It will be fine not minding the horns behind him as he creeps along. He takes the breezeway to the garage, starts up the Caravan without raising the door, and, in the moment before hitting the opener, he smells the exhaust buildup and lets it idle a minute in the closed space because the odor is not as repulsive as you'd think. Breathe deeply till you fall asleep; it might quiet the voices of a phantom ear. Then his mom's face appears in the breezeway window, he hits the remote, and the door lifts. The air displacing the carbon monoxide now carries the scent of ocean salt.

He's turned 180 degrees in the bucket seat looking backward and there's Flicka noiselessly barking just beyond the Harrises' low fence gate, and then Dupuy's halfway out of the roof hatch with his whole body exposed and Nick lets go of the steering wheel, spins around and grabs both his legs, dragging him down to safety, but a rear wheel slips off the driveway onto the wet lawn and the car tilts and he's spinning his tire trying to get out. "Rock it easy, dude, Drive and Reverse," says Ramos beside him, and with a delicate touch on the shift lever he's back on the pavement. He pulls the Caravan into the garage again, shuts the engine off, and shaking his head *no* he hands the keys back to his mom. He won't be needing them anymore.

His grandfather Guido was another disabled vet from a distant war, and there's still a rack of his canes and sticks by the garage door. He grabs a stout old bronze-headed cane for support and confidence, then he's out the side door and stumping around the long way to avoid a dog who was mistreated by an old friend but keeps coming back for more.

He's starting to walk a straight line as he learns to compensate for the loss of his ear canals. He can prop Nonno's cane on his right shoulder like a rifle and march down the long hill of Bell Street, into a hometown that even in September's still in full tourist mode. Bus-sized RVs jostle and jam in traffic and senior citizens browse the galleries and latte bars that are making this once-proud little city into a lapdog of New York. Then suddenly without warning this fucking poodle sticks its grotesque shorn snout out the window of a parked car and he throws himself across the sidewalk against the brick wall of Rosen's Jewelry the way they were trained to treat urban explosives. A foot over and he would have been through the plate glass into the necklace display. A couple of people look shocked and back away from him but the younger ones smile, maybe thinking it's street theater, and they look around for the other actors, or what are they? Mimes. That's another thing he could do.

The dog still pumps its jaws as if barking but the window opening's too narrow for it to get out, or for that matter to give it a crack across the snout with Nonno Guido's cane. He might want a sidearm, just in case. He could get a concealed-carry and even if they didn't see it, the dogs would smell powder and back off, or if not they would take a hit right down their yelping throat.

He works his way along the sidewalk to Aaron's Drugstore, chilling down until he spots the outside paper stand. Right there on the front page of the *Ledgeport Weekly Herald* is his own face: DISABLED SOLDIER HOME. He doesn't read past *shattered the bones of his inner ear.* The interview's with his parents, of course. Old Aaron, who was in some war himself back in the day, comes out from behind his counter and shakes his hand, smiling, frowns at the cane, then recognizes it from his grandfather's time, puts an arm around his shoulder, one soldier to another, and takes him into the old-fashioned drugstore with its wood drawers and Coke spigots which Aaron maintains like his own self as a relic of the past. He rips a guest check off the pad and writes, NO CHARGE—.

COFFEE, Nick writes. BLACK.

Old Aaron brings the coffee and opens the donut jar, then the pie case, points questioningly to the milk-shake blender, the jar of bagels, the row of four ice-cream flavors, vanilla, chocolate, strawberry, coffee—no wonder he only has one customer, he's competing with Ben & Jerry's 54 flavors at the mini-mall. He writes VANILLA and Aaron puts two small scoops in a silver bowl, then writes, STAN FISCHER ASKED ABOUT YOU.

His old English teacher's name takes him back to Ledgeport High, a brand-new consolidated school located on a remote, barely orbiting planet whose clocks move slowly or sometimes not at all. Mr. Fischer's class was the one bearable activity. Of course he might hold Mr. F responsible for the world's silence; it was a war book called *The Things They Carried* that planted the idea of signing up, though it didn't take root till they attacked the World Trade Center on 9/11. Mr. Fischer said all those stories—*The Red Badge of Courage* and *All Quiet on the Western Front* and *Farewell to Arms*—were antiwar books, but they had the opposite effect on Nick. He wanted to see and hear what had caused in these writers such explosions of words that you could feel them like ordnance in your spine. They were not just imagining. They'd been there and seen combat and knew how to bring the sights and sounds of it to the silent page.

He tries to pay old Aaron but the druggist won't hear of it and instead thrusts a few copies of the *Herald* in his hand on his way out. He looks at his image in the paper, with a couple of trombones and a tuba gleaming in the background, and, down in the lower left corner,

Flicka the dog, who even in the photo freezes his heart tissue like Novocain. They say the Taliban cut the pictures out of every newspaper in Afghanistan, which sounds as whacked as all hadj behavior, but he can understand. His own likeness in the paper under his arm is irritating his skin and he throws the *Herald*s in a wrought-iron trash basket wired to a streetlight pole. He takes a few steps, then looks back, and there's some guy fishing one of the papers out, glancing down at it, staring at Nick, and a couple of high-school kids peer at it and gape as well. This is what fame must be—to have an existence in other people's eyes after you've thrown yourself away.

The Ledgeport waterfront forms a circle from the breakwater to the old fish houses where the clouds of seagulls once screamed their beaks off but have now gone silent in honor of those who served. One wharf holds the gold-plated cruisers belonging to MBIC, the credit-card bank that laid off his mom though the size and splendor of their yachts did not decrease. Next is the Coast Guard headquarters with huge red and green barnacle-coated sea buoys hauled out, waiting for repair. The bell buoys have twice as much under the surface than you can see above, and their beached silence is like his own: Like the king who turned everything to stone, whatever noise a thing once made, it ceases as Nick comes near.

He looks at the boats for sale in the Ledgeport Marina first through the chain-link fence, then goes inside. If he buys a boat like her old man lent them and camps in the same place on the same island, that might remove the live ghost of Brenda Campion, though he doesn't know what vessel or journey would release him from Ramos and Dupuy. The salesman's an old dude he's seen in a few bars but doesn't know—Bill Stivers, his desk plate says. When Nick walks up, the guy does a double take and dives into the office wastebasket for the morning's *Herald*. Stivers looks at the picture, back at his customer, says something through a big patriotic smile with his teeth white as flag stripes, then puts his hand over his mouth to cover the mistake.

Nick picks up a yellow pad from the sales desk and writes, DOUG CAMPION'S BOAT?

Stivers leafs through his brochures and finds the one, a Grady-White 19, then leads him outside to the row of outboards and there it is, an exact copy of the one he borrowed to take Brenda to the island: $7,000. Money is a language you don't need hearing for. They sit down on an old wooden dory outside the office overturned on a pair of railroad ties, planted with nasturtiums all around. Must be their negotiating bench. Stivers scratches out the price. AFTER VETERAN DISCOUNT, $5,500.

PAY YOU TOMORROW, Nick writes. I WILL BE HERE.

The deal's over, hands shaken, newspaper brought out once more to show the employees, who gather around, give him a thumb shake, a friendly punch in the biceps. He pats the Grady-White on its trailer as if he's bought the most awesome yacht in the place.

He pauses in the marina parking lot to look past the breakwater at his destination, Amber Island glowing like its name, honey-colored granite that shimmers mirage-like over the bay. The other islands off Ledgeport have lighthouses, mansions, cattle herds, fish piers, campgrounds, airstrips, aquaculture pens with blinking strobe lights, survival schools—humans have possessed and marked them. Amber is different. There's nothing on it but the overgrown granite quarry where his grandfather came to cut stone as a young boy, sixty immigrant Italian laborers living and working out there, another world in another time. Nonno Guido was also a disabled vet: He gave his left knee for a country he wasn't even born in, and when they went out to Amber he'd lean on his little grandson like a crutch.

He feels the presence of something at his back, turns from the sea view to find a beige Volvo station wagon only a couple of yards away, inching toward him, bumper about to make slow contact with his knees. The driver inside tightens his lips, clearly poking the horn button, baldheaded old fart. How many good soldiers got wasted for his right to drive with the windows open, kids strapped into the backseat, free from death and fear? That's what they died for, words like *petroleum* and *freedom*. He's glad he'll never have to hear them again.

Back at his own house there's a strange car in the driveway, an old pea-green Land Rover with a white safari top, which he's seen where? Ledgeport High, faculty parking lot. He looks in the back and there's a two-bladed airplane propeller taking the whole length of the vehicle on the diagonal with its varnished wood tip sticking out the window on the passenger side. That has to be Mr. Fischer's; he was the only teacher he's ever known to fly a plane. Why is it here? Mr. Fischer's not a friend of the family and Nick wasn't exactly part of the intellectual elite.

Mr. F's squeezed into the narrow kitchen dinette having coffee with his mom, but when he sees his old pupil he jumps right up and offers a handshake, then a hug, which is the first ever from a teacher. He's surprised how solid and flabless his thickset body is, considering all that time behind a desk, correcting homework, memorizing all those books. He takes out a laptop and motions for Nick to get his own, while his mom jumps up to brew more coffee so teacher and student can face each other over the dinette table. Mr. F types like a machine gun with all ten fingers while Nick still hunts for the letters one by one.

U STAYING AROUND OR SHIPPING OUT AGAIN?

HERE FOR A WHILE.

TOMORROW LOOKS LIKE GOOD FLYING WEATHER. HOW ABOUT GOING UP WITH ME, TEST-FLY THE NEW PROP? OR MAYBE THERE'S TOO MUCH

ON YOUR PLATE.

   NO PLATE.

   SURE?

   BUYING A BOAT, MAYBE.

   BOATS CAN WAIT. I'LL COME BY TOMORROW, 0730. MEANWHILE, CHECK OUT THIS BOOK.

He points to a small thick paperback between his laptop and empty cup. It's called *The Portable Thoreau*—as if you could fold a guy up, a dead guy, and carry him around. It's all beat-up, the binding taped. Mr. F's probably read it a hundred times; it's what he does.

Nick leafs through the contents but the only chapter he's ever heard of is "Walden." There was a guy in the hooch from someplace in New Hampshire, Peters, who was always saying that when he got out, he'd make a cabin and live like Henry D Thoreau, survive off of coons and woodchucks, grow marijuana and hoe beans. He said Thoreau had to be smoking something to have the ideas he had. Peters was the top marksman in the platoon; he could live off the shit he shot and sell the rest. Then they pulled him up to Mosul 'cause they needed snipers and sent him back minus his left arm.

He tries to say "Thanks," though who knows what it sounds like; from now on he's going to stop words before they can escape. Mr. Fischer makes his hand into a plane to confirm about tomorrow morning.

Sure, Nick nods, thinking they could fly out over Amber Island and view the old tent site from the air.

Up in his room he turns to a chapter already marked with a paper clip, called "Sounds." Why not? If you can't hear, you might as well read about it. The whole book is scarred with clips and dog-ears as if Mr. Fischer hacked a path through it for him to follow. *I long ago lost a hound, a bay horse, and a turtle-dove, and am still on their trail.* Mr. F put a big question mark on the edge. It's not hard to figure out.

Their names were Ramos, Williams, Campion: salsa hound, chestnut-brown horse, dove flown away. He's on their trail but he'll never find them because they've either gone feral or died in the wilderness. He stops and builds a cabin so even if he can't catch them he'll at least be closer to where they are.

Simplify, simplify. Mr. Fischer highlights that passage, though it's not clear he lives by it. He's got the Land Rover and an airplane and a teaching job with a principal on his back and fifty kids who don't always give a shit. He thinks of his old man with his tombstone profession and his mother still sleepless over losing the bank job and old Aaron trying to hold on to his mom-and-pop drugstore with his wife dead and the guy in the Volvo honking and honking at someone who doesn't even turn around. Nobody simplifies. Nick himself is going the next day to buy a boat with a motor big enough for a car because it looks like one owned by the father of a girl who doesn't exist anymore, if she ever did.

He saw what *simplify* meant in the Arab streets where he'd walk in Kevlar armor, radio helmet, M16, Night Vision Goggles, field pack, sidearm, ammo belt, twelve-inch boots, Ka-Bar; meanwhile, the insurgents went light as animals, just a white toga to conceal the AK-47 up against their dicks, not even underwear. Fucking terrorists walk barefoot while the load we carry gets heavier every day. If you don't have the discipline to simplify, somebody will do it for you, homicidal insurgent or just a devious companion you mistook for love. By not hearing anything he's already halfway there.

He closes the book and turns out the halogen desk lamp to listen, and there is a sound, like an unending waterfall or air rushing over a plane's wing, and under that sound the slow steady beat of his own pulse. Maybe he can learn something in this cave of silence. He didn't pay much attention when he could hear.

4

In the dream, a uniform without a man in it. It's got an E2 stripe and a nametag that says WILLIAMS and it's walking in the wrong direction toward their house up Bell Street, which is one-way in the dream, and the punishment is electrocution by car battery the way they did it at Abu Ghraib. Nick runs out to stop him, pointing at the sign, telling him to turn back before it's too late, Flicka barking the whole time, and he hears her perfectly. The empty uniform keeps coming and as it approaches the door everything starts to glow with radiation and the light brightens and brightens till the sound is deafening and the whole sky's a solid white flame like the nucleus of the sun. It must have even awakened his mom because she enters his bedroom and kneels beside his bed with her forehead touching his shoulder as if he's in kindergarten. He holds himself rigid till she gets up and goes away. The first rays of sunlight score an orange line across the Winchester .30-30 standing loaded and ready beside his bookshelf. *Rise free from care before dawn, and seek adventures.*

He never had a black friend before Dupuy. There were zero black kids in his whole school system except one year, an African exchange student, but her host family owned the Stonehill ski area, so she hung out with a higher clique. Henry David helped a runaway slave on his way to Canada, and Mr. F highlighted it. *Whom I helped to forward toward the north star.* Spc. Nicolas Colonna did something—he wakes every night in a hot sweat trying to remember it—not to help someone survive, but the opposite. The only survivor was himself. Maybe in heaven Dupuy's getting to know 2Pac Shakur, his main man gunned down when Moby was ten years old. Thug for Life. I will be. *A life of crime I will lead, If you play the game, you play to win*; he'd always be singing 2Pac's "Ballad of a Dead Soulja," and now he is one—one more dead motherfucker, as he loved to say.

He wakes to a voice in his left ear as if the speaker's right beside the bed, but there's no one there. It's like Mr. F's voice but it's not, it's a man with a foreign accent like someone from Massachusetts. *Only that day dawns to which we are awake.* What the fuck; it's clearer than any voice when he had ears. He tries to envision Henry D standing over him, the bearded dude on the book jacket looking like Abe Lincoln as they all did in that time, but the image that comes to mind is of Sergeant Trefethen, six-four, even blacker than Moby, rolling them out with the voice of a sousaphone.

He touches his toes five times lying on the bed then hits the floor for twenty push-ups, but then comes Henry D's accent right in his ear: *Simplify, simplify*, and an idea strikes him before he reaches ten. His grandfather once told him he left the island and rowed across the ship channel to see a Ledgeport girl. Fuck the Yamaha outboard and the Grady-White, he'll see if he can buy the old overturned dory outside the office and get a pair of oars. On a calm morning before the wind comes up he could make two miles an hour, easy; leave at six, row diagonally four miles across the channel, be at Amber Island by eight or nine. A plus to that method would be getting his body back before it goes to flab; besides, that whole fucking plastic hull is made from petroleum, not to mention the gas it burns. He was all for revenge on Saddam for 9/11, including Uday and Qusay, bloodier little butchers than their old man, but wasting Ramos and Dupuy for the price of oil is another question. *We do not ride on the railroad*, Henry says. *It rides upon us.*

His father has already left for work when Nick comes down. His mom's pimped out the kitchen for Mr. Fischer, yellow plaid cloth napkins and Grandma Edna's real silver from the wooden box. The table's set for two with squeezed orange juice, sweating plums, open box of Dunkin' Donuts holes with the waxed paper perked up around the sides, along with a small clipboard and a yellow pad on which she's already written *FINE FLYING DAY*. He looks outside and it is. The sun is evaporating the last dew from the garage roof in clouds of mist. A pair of red squirrels chases each other up and down the rose trellis while crows flap and hover like sand vultures over the Harrises' yard; maybe something happened to Flicka. He hasn't been in a plane since landing in Portland when the pressure drop burned like two soldering irons in his ears. But you can't be a pussy about pain when others have had their feet blown off or they're not even alive.

Mr. Fischer's Land Rover shows up before 0730 and he comes right in, wearing a camo nylon flight jacket and a Red Sox cap. Under the cap he shows gray hairs which he didn't have when Nick was in high school, and gray strands in his summer beard. His mom offers coffee and the donut box, her mouth moving with gratitude that one of his teachers has remembered and taken such an interest in her wounded son. Mr. Fischer stays standing and scarfs the glazed hole in a single smiling bite, licks the sugar flecks from his beard, blows steam off the coffee; after all those years of flying he's still excited to go. Nick grabs the clipboard, kisses his mom, takes a chocolate followed by a coconut hole, and they're out the door. On the Harrises' side, Flicka is jumping and mouthing barks but the gate's been latched solid since the parade. He slips around the Land Rover, keeping his exposure low, gets in on the double, locks the door while keeping a close eye on the Sheltie's foaming mouth.

He hasn't been in a car since his attempt with the Caravan, whose sheet metal wouldn't stop a BB and if it caught fire you'd be trapped inside. The Land Rover's made of solid aluminum plate with a double roof in case a rhino upends it, but it would be like cardboard to an RPG. They head away from the ocean and go right past the airport turnoff on Route 13, same road that goes to the VA—and that's when he suspects that it's a trick. Fischer's an agent and he's taking him back to the hospital, and if so, Nick's trained for high-speed rolls and ready to jump out and chance it in the woods. But just then they slow down and turn off into a random farmer's field with a barn and a feed silo, and out back there's a wind sock and a long low hangar for maybe a half-dozen private planes. They're lined up in two rows so they must have to move the front planes if the back ones need to get by.

As soon as they're parked, Mr. F takes the clipboard and writes, LOOK AT THOREAU? He writes in the same thick scrawl he used to correct papers, but handwriting is like a voice and the Land Rover fills with the words of his old teacher as if he were in class.

Nick borrows the pen. SOME. WHAT WAS HE RUNNING FROM?

GIRLFRIEND DUMPED HIM, Mr. F replies. BROTHER DIED.

Chestnut-colored horse, fugitive dove. Brenda and Dupuy. Halfway around the world to find a brother, and while you're over there you lose what you left behind. But if she hadn't dumped him he would never have built the cabin or discovered the book hidden inside. *You can't always get what you want—you get what you need.* The Stones were Mr. Fischer's generation, Vietnam such a bloodbath that it took a year just to engrave the names on the black wall, but sometimes it takes a war to make you see.

There are still big puddles around the airport left over from the hurricane. They skirt between them to a green-and-white plane in the first row. It has the new varnished propeller and the word CESSNA over the engine hood, and by coincidence bears the tail number of Brenda's birthday, N1002—less than a month away, and he hasn't thought of a present or anything. Then he realizes he doesn't have to, and should delete that date from his memory if he can.

Mr. Fischer releases the wheel chocks and two tie-downs, opens the unlocked right door, guides Nick's foot to the strut step, and he's up and into a seat with its own steering wheel and controls. Angela's old boyfriend Dana had a Piper Cub and gave him a few lessons, but they broke up and he never got to solo. Now it comes back to him as he surveys the instrumentation and settles in. *Push the fuel valve to the* ON *position.* He hears Dana Burke's voice as if he were in the cockpit, but when Mr. F moves his lips nothing comes out. Memories of speech come alive in the vacated space.

The Cessna's pretty much the same except in the Cub he sat in front of Dana Burke, while here he's side by side with the pilot, like a regular car. Mr. F goes around the tail, pauses to shake the elevator a bit, which moves the controls in front of both seats and shudders the whole plane. He hoists himself into the left seat in a pretty spry jump for a graybeard with glasses who spends his life in a book. He reaches into his pocket and pulls out a few well-worn sheets of paper, folded and stapled, with the heading *Cessna 172 Start-Up & In-Flight* on which he's written *KEEP THIS AND STUDY IT IF YOU WANT.* Nick tries following Mr. F's actions with the printout but it's easier just to watch him; he's not here for a lesson anyway, just for a flight with his old teacher on a clear September day, hoping to fly over the old campsite on Amber Island.

Mr. F moves his hand toward the magneto switch, then stops, hits his knee and laughs like he's forgotten something. The key? He gives a thumbs-up, reaches way down under the threadbare gray left seat, and pulls out one of those hide-a-key boxes with the spare inside. In quick succession his fingers hit the red master Alt and Batt switches, Fuel On, BCN and NAV switches, mixture control turned up to Rich, as with the Cub, primer pumped three times just like a lawn mower. Then he twists the key over to Start like any car and the prop throbs around a bit, then really catches, and though it's completely silent the wheel and pedals vibrate as the rpm edges up past 1,500 to 1,800 and the plane tries to pull itself forward out of the hangar. Mr. F moves a lever called "pitch" to T/O and the flaps lever to 0 degrees; the corresponding lever on Nick's side moves at the same time. He pumps the two foot pedals a few times as the co-pedals force his own feet up and down. He swings the control yoke forward and back with a duplicate movement on Nick's side, pointing to the wing flaps and back around to the tail elevator, then he lets the rpm sag and hits a black handle over by his door that seems to release the plane as if the brakes had been let up.

His feet sense the rudder turning as the wheels bump over to the runway, just a grassy cow field with much the same feeling as any 4x4 on rough terrain; then the rpm rises with the throttle and they move faster, past the silos, the wind sock, and the Land Rover, scattering some seagulls in their path. His hands on the copilot's yoke are moved backward, the bumps cease, and they rise into the third dimension as the Cessna feels its way through the unseen chop and contours of the air, and then he's lashed to a stretcher in the shaking Blackhawk, he's twisting his neck to find his vehicle team with the chopper door wide open beside him and there's no one, nothing; he turns to jump the fuck out of there but he's strapped in and the female medic puts her hand on his forehead to keep him down. As the plane gains altitude now over a Christmas tree farm, it would be so easy to flick off his seat belt and flip the door latch and roll out sideward into the empty air, halfway already to Ramos and Dupuy.

Mr. F taps Nick's left knee, points at the horizon gauge with a red dot on the second line over the center, then settles to the lower line as he lets the yokes forward and the steep climb eases off, soundless as an electric car. They're already over the smokestacks of the Ledgeport cement plant, the antique airfield under their right wing with an old-fashioned Spad on the tarmac and a World War II Mustang coming in. War is the whetstone of technology. If not for the theater of combat, people would still be in Wright Brothers biplanes with their heads in the open air. Mr. F turns down the mixture control and the yoke pivots as they bank left; you can see the aileron rising on the downward wing as his left foot sinks with the pedal while the town clarifies below, the live elms of Bell Street like broccoli stalks in the salt mist drifting from the sea.

The altimeter reads 1,100 feet when they overfly the breakwater lighthouse with its red blinker, the island ferry with a load of cars, a few hopeful sails upright and hanging in the windless air. Now an amphibious seaplane from the aircraft museum crosses under them on a northward course. Mr. F banks in another direction and Nick's own pedals move with the rudder as they wheel over one island after another to the open Atlantic. His teacher is reducing his foot pressure on the controls, so Nick can do some of the rudder work himself. A few minutes over the light-struck surface of sea and ledges, then they reach Matinicus and Mr. F turns the yoke side to side above its small island airfield, the plane wags to the single runway, and they bank and turn left over a supertanker loaded with Arab oil for the Coveside tank farms, waves breaking occasionally on the water, the little plane surfing the air currents aloft.

Mr. Fischer lets go the controls and now it's Nick tipping the yoke gently leftward while he presses his clutch foot ever so little at first but more with increasing pressure as the pilot raises the tach a few rpm into the maneuver. The silence and steadiness of this turn feel so smooth that he keeps going, a full 360 degrees over the cusp of Saddleback Ledge beneath him like a kite tethered to the lighthouse below. He lets his feet even out on the pedals and levels the yoke off so the plane flies straight up the shipping lane toward Mark Island, then Bridle and Amber, only it's not Penobscot Bay under the plane but the city of Samarra with its streets on fire from tracers and RPGs and they're right over a mosque or school which is blown into a white cloud of dust as the Blackhawk yaws left and strains away from a bomb blast that sucks the rotors down.

Mr. Fischer's tapping the central gauge and pointing skyward, so Nick pulls back gently, eyes on the climb rate as the dial moves through 1,500 and they're over the Fox Islands ferry trailing its white wake below. Mr. F signals to descend; Nick eases the yoke forward and Amber enlarges beneath them like an atoll just now originating from the sea. Only a small spot of red spills over its honey-tinted shoreline at one point on the eastern shore, as if blood dyed the granite from a firefight in the dense woods. They're over the tent site where he camped with Brenda, then the abandoned cabin on the tip of the north point, where, according to Nonno Guido, once upon a time a sheep farmer lived.

He's been flying for twenty minutes now and Mr. F's giving him more and more command, so he's not meeting the helpful pressure of someone else on the controls, but the response of the plane itself as the pilot gradually withdraws. If he thought he was going to be the passive passenger, he forgot Mr. F has a teaching disorder and can't help himself.

The fall air's so clear they can see a hundred miles to Mount Katahdin and Mr. F writes on the yellow pad: THOREAU CLIMBED IT. Nick climbed it too with his father and sister but Angela got scared on the Knife Edge and they didn't reach the summit. They said they would try again, by some different approach, but they never did. Angela went west and he went east, both into the desert, and they came back changed, one swollen with new life, one with a cavity the size of a human being. Everything around him changed and coming here hasn't restored it. Once you leave the place where you started there's no turning back. The person arriving home isn't the one that left.

Now they're over the vast orange deck of an oil tanker in the channel between Amber and Ledgeport, and Mr. F gestures left and downward in the direction of the small town beneath them and the airport beyond. Nick himself starts the slow banking turn, carefully trims the flaps and eases the rpm to descend slowly westward toward the lighthouse, the fishing fleet, and the dense circle of wharves. They skirt Mount Amatuck at 1,500 feet and drop to 850 as the runway grows visible, then the wheel begins to move on its own as his old teacher takes control.

Back in the driver's seat of the Land Rover, Mr. F takes the yellow pad and writes, *SHEER TALENT. WANT TO LEARN?*

CAN'T HEAR RADIO, he writes back.

NO NEED. DIDN'T USE IT THE WHOLE TRIP.

I COULD GET A LISENCE? Oops—English teacher. He crosses it out. ~~LISENCE~~. He knows it's wrong but he doesn't know what's right.

THERE'S AN ASSOCIATION, Mr. F writes, *FOR DEAF PILOTS; CAN ARRANGE IF YOU LIKE.*

MAYBE. THANX FOR A QUIET FLIGHT. He pauses before his next question, then asks it. *HOW COME YOU TOOK ME?*

I NEVER SERVED, Mr. F writes. *I WENT TO CANADA.*

THAT'S OK. CONG DIDN'T DO 9/11.

NOT OK. SOMEBODY TOOK MY PLACE.

Mr. F's stuck in the Vietnam days when men went and got killed and he survived. He visits the Memorial every year; that's what he said in class. He feels responsible for every man that died 'cause they weren't him. Nick would like to remind him Tonkin was a hoax—he'd told them that himself—so he shouldn't feel bad about draft dodging. Saddam was different; his elite guards were asshole buddies with Mohamed Atta. They met in Europe and planned those flights like a travel agency. That day was worse than Pearl Harbor; payback was mandatory. A nation must stand to its full height in a hostile world. If Mr. Fischer was Nick's age he'd be over there crossing from the Gulf in an F-16. He reads about Nick in the paper and offers a book and an airplane; how could he know that nobody can help? Nick was the vehicle commander, his best friend had one hand on his Deuce .50 and the other tossing Mr. Goodbars to the street kids; then there was nothing, not even this silence that he wears every waking hour like a chemical-weapons suit. He knows why Mr. Fischer took the deaf vet flying. Forty years back someone got wasted in his place, and he still doesn't have the right to be alive.

Now they're turning into the driveway where Jenna Harris hustles Flicka back into their sunporch and shuts the door. Mr F pulls up and writes on the pad, *READ THOSE PRINTOUTS BEFORE NEXT LESSON. MEMORIZE THE START-UP SEQUENCE. WE'LL KEEP THIS GOING IF YOU WANT.* He hands over a thick envelope with a full-width grin through his beard as if Nick's finally one of the AP kids.

His mother's away somewhere when he goes in, so he heads upstairs to look over the contents. A pamphlet from the Stone Deaf Pilots Association. *Overcome your handicap and become a licensed pilot* (ah—it begins with "lice"). And here's an e-mail printout to Mr. F from the Owls Head Pilot Instruction Center saying they'd heard about Nick, that non-radio certification was possible, and they would work with a disabled veteran at reduced rates, and maybe the VA would cover part of it. Also, a flight manual for the Cessna 172.

He's sprawled in the window seat reading a chapter in *The Portable Thoreau* called "Conclusion," because Mr. F marked almost every page with stars and highlights. *If a man does not keep pace with his companions, perhaps it is because he hears a different drummer.* That's what Sergeant Trefethen used to say when they got out of step in Basic—"You hearing some other music?" Now the different drummer is all he hears, heart churn and artery rush when he presses his hands over his ears; the only beat he can keep pace with is his own pulse.

He's got a mirror rigged over his bed so he can face out the window and still see if the door opens behind him. His .30-30 stands unseen but instantly reachable behind the curtain. Someone could whale at the door with the fireplace poker and he wouldn't know, so they flap it open and shut if they want him. He sees its reflection or feels the slight wind on his skin. It's true, the other senses ramp up when you lose one. He can tell movement even when he can't see it. He's getting a doglike intuition; his neck hairs rise if someone even approaches the house.

Now he feels and sees the door move at the same time. He swivels around from the mirror to reach his weapon but it's his mom, holding a UPS package as if it's his birthday. His Ka-Bar's strapped to his leg as always and he cuts the ribbon and slices the striped paper with its razor edge. The box says One TTY Telephone. They gave him the word on that in the hospital, but it's the same as the internet—you call someone and you can type into it and they can answer on its little screen.

He writes on the pad, THANX, MOM.

THIS IS A SPECIAL ONE, she writes. YOU CAN TALK TO SUSAN MERCHANT.

?

HER MOTHER WORKED WITH ME AT MBIC. WE WERE LET GO IN THE SAME ROUND. SUSAN IS YOUR AGE; SHE'S HEARING-IMPAIRED, TOO. BUT VERY ATTRACTIVE! THEY LIVE IN LAKEWOOD—LOVELY HOME!—SHE WANTS TO CORRESPOND.

NO, MOM, I'M GOING OUT.

OUT? OUT WITH SOMEONE?

OUT TO BUY A BOAT.

She opens her eyes wide with a proud smile and a forehead kiss. He re-snaps the Ka-Bar, extracts a few hundreds from his locked cashbox, and gets his combat boots. She taps the knife handle on his leg with a twisted look, like, *Do you really need that?* He shakes his head yes, shaping his hand into a pistol to say he should carry a sidearm too. She doesn't know how the world's changed; it's not her century anymore. Only the vulnerable go unarmed.

The Saturday-afternoon blues concert fills the small park between the ferry terminal and the Ledgeport Marina. It's still a shock to him to see girls dancing short-skirted and unveiled with their hair flying and no morality cops hassling them, grinding at guys in broad daylight or grinding with other girls, which would have got their throats cut in Shariaville, their heads tossed to the carnivorous street pigs.

Following the seismic bass line with his feet, he lets himself drift toward one of the big outdoor amps with the top cone right at the level of his ear. Nobody's anywhere near this close to the speakers and the band guys stare at him pausing to headbang in the line of fire like he's a zombie from the walking dead, but for the first time since Iraq he can feel the music as it comes from the pulsating ground directly through his spinal column so that he's not just the listener but the instrument. He imagines himself as the audience sees him, a big shavehead soldier with tattoo and muscle shirt, camo pants, Ka-Bar on his calf. A bit fat and out of shape from too much bedrest, but no one to be fucked with either, though he won't hear you coming from behind. How does a man live who can't defend himself? Henry D might know.

Most of the dancers are out-of-state tourists and rich island kids waiting for the ferry. Then he sees Maggie Lyons and Bert Theriault, a couple he knew from his class, out of college and by the looks of it, living off food stamps while they figure things out. They're laughing at him and covering their ears 'cause he's so close to the speakers, headbanging deaf hero in the line of fire. The band too is local, the Diggers; they read the papers and know who he is and wail it out for him with the sound guy maxing the bass out and everyone backing off further but him. He goes for a few moves and high-fives with Bert and Maggie, who engage their mouths in excitement, forgetting it doesn't get through, then they laugh and shake their heads, sorry, and he can lip-read Mag saying, *Fucking war*, with her upper teeth dug into her lower lip so he can see the *F*. They're indicating the Black Pearl Tavern as they lift invisible beers, as if they want him to join them for a drink. He couldn't sit down with them; there's an abyss between them that's deeper than language—between who has been there and who has not. Maggie hated Operation Iraqi Freedom, he remembers. She's Brenda's friend; she marched with a peace banner in March 2003, and so did Bert, as if they could prevent it with signs and slogans, but it was too big to stop. The time was over for the free choice of yes or no; it was in too many hearts like a dog that's been chained or hidden but has now come out.

Bill Stivers stands in the doorway of his marina office mouthing a big *Hey, where you been?*

Nick writes on a blank sales check, Not the outboard. I want the dory.

Dory?

He points to the old upside-down flat-bottom rowboat surrounded by nasturtiums and goldenrod stalks, slaps its side like a sea animal, and tries to rasp, "How much?" but who knows what comes out?

Bill shakes his head, grins, writes on the sales pad, This is our deal bench. It's in retirement. Not for sale.

Everything's for sale, Nick writes. How much?

Bill puts the pad down, reaches into the nasturtium bed to pull up one side of the dory, but stops short. It's heavy. Nick gets a hand under the gunwale and the two of them raise it to reveal the long unpainted oars beneath. Bill runs a penknife along a caulking seam; it seems to stop rather than go through, a decent sign. He holds three fingers up, then writes it, For you, $300. He draws a ribbon and adds, Support the troops.

5

Nick and his dad take the old Trek mountain bike down from its pegs in the garage. A decade ago it was his transportation and his freedom, but since he got his license it's hung there like a painting of a kid that once lived here but disappeared. The bike will get him out of his room and kill some time while the wood of his dory swells and the seams close tight. It will help him get his strength and wind back, plus his equilibrium. Amber Island is at least a two-hour row over open water, but if his grandfather could do it, so can he.

His dad steadies the six-foot stepladder beneath him as he pulls the bike out and hands it down, then heads for the cellar and returns visibly laughing with the old set of training wheels. Nick jumps on the bike and goes for him but his old man steps aside like a matador and he's wobbling down the driveway then oversteering into a low-speed crash. He gathers himself and pedals up Bell Street with kind of a corkscrew motion, but his legs feel like they're recovering from hibernation and though he comes close to falling he doesn't. He used to ride way up on Mount Amatuck and pitch off like a dive-bomber down the summit trails. If he can stay upright, this is the way to get his stamina back for the long row.

He U-turns again and coasts down Bell Street toward the waterfront, where his dory floats proud and upright at the dock, a couple of workmen pounding the oar pins in. They're older, but he knew one of them from Pat's Pub back in his drinking days, Frankie Ruohoma, who grins and salutes him. He's a vet from some war, and one of the

Limeville Finns. There's an anchor and a length of rope coiled in a careful spiral on the floor slats, and across the seats the oars are painted satin gray, with the handles left bare.

He climbs into his new vessel, they cast him off, and he rows straight for the open sea. There was a sense of freedom in Mr. Fischer's plane, a bird's freedom from gravity and distance above the suck; but as the boat pulls past the calm water around the float and into the light harbor chop, he feels not only free, but home. Water's seeping in at every seam, but he can sense the planks' thirst and feel them already swelling with seawater and clamping themselves tight. He turns and rows back to the pier, letting the strakes soak for a bit while he puts some miles on the mountain bike.

He cranks up the Bell Street hill past the big white shipowners' mansions of the Historic District, now owned by doctors and bankers, that always seemed dead and unoccupied because the kids were shipped off to private schools and you never saw them again. They were like salmon that spawn upstream in the woods somewhere then go to sea after they hatch and never return. None of their offspring joined the service nor do they consider that their homes are mortgaged in blood on the other side of the world. The smallest IED could level all the French doors and porch columns of lower Bell Street, Audis and BMWs gutted and overturned, overhanging elm branches engulfed in flames. Kids not in the AP classes traveled eight thousand miles to protect these trellises and gazebos, and they did not always come back intact. Next time the fight could be at home.

He pauses at Dr. Savage's big brick home for a moment of pride and admiration of the new stone chimney, built by Nick and the crew at Davis Stonecraft before he enlisted, when it still meant something to work and live. He starts up again and downshifts and pushes his legs through the pain threshold to climb past his own house, where his mom smiles and waves from their small piazza as if she'd been waiting for him to appear. Then the hill steepens and he drops to the lowest gear as the road climbs through a maple grove on both sides, half the leaves already orange or blood-red. By the time it levels off it's like another culture, rust-bucket trailers and little wood shacks, most of them with junk cars on the lawn, piles of worn-out backwoods shit like ATVs, log splitters, busted snowmobiles, while their own sons are in-country dropping and perishing for the fuel to run those things. They are the warriors of the earth up here; they take their rifles apart Sunday mornings and lay the parts out on the workbench while the women dress up for church. They were soldiers and their kids are soldiers and yellow ribbons hang like September apples from the trees.

The bike's in top gear now, his legs are unwinding and he's catching his breath again after the hill. He's cruising past some farmer's field thinking if you took a headshot from one of those windows, you'd hear the discharge just before the round hit you; but in his case it would be silent as an arrow. He's not afraid of it; he has no family to protect, just one more lost vet on the border of here and oblivion, no preference for this side or the other, cycling through that space with the spokes of time.

Then suddenly a mailbox with a bullet hole through it, no name or number, in front of a beat-up double-wide. It makes him cross to the left lane. Anything could be in that rusted box with some redneck jihadi behind the curtains of his trailer window, a remote detonator in his hand. There didn't used to be any but now they're everywhere, they're tuned in to Al Jazeera and waiting like time bombs in their sleeper cells. But who was the motherfucker that wasted the Humvee? He tries every hour of every day but he can't remember, just Moby throwing the Mr. Goodbars and then the hospital with his skull on fire and his capillaries clogged with drugs.

He's cruising at maybe twelve miles an hour through the friction-less air when out of nowhere there's a streak of dark fur like a Scud missile incoming at leg height across the road which he tries to kick at but the bar grips twist out of his hands and he's down hard on the right side, head flat against the roadway, leg under the chainwheel and the bicycle on top. It is a big black German shepherd with its mouth opening and closing but not making a fucking sound. The dog's over the bike and his leg's pinned under the rear wheel. It thinks it has him cornered and trapped and it's pointlessly barking while it waits for that cocksucker to come out. He tries shouting *back* and *heel* but even an animal can't understand him and the dog has its eye on his right arm, just the distraction he wants because his left is going for the Ka-Bar and it's very easy to slip it out so he can't see it. Just as the dog goes to lunge, the Ka-Bar comes down as he was trained and it's instantly jammed to the thumb guard in the animal's black hairy spine just before its jaws could break his arm.

For a moment he holds the dog still with the Ka-Bar in its back like a tank control, then he jerks the knife out and the dog limps homeward a lot slower than it arrived. It's lost all interest in defending its territory and when he looks up again it's out of sight, but there's a bright trail of blood marking its retreat. The bike's in a pretzel twist; he spins the handlebars 180 degrees and it straightens out. He threads the chain back on both sprockets and lifts the rear wheel so he can crank it and believe it or not, it spins. Mountain bikes are built to descend like wild goats, crash into trees, and keep going. Which he does himself, moving on now past that obstacle, toward Mount Amatuck State Park where there are no houses or unleashed dogs. He's waxed the enemy both distant and close range but never used a knife on a living thing. He's kicked Flicka and now stabbed a shepherd, and each time the anger blinded his vision like a flamethrower.

The adrenaline and canine stench recede in the green hills with the sea view opening up before him as the park road ascends. The infinite parched desert makes people crazy, psychopath Arabs in their eternal Sandbox with grenade launchers under their prayer robes, stopping to face the oil fields of Saudi Arabia five times a day, slitting each other's throats over Muhammad's uncle a thousand years ago, not to mention the Jews and the infidels, mad fucking Ayatollahs severing people's hands, Taliban drug addicts blowing up statues and sawing girls' heads off in soccer stadiums. It's not their fault; they're born into a place without water where the sun parches everything out of them but the rage of God. Fast for a month, then fly a plane into a high-rise packed with three thousand human souls. Even our guys caught it in the FOB; you'd hear a scream in the night, some poor son of a bitch with a sand nightmare till they shoot him up with sedative and ship him to Kuwait. They are the Earth's deepest believers and death is what they believe in. Their calls to prayer were answered by Ramos and Dupuy.

The chain grease on his hands is streaked with dog blood. The scalpel-sharp Ka-Bar went right through the marrow of its spinal cord. He stops his bike here at the park sign where five Belted Galloways crop the September grass and beyond them the ocean is laced with white fire from the afternoon sun. He tries to recover his hatred for the black shepherd coming out at him but he can't, it's lost in the cattle and the green hayfield already misty from the cooling air. It comes and goes, but in the desert it never stops, the people are made of it like those twisted sculptures in the middle of fucking nowhere that the sandstorms make. To live in such a place must be like being deaf, generations of deafness, till the only voice comes from inside and you can't tell if it's Allah or the Other One.

He could have stayed with Brenda in the blue tent of marriage for all time, but now he's free. He's cranked past the dog and the trailers and a thousand feet above the village, the far ocean below him, its distant boundary etched sharp as the razor line separating death and life. The hadjis believe the world is flat, but if they ever climbed to this altitude with their eyes open, the long curvature of the horizon would declare the truth. A powerful south wind rises and bends the trees over, bringing pure air created so far out at sea that it contains no breath of any living thing. He gets back on the bike and takes the left fork up the summit road, then shifts to the hiking trail and drops into the lowest of twenty-four gears as the climb angle sharpens and the fork springs flex over the rocky ground. It's thick spruce trees for a while, then at the peak the view opens again in a panorama of the windswept bay and islands, as it did in the Cessna. He picks out Amber with the small southern islet that forms its protected cove, uninhabited as in the days before human beings when there was as yet no evil mutation on Earth.

He turns the bike around to plunge down the steep trail as the front wheel bounces off rocks, brakes barely holding on the soft needly surface, overgrabbing on granite shelf. He rode this as a kid on the bare margin of control, a boundary lethal at its outer edge. Lacking the cues of sound it would be easy to let go, one bounce into irreversible free fall, but he brakes down, pulls back from it. This isn't the time and place. Not yet.

Back on the pavement he slips the chainwheel into high for the long descent to town, luckily by a different road so he won't have to pass the bloody dog. It's almost like flight when he stops pedaling and gives the bike over to gravity, his balance still shaky at that speed, but he actually passes a little Mini Cooper with the top down and two senior citizens driving slow and gazing at the cows.

He doesn't touch the brakes till the Connellan Lane cutover that forks into Bell Street and pretty soon there's his house, a police car out front with its blue light flashing, an olive-drab Ford Escape in the driveway with US government plates. Everything tells him the dog didn't pull through.

6

They're burying the dead shepherd only it's in Samarra and its body is hairless so its black venous skin is like Dupuy's. The spades are handled by Ramos and Sergeant Trefethen, and there's a girl holding a camera so you can't see her face and the grave opening is the color of an untreated wound. In this dream as in every one of them he can hear and speak perfectly and the girl's whispering *Don't bury it, it's still alive; look, its eyes are open*, and a low rasping growl escapes its throat.

He wakes in a bed of sweat and strips off his underwear so he can feel the reality of the sheets. He fights going back to sleep but it envelops him like the blind hood of an assassin and drags him down. Now he's in Abu Ghraib where the insurgents are harvesting organs from the backs of a long line of living soldiers till they come to Brenda Campion, who has a huge swollen belly under her uniform and they turn her over and instead of a kidney they cut a child out and throw it in this enclosure where the street pigs live. Sleep is a prison of no escape till the sun comes and he wakes again wet and breathing as if brought up from the black Euphrates.

He went to bed before sunset to get away from the extreme suck that came down over the dog. His VA minder Dr. Borque showed up at the house, which was no sacrifice because he lives on the Ledgeport waterfront only a mile away. Along with Officer Bassett, who used to be an ordinary town cop but now flashes a detective's badge under his windbreaker. They already had three laptops lined up on the coffee table with Dr. Borque on one, his parents on another, and the third for him. His father wrote some stuff with his slow one-finger pace like carving letters into a headstone one after the other, keying in SELF-DEFENSE and WHAT SOLDIERS ARE TRAINED TO DO WHEN ATTACKED while his mother nodded semi-approval with her lips tightened into a straight line. Before long they stopped typing and mouthed words among themselves as if he were absent from the room, like grown-ups talking about a sick child while the kid lies there listening, only this child has centered his laser sight on a man's neck and blown the head off like shooting a powerline insulator. His old man served the Vietnam years plying his trade in Georgia where they sandblast the military headstones; Officer Bassett's a small-town cop who has never used lethal force; and Dr. Borque's taken no one's life unless you count ODs and suicides. If you're the only guy in a room that's deliberately waxed someone, it's worse than not hearing; it's like you're of a different creation, an animal that belongs off somewhere to itself.

At one point they all excused themselves and went into another room to negotiate, and he figured they'd be dragging him to the locked wing of the VA, if not to jail. He thought about making a break for it through the parlor entrance that no one ever used, but when they came back smiling it looked like it would be limited to house arrest.

The cop wrote, THIS TOWN IS HELL ON ANIMAL CRUELTY. GUY CLAIMS IT JUST BARKED. RECOGNIZED NICK FROM THE PAPER.

His father wrote, CRUELTY? IT WAS SELF-DEFENSE. DOG SHOULD HAVE BEEN CHAINED.

Dr. Borque wrote, TAKE YOUR CELEXA 20MG MORNING AND EVENING. ONE ONLY. YOU CAN DROP BY THE VA NEXT WEEK. WE'LL ADJUST THE DOSAGE OR MAYBE TRY SOME OTHER MEDS.

Translation: *Drop by the VA and we'll never let you out.*

Then Borque and Bassett left in their separate vehicles and he was safe—safe for a while, anyway—but who knows when they'll return or what the next step will be.

His parents looked grim during dinner, like they knew something their son did not. He's not sure whose side they're on; his dad seemed to defend him, but they could change at any minute and turn him over to the authorities. A mental institution. *Asylum.* Fucked up word. Sounded like a place to rest when it was just another trap.

He went to bed early thinking he'd better skip the planning stage and make his escape while he still had freedom of movement, if in fact he still did. Next day, for sure, they could be tooling him back to the VA in plastic cuffs. First he thought about spending a couple of days on Amber Island, see if his dreams would let him alone out there. Now he's thinking that if the island's unoccupied, maybe he'll stay awhile. There's no limit to the suck that might develop over the dog, which was justified homicide because the thing came out at him like an RPG with lethal intent. Only in stateside America would they lock a guy down for self-defense who has put his life on the line for his country.

He woke between one dream and the next and opened Mr. Fischer's book: "Where I Lived, and What I Lived For." *I went in the woods to live deliberately.* No one to hassle him, and no dogs. 'Course you couldn't just build a cabin in the woods anymore; it wouldn't get past the zoning board. An uninhabited island would be different, like going back to Henry's day when freedom still meant something. You could live deliberately out there, unhassled, one step at a time, as if learning to walk again.

Simplify, simplify. He'll throw some stuff into his long army duffel and clear out of the house before they wake. He gets up and hits the floor for a quick twenty on his fingertips, unsheathes the Ka-Bar, and takes it to the upstairs bathroom to scrub the dog blood off. His spare knife goes into the bag, then he looks at his three guns to pick the shortest, which is the Winchester lever-action .30-30. Maybe not an M16, but it's serviceable protection with a nice comfortable feel, and he's got two boxes of cartridges with twenty-four rounds each.

He double-wraps it in a green contractor bag. It's a tight fit, but the worn canvas duffel stretches to receive it on the diagonal. No tent this time; it would be spotted, and he wants to stay concealed. When he and Mr. F flew over the island he saw the old sheepherder's shack at the north end, roof rotted through. If nobody is living there, that's where he's going to try.

Henry D went to his cabin on July 4—*by accident*, he writes. Mr. F told them there are no accidents in writing, so he must have intentionally chosen to start on his nation's birthday. Then he stops cold with his hand deep in his closet and realizes it's September 10, 2006. He'll wake up on Amber Island on the date of an explosion so loud it could split a man's eardrums five years after the event. On his long desert convoys he'd imagine Mohamed Atta in the pilot's seat, the moment before he hit the tower, his heart bursting with black-blooded Arab hatred and the joy of death. He'd never given Muslims a moment's thought till they weaponized airliners and invaded the United States; now they could waste the whole population of Iraq and torch their oil wells like the Last Fucking Judgment and it would not cover reparation for that flight. The guys he worked with at Davis Stonecraft used to sit in Travis's basement and play the 9/11 tape with the sound off, then in reverse so the planes would back out as the flames sucked down into the building and the people sprang back up to their office windows like grasshoppers. Then they'd crash it again till they got tired of it and they'd play Texas Hold'em for Saddam's body parts. For three years he replayed that image on his computer screen, trying to purge it from his system, but it would not diminish till he went to the recruiting office and signed up.

He packs the duffel with his camouflage hooded field jacket and combat boots, a few socks and boxers, a carton of Camels, a collapsible water jug, what was left of his old stash with some Zig-Zags, stove matches, Henry's book, and a flashlight to read with as long as the batteries hold out. Henry knew all about birds, so he finds a little paperbound bird guide from his mom's kitchen bookshelf, though it doesn't appear to have recipes; and while he's in there he grabs one called *A Foraging Vacation* with plant lore for eating off the land. He won't need the old hurricane lamp yet; maybe later when the nights get long. Tuna fish, Spam, maraschino cherries, Hormel chili, Dinty Moore Stew, B&M Baked Beans, canned Bartlett pears, deviled ham, Vienna sausages, corned beef hash, canned pumpkin, applesauce, featherweight sleeping bag, Ultra Soft two-ply toilet paper. She's got her kitchen equipped for the end times when the poles melt and seawater comes up Bell Street like the Flood. She's not going to miss this three-pound sack of rice. Henry D grew his own food but he didn't start out in mid-September.

He pats his pocket for the Dexedrine bottle but it's still in his drawer upstairs. He left the desert with a habit like everyone else. He took one before the Cessna flight and before the bike ride with the dog. He could use one on the row out with the wide empty ocean so near on every side. He wonders what they took in Henry's day. Peters was right; he must have been on something to lie in a boat's hull for five hours staring at the sky. Hashish and opium from the China trade. He wants it but he doesn't need it. If he can leave everything else behind he can leave that. He takes the half-empty bottle of Jim Beam which he would have killed anyway with his dad in the next couple of evenings, playing cribbage and reading the closed captions of *NYPD Blue*.

Sundays his mom usually sleeps in till church time, but his father's an early bird, so Nick has to keep moving. He scrawls a quick note on one of the yellow pads, so they won't start a manhunt and put the dogs on his trail.

OUT TO AMBER

Taking just a few things
Simplify simplify
Thanx,
Nick

For his mom he adds *Love* before his signature, though he's not sure what it means, if anything, in a degraded world. He leaves his watch on the note as a paperweight. He won't be needing the time of day out there.

He sneaks the duffel down the basement stairs to leave through the cellar bulkhead so they won't hear. On the way out he hits up his dad's basement toolbox for a few spares: hammer and pliers, hacksaw blade, handline from the fishing box, roll of duct tape, the olive-drab compass they used on hunting trips, and a fistful of two-inch nails. Henry spent $3.90 on nails, which must have bought thousands of them in those days. Duct tape was not yet invented; there's not enough room anyway, and he puts it back.

When he reaches the sidewalk and looks up, their window is still dark. No cars are moving on Bell Street and behind him the half moon is about to sink down behind the profile of Mount Amatuck. The duffel outweighs a body bag but it sits solid over his right shoulder, thanks to the rifle inside that keeps it stiff. Downhill over the Ledgeport rooftops the sky's just getting light, a bleached yellow-gray the same color as the two skinless pears on the Del Monte can. He can recall the exact sounds of this hour from the cemetery of his hearing: chatter of street sparrows, black-faced red cardinal that whistled way before it was light enough to see it, foghorn on the breakwater, Catholic church bells tolling for early mass. Memories of sound surround each visible object like a pulsating shimmer in the air.

In the empty park where the dancers and amps were, a couple of white gulls pick at the leftovers while a third throws its head back and opens its mouth wide in a voiceless screech. Birds used to wake him but now it's thousand-decibel nightmares in which his ears spurt blood. It's light enough to see the car ferry waiting at its green steel pier and, down through the chain-link, the float where his dory has hopefully finished swelling up. It looks at first like the marina has fenced him out, but the padlock's at ease with its hook, just tucked into the hasp. He slips through and there's the gray dory floating proud and dry. Time to haul ass; people are up and they can see. If his folks find his empty bed they'll call Borque and Bassett and the blue strobes will start flashing on the waterfront. Beyond the breakwater lighthouse there's a wall of white fog and if he can make it that far he won't be seen.

He lays the duffel gently on the dory's stern seat, undoes the lines holding it to the float, and pushes off into the growing light, no time to lose. His own weight in front balances his gear and the freshly painted gray oars slide easily forward along the floorboard. He hammers the pins in place with the butt of his Ka-Bar, centers the oars on their leather collars, leans forward, and submerges their blades in water that's black as night and brimming with phosphorescence like the Milky Way. With the first stroke his course alters from random drift to purposeful escape. His eyes face the waking shoreline as his back strains forward into the unknown. Soon as he rounds the breakwater he gets out his dad's compass and sets the course needle to NE, diagonally across the ship channel toward an invisible island on the other side. Muscles kick in that have been sleeping all their lives and his hands are already chafing from the unsanded grips. Back on the waterfront the cops, lights flashing, have pulled to the terminal and departed, maybe looking for a fugitive from his own existence, maybe for someone else.

The fog coils its thick fingers around the boat, up from the water and down out of the air. A seal pokes up its helmet like a sentry between this world and the other, its eyes following him as he rows past, then the fog dissolves the world behind him and he's safe inside. The fog and water and the dory and its occupant are made of one colorless blind material and every dimension is the same. He stops pulling and lets the oars rest between their wooden pins. It's quieter than death within the fogbank despite the breakwater whistle that must be right on top of him. He places his watch cap over the compass and rows through the wet air until he has no idea where he's at or what his direction is. Henry's voice speaks from the bow behind him. *Not till we are lost, do we begin to find ourselves.*

The shock of a gull's whiteness pierces the curtain, then dissolves, and the world's once again formed from the same color, as in the beginning before the separation of sky from sea. His wake disturbs the glasslike surface for a few seconds, then all trace of his passage disappears. A black shag enters his tiny circle of vision, making a low-altitude flight just inches from the water, then a green bell buoy appears out of nowhere, towering huge and silent as a house. White lettering of "PB" on one side. He has to jam his right oar in the water to keep from hitting it. Only now does the deep ocean swell grow visible as it lowers and lifts this buoy whose bronze hammers noiselessly strike the central bell. His spinal cord reads its vibrations through the wooden hull. He eases up to its gently heaving side and ties the bow rope onto the mooring ring, and with chafed and blistering hands hauls himself up the steel rungs of the buoy. He stands on the rounded base and leans his spine on the green metal frame so the bell enters his nervous system directly, and though he can't hear a syllable, he sings Brenda's favorite verse from Def Leppard's "Pour Some Sugar on Me,"

> *I wanna be your hero*
> *I'll be a trick of the light*
> *I wanna be your hero*
> *I'll be your heat in the nite*

They're in the Humvee again and Dupuy's throwing candies, then suddenly he rotates the Deuce .50 and waxes a pickup full of ragheads that ran a checkpoint. Doors open, people crawl screaming across the sand. Here, in the middle of the ocean, one body appears blown open with a cavity like a Thanksgiving turkey. He almost falls into the dory, draws it close to the buoy to untie the painter, uncovers the compass, and pulls for a solid hour straight NE, the fog closing behind him as he rows. The only truth comes from a quivering needle attuned to the Earth's iron core.

He must be in the shipping lane by now. He remembers the super-tanker they watched from the airplane, fucking thing could appear out of the pea soup blasting its foghorn and sink a wooden rowboat anonymous to their radar and no one would ever know. It would be nothing to the crew a hundred feet over the water and, Nick realizes, it would be nothing to him either. Time would keep going like a thousand-foot fuel carrier and nobody would hear a sound, blood-streaked Arab oil from the Strait of Hormuz running down everything in its path. The college guy Evans kept saying Saddam Hussein was a fucking pretext, there were no weapons of mass destruction and there never were, it was all petroleum; but Evans never understood the necessity of revenge. After three thousand sacrificed in the Twin Towers, every hadj killed was eye-for-eye justice in a just cause—only why did they have to take Dupuy?

The flesh of his palms has scraped off nearly to the bone when the fog lifts like an eye opening on the granite shore. He's coming abreast of the field where he camped with Brenda, then a dense spruce forest that tapers northward to the island's tip. It's an easy tideswept pull around the northern point and there's a small cobble beach interrupting the wall of sloping bronze-tinted granite shelves, with the old vacant sheepherder's shanty above it, windows shot through with buckshot holes, roof half caved in. His burst blisters have stained the oar handles a deep vascular red; he stops rowing to plunge his hands in salt water and drown the pain. He turns the dory 180 degrees and with the last layer of flesh on his palms and fingers he plows through a cluster of sea ducks that could be a source of protein if he had a bird gun, then grounds out on a runway of round stones.

Beside the cobble beach is a deep tide pool only half-penetrated by sunlight; he lies down full length on its sloping granite rim to soak his hands. A brief flash of shadow darkens the surface for an instant as a huge-winged blue heron flaps over to light on long jointed legs at another pool less than twenty feet off. He shows no fear of the invader as he swallows a fish headfirst, then throws his neck back so you can see it swimming down his throat. This is his territory; he has a snake's neck, he's fished in this tide pool for a thousand years.

Nick digs out an exposed tree root on the shoreline to secure the dory, then picks his way over seaweed-covered rocks to the neglected and rotten-down structure that from the air seemed like a feasible shelter. The door's just swaying on its hinges so he walks right in. It would almost be better to find someone living here than see a good cabin in such fubar shape. Squatters have come and gone, duck hunters and fishermen: empty beer bottles, twelve-gauge shells, a ragged maroon-stained mattress that looks like someone was repeatedly stabbed on it and left to die. The big rain found its way in here and left it with the dank humidity of a swamp.

He hauls the sodden mattress out on the slanted porch; he'll sleep on the plank bench underneath. The ripped-out roof section looks like a tree limb might have fallen on it, with an old half roll of tar paper sitting directly beneath, which Allah dropped right through the opening for the repair. Half of the windowpanes are missing, filled in with copper screening oxidized to a green crust that's more opaque than the antique swirled glass. He'll scavenge the island for materials, seal this place up and save the floorboards before they rot. The most human object in the place is a broom with the handle split and duct-taped and the bristles worn diagonally from longtime use. He sweeps the broken glass down into a flooring hole, then clears the wild turds out of a corner where an animal's been in residence, but not anymore. The occupier has arrived.

He pulls the carbine out of the duffel and checks for seawater corrosion but the 5-mil contractor bag has kept it clean and dry. He opens the chamber, blows the dust out, and loads six hollow-points that could drop a deer on the other end of the island and give him a winter's meat. Henry slaughtered a woodchuck once, which Mr. F underlined, but the weapon was not described.

There's a couple of stew pots and an old woodstove rusted from being under the roof hole but the pipe is galvanized and the stove can be cleaned up and made to work. The whole place is waterlogged from one rain after another plus constant fog, and though it's not cold a fire would dry it out. There's fuel enough in scrap wood around the room. He gets the matches out and starts it going with the Hormel chili in the smaller stew pot. Soon he's swept the porcupine shit off the old table and found a corroded spoon and the chili is simmering on the stove. People have come before him, the sheepherder from the farming days then hunters and clamdiggers after that. Under the plank bed somebody left a bunch of *Playboys* that are so mildewed and rotten the models have congealed into a single flesh-colored wad, also an ax which is rusted but usable, and a big beat-up railroad lantern you could eat and possibly read by but nothing to burn in it. Kerosene goes on the list: entitlement for liberating the oil fields.

He has to find planks to support the roofing and some kind of source for his water jug. He makes a small woodpile beside the stove and away from the roof hole so it will start to dry. He can pull roof boards from the old tent platforms where he camped with Brenda in the middle of the island, near the overgrown ruins of the quarry dorm where his grandfather lived as an apprentice stonecutter, just off the boat and younger than Nick is now. It would be good to have even a sliver of a plank the old man had walked on, or slept on, maybe, as a young guy lonely in a new country where he couldn't understand a word.

He rips some fabric off the old mattress to bind up his palm blisters and sets out in the direction of their camping spot. Behind the cabin there's an open clearing for a couple of hundred feet, then the ruts of an overgrown woods road through dense old-growth spruce trunks where the sun streams through foliage to spackle the trail with light. Layers of dead limbs ascend like a standing boneyard toward the living green canopy above. It's still slightly misty in here so the sunlight comes down in visible shafts illuminating insects at all levels of the air. He tenses and hits the ground when a partridge silently rockets into the air almost from underfoot, then waits, flattened, till he realizes where he is. He'll bring the bird gun if he ever goes home again.

The dark cool conifers open to a sundrenched island field as the path slopes upward, bordered by clumps of blue asters and golden late-summer vegetation cropped close as if mowed or hayed. Suddenly it's last August again and Brenda's beside him on the old tent platform passing a smoke back and forth till they lose all sense of time and it could be another dimension as well as now. They unpack the nylon tent and thread the stiff fiberglass arches into their nylon sleeves, then lie in its blue interior looking across the ship channel toward Ledgeport and the hills beyond. They clean the sleek mackerel they caught on the boat trip and fry them in bacon fat for dinner, then lie there naked and toke with the door zipped tight so every breath they draw is another hit. They visualize a future with their smallest fingers entwined because those are the only parts that can still move. He tells her of Nonno Guido and the sixty Italians who sliced raw granite from the quarry walls and polished it to the sheen of Carrera marble.

She asks, "Who owns it now?"

"Some rich architect from Massachusetts. My grandfather knew him. They were friends. He used to take me here. The whole family lived in canvas tents. It looked like an encampment from the Civil War."

"If he's an architect, why doesn't he build a house? I would. I wouldn't mind having a house out here, just us." She sits closer and cradles her head against his shoulder and for a moment it all seems permanent, but it's as fraudulent as a dream.

Two insurgents in a white Toyota pickup peel through an intersection and Ramos says "Chase the motherfuckers," so they keep on their tail till they dodge into a tight alley and he cuts in there behind them with the Humvee. When the driver jumps out, yelling, Dupuy wheels the .50 on him and fires a burst that goes through him and craters the pavement underneath. The impact tears his robe off and reveals the long desert body already thin as death from living off hatred and prayer. He tries to purge it by the thought of Brenda in the half-zipped sleeping bag, but still there's the dead hadji, eyes staring open, as if through the tent window, watching everything they do.

He stands there alone and sweating in the yellow field. An old man limps past holding a cane in one hand with his other hand on the shoulder of a little boy, no more than seven or eight, and they continue that way, one gently leaning on the other, over the top of this field to the old quarry where he used to work. The pit's now a rockbound pond thick as guacamole with green frogspawn and iridescent slime, with an old rusted crane still dangling a large squared-off granite block that's hung there since his grandfather was twenty-three years old. He dips his bandaged palms in water capped with gelatinous pond scum and warmed by the late-summer sun. It feels like the exact center of the island, the hollow of its stone heart brimming from a thousand rainstorms, huge cubic rock suspended like time itself. The field slopes gradually upward toward an old foundation barely visible above the grass, remains of the boardinghouse where the Italian quarrymen lived.

On one of the cornerstones Nonno Guido sits down to rest his leg; the kid paces out the buried rectangle: a three-story house where twenty men lived on each floor. "Five in a room," the old man says, "all at the supper table like sixty pigs. The Depression comes, no pay, everyone disappears for New York. All but me. Then the crazy man, *pazzo*, burns it down. They find him hanging in there after the fire, by a rope."

"Was he a stoneworker, Nonno?"

"No, that was after the quarry closed. He was the shepherd that lived in the old cabin by the shore."

"Nonno, did the animals burn too?"

"No, Nico. The sheep went free."

They peer into the shallow wellspring where the working men drank. He dips a rusted pail to raise up water he can scoop out with his cupped hands. He cups for himself and cups again to hold against the old man's lips, who drinks and stoops and leans his left arm again on the boy's shoulders and they walk back to where Peter Colonna's waiting at the float.

Now the well's hidden by alder saplings with the top course of its stone circle almost gone. He pries up a plywood cover by no means old and it seems dark and dry, then as his eyes dilate, there's freshwater two or three feet down with mosquitoes hovering and a couple of Jesus beetles skimming the surface. He'd like to try it but there's nothing to reach down with. His grandfather dipped and tasted as a young kid, not even twenty when he came. He looked out from here across to the small city that once had a Catholic church and a whorehouse, which is now just an old ladies' nursing home. He tries to imagine Nonno Guido among the hookers with his faraway moist eyes that seemed to see past this life to another. He too was a young guy with the pressures of seed and hunger; the ninety-year-old ladies on the nursing home sunporch were once for sale.

He senses something at his back, low down and moving, dog possibly, and spins around fast, wishing he'd taken the carbine. He breaks out laughing at a black-faced sheep, unshorn and shaggy as a yak, that spooks and takes off into a cedar swamp. The shepherd killed himself, the flock went feral; must be a hardscrabble life, chewing through snow and ice for a few blades of grass. He follows after it. The low, shit-studded sheep path through a dense cedar brake forces him into a four-legged crouch, following the sheep track on his knuckles like an orangutan. He almost steps on a mass of spherical chocolate-green sheep turds, then the path stops as the thicket abruptly opens on a small gravel ravine that might have run serious water in another time when floods and glaciers savaged the Earth, but now it's a barely visible trickle coming down from the well source, rust-streaked but maybe drinkable winter or summer by the flock. There is a high-water line of leaves and branches so it must have flooded again over the past week.

He takes off the old mattress-strip bandages and cups his hands to taste. Though thick with iron oxide it feels so cool after the sweaty and brambly passage that he lies down slantwise on the bank, buries his face in it, and drinks. It's as if something led him directly from the broiling homicidal desert to this place, all things intervening just the waystations of a dream. He takes off his camo jacket to slake the back of his neck and sluice his arms up to the shoulders in the cold mineral purity of its source.

The stream stops and runs underground at a huge blowdown spruce whose upright and tangled root system was ripped out of the gravel bank like an impacted tooth. The roots reach three or four meters into the air, grasping at earth and stones as if alive. Its fall tore out a raw crater in the streambank, streaked with a dense rust color from the ferric soil. It's still moist from the big rain which must have eroded the topsoil so the exposed gravel bank bleeds out like a bayonet wound. It's veined with packed broken mussel and whelk shells as if it had been a clam flat in another time. The sea level rose over this whole coast in the past and they say it will come again by our own hand. When he pulls at one of these shell layers it flakes off and slides down the embankment like the remains of a clambake or the dumpster behind an oyster bar.

The cool moist russet-tinted earth soothes his raw palms as he cups and wedges his fingers into the gravel bluff, then they strike something hard and can't go further, probably a stone. He unstraps his knife to clear away the clamshells and dig it out, then gets his fingers around it and gently pulls. An elongated shape comes out the size and shape of a large razor clam and coated with packed earth. He dampens one of his bandages in the groundwater at his feet and rubs the soil off. It's not red granite but a local green chlorite slate he recognizes because at Davis Stonecraft they slice and polish it for countertops. Its shape seems honed and tapered by natural erosion and abrasion, but when he rubs it cleaner its texture seems deliberately worked, tapering to a rough point at one end and one edge defined and knapped like a distant ancestor of his combat blade. As a stoneworker himself he senses the touch and presence of someone of his own vocation.

He tries the edge on the thin sensitive skin on the back of his hand. A little work with an oilstone and it could shave through the sparse wiry hairs to the veins beneath. One side of the blade is smeared with a red pigment that does not rub off, so it looks like a murder weapon or a killing point, for food or defense against violation or disrespect. Under the red coating it looks like an X has been gouged and stained into the handle like the first letter of a written tongue. His history teacher Ms. Barron mentioned a race of prehistoric natives on Dix Island with their tools dyed red as if dipped in blood, and a cemetery of red-ochred bones from ice-age aboriginal humans that were seven feet tall. Ms. B could get carried away by history, but this thing's a serious weapon that could have stood up to his Ka-Bar blade. It feels like a message and talisman from the first inhabitants. If they could live here unhoused under the breath of mile-high glaciers, he can survive in a wood-heated cabin with a climate that's growing warmer every year.

He reaches in even deeper with his blistered hands. Sharp shards and shell edges mix with the fine gravel as his own blood mixes with the hematite of the earth. Quahog shells, unbroken whelk shells, half-formed mineral fragments stained with the same crimson as if the only color they knew came from the Earth's dense iron heart, no different from war blood and the blood of homicide. Every weapon people have ever conceived for game animals has been turned on their own kind.

His fingertips find and carefully encircle another object, this one softer than stone with sharp delicate points. He draws it slowly back through the tunnel his arm made. It's as long as the slate blade but thicker and lighter, not rock but some kind of bone, with the tip dulled from usage or erosion or just time. He dampens his bandage in the rusty flow and wipes it off: a point with six angled barbs on one side in a row, not enough teeth to be a saw, but it would bury itself in flesh and not pull out.

He stands up to stretch and his eyes are level with the top of the exposed bank. This is an island you can see from the bleachers of the high school football field. Didn't Ms. Barron know these things were here? A field trip might have broken the deathlike monotony of history with every human century replaying the same dumb blunders and mistakes, while layers of time and vegetation buried an offshore community that once hunted and fought and prepared food using these tools. The huge spreading base of this spruce growing over the accretion of fallen and rotted trees before it must have provided sanctuary and concealment. Then it came down, maybe over the winter when he was deployed or even the ocean gale he saw from Mount Amatuck.

He can't imagine the shriek of the windstorm or the rending of trunk and branches as it tore from the streambank like a deep-rooted tusk or molar, followed by the rains of Ernesto eroding the surface off. Nobody seems to live here on Amber Island, no human presence or habitation, just the rotting tent platforms and the abandoned shack; he may be the first to have reached this spot since it was unearthed by the wind and rain. He came here driven by lost instinct and coincidence of time, but also a sense of intention, as if he'd been walking or rowing toward it all his life. What did Henry say? *Speech is for the hard of hearing.* Maybe it's the privilege of silence to witness the unspoken and unheard.

With the stone blade and barbed point wrapped in the two bandages, he works his way down the stream cut to the red-stained shore. He walks north along a sloping granite shelf that turns pale amber, then light gray as he rounds the tip of the island, and there's his cabin and his tethered dory floating on the tide.

7

He's just dug Dupuy and Ramos out of the shell bank, now he's trying to crawl into the vacant grave. They're yelling *Get your ass out of there, it's going to blow*, then the determined sound of an animal trying to chew open its old passage through the roof. Brenda Campion is a DJ on the army channel playing Radiohead: *You broke another mirror; you're turning into something you are not.* He cranes his head around trying to see her but all he can do is hear. Then he's entering a beaded Samarra doorway and when his eyes adjust to the cave light he sees Ramos and Williams standing there holding their rifles with the furniture around in broken pieces, the kicked-in TV still smoking, and there on the sand floor is a whole family sprawled like lost swimmers in a lake of blood.

He wakes up soaked in perspiration with his bunk slanted onto the floor and his head down in the foot of his sleeping bag, trying to reach his companions, but it's daybreak and they're disappearing at the speed of light. When he climbs out he grabs a Camel and maybe the smoke rasp in his throat says *Stay here, this side is the real one*, but how would you fucking know? There on the old sheepherder's table are the results of his three visits to the shell bank, which is all he's done besides patching the roof with tar paper and outhouse planks. He deepened his tunnel into the wall of ochred gravel and shell layers till his blisters reopened and smudged his own blood on the things he touched. He pulled out a two-foot-long spear-shaped object tapering to a point fine as a knitting needle. He'd seen the exact thing before, same length and shape, and that was over the bar of the Black Pearl Tavern on the Ledgeport waterfront. It was the beak of a huge lacquered gamefish mounted so fishermen could fantasize as they drank. Sailfish or marlin, fish from far offshore in the Gulf Stream, its spear glazed with red pigment as if from combat and laid to rest deep in the island soil.

He found what looked like a leg bone, brittle and half-decomposed, a few russet paint smears but mostly brown with decay. It could be a deer or coyote bone, or from a half-grown child. He once drove an M113 for a grave detail at one of Saddam's death pits where the Republican Guard had used lye to strip the bones. He cranked down the window and watched them load bleached, broken skeletons into the cargo bed, thinking *Good riddance—a trainload of them wouldn't repay for 9/11.* Then he saw one of them was an infant and someone said *Jesus, they're human.* He looked off into the distance and it was all desert, no reason or end to it, it just went on.

He groped back in there for one last item among the stone fragments and clots of hematite: a thin, slender shaft he could hardly touch for fear of snapping it, worming and wiggling it free from soil that had held it for a long time and did not want to give it up. This was a carved, hook-shaped bone, with a squared-off U-curve, wicked barbed tip, slim oval hole through the upper portion for the thread, the same shape and proportion of any hook you could buy at a saltwater bait shop, affirming the constancy of prey and predator throughout time.

With an unformed prayer or apology he inserted the fish beak back in its cavity and laid beside it the child's bone. Then he replaced the chlorite slate blade he had honed to a fine edge, since they may need protection in the underworld. He repacked and tamped the clay and mussel shells over the hole and the red seepage so no one trespassing there would ever know. He bouldered his way back to the cabin by the rocky shoreline, knowing the first owners of this island were not foreign mercenaries mining its granite core but those who had lived before history without compromise or reserve.

Hazed sunlight falls from his one sooty window onto the old table, the bone hook and the six-barbed point. He's borrowed them from time to have the physical evidence of their existence, and of his own. Their red stains are the color of life in the gray air, buried for centuries till a grave robber from the blind future violated their sleep like an invasive dream. One day in Samarra an insurgent took refuge in one of Saddam's museums and when they blew the door open with C-4 it revealed things from the Old Testament when Babylon ruled and the Israelites were in chains. Papyrus scriptures and tall painted vases depicting the slaughter of calves and goats, labeled "4000 BP."

When they returned the next day nothing was left but shattered glass cases and empty shelves. Who knows who looted the place that night, them or us; but it's not going to happen here. He'll fill in the whole root crater with a layer of fresh gravel and replant it with seedlings and vegetation from the forest floor. Never to be reopened or desecrated because no one except himself will know.

He came to this island as a refugee from injustice and within a day followed a stray sheep to these objects as if it had all been prewritten in some book, as the hadjis believe. He dreamed he would marry Brenda and have kids but the script was otherwise. You think you're writing it yourself but the words are on the page already, or in the paper itself like a watermark, sentence by sentence, your hand directed by something you can't see. He blows the coals in the woodstove and stuffs in a few twigs and scraps to warm the Dinty Moore stew in its can. The barbed spear point rests on the table while he eats, one eye on Henry's chapter, "Former Inhabitants." *I sometimes expected the Visitor who never comes.* Three days without seeing a human being except for the outlines of sailors and fishermen in passing boats and the red ghost of a bone from another time. If he stays up late enough, beyond midnight with no source of light, maybe the visitor will show up at the cabin window, looking in, invisible three-hundred-pound spirit the same exact color as the night.

He's staring out at the gray dawnlight whose vapor particles stream through his corroded window screen when the heron takes off abruptly and disappears into the perimeter of fog. A big cream-colored Boston Whaler with a radar mount emerges from nowhere in total silence and stops short. The boat tilts its twin outboards and coasts up on the small patch of cobblestones where his dory's beached.

His first thought is to hide the objects. He stashes the spear point and bone hook in an old wooden ammo box left by the duck hunters and slides it under the sill where the floor's rotted out, covers it with one of the outhouse planks. Huge-rooted trees have risen to conceal these people since their interment. He found them and now they're his responsibility. He has to shield them from the shame of excavation and display.

He swings the door open on its one hinge and steps out to watch his father and Mr. Fischer and climb out of the outboard like apparitions in the orange fog.

They both give him big smiles and hugs and a few words lipped grossly so they can be seen. They drag their Whaler next to the dory and put a small anchor out. It's got more shit aboard it than a Wal-Mart semi. His father unloads a brand-new Husqvarna chain saw plus an ax and shovel that still have the barcodes on their varnished handles, a hurricane lamp to replace his rusted one, two gallons of kerosene, a thick yellow legal pad, two cartons of Camels, and his .410 bird gun to back up the Winchester.

Direct from his mother comes an aluminum cooler packed with two jars of white chowder, the last of the sweet corn, and his brown fisherman's sweater topped with a strawberry pie on a glass plate wrapped in cling. The pie is as he preferred them as a young kid, with a layer of halved strawberries both above and beneath the thick hand-whipped cream that somehow survived the crossing.

He picks up the chain saw and shovel and follows the two men up the beach. When he gets up there Mr. Fischer's looking at his old ragged Thoreau book and smiling when he sees the pages are coming out and a couple of them are spiked to the wall with two-inch nails. His dad's knocking creosote from the stovepipe, examining the roof repair. They both look like they feel sorry for him in this forgotten shanty, but they have no idea of the revelation stashed under the cabin floor.

His dad gives him an envelope with his name on it in his mom's super-legible cursive hand. He has vowed not to live by time but he can't help looking at his father's watch as he takes her letter. Only 0700; he would have thought eight or more. But maybe it's a school day for Mr. Fischer; he's already late and probably has to get back.

His mom writes "Dear Nicolas" and "love" and "take care of yourself," as you'd expect; then comes the unexpected:

> *Mrs. Fletcher welcomes your stay on the island in memory of your grandfather Guido who was her late husband's old friend. As you know, Guido worked in the original quarry there. Mrs. Fletcher mentioned improvements to the island and hopes you can work on them, as well as serve as an informal caretaker while you are there. Her kindness provided the saw and tools, or her eagerness to get started on her project! They seem to be considering some kind of development after all these years of leaving nature to herself. She hopes you will start by clearing the spruce trees that have grown up on the high point of the open meadow above the old tent platforms. We think it generous of her to let you stay there, though of course we eagerly imagine you will return as it gets cold. You will find a place here always, in our home and hearts.*

Dr. Borque was startled to hear you left home, but I feel if that is where you want to be, he will go along. He has too many to care for as it is. He told me Maine has the second-highest casualty rate of any state. We are fortunate to have him as a neighbor and someone who takes an interest beyond the call of duty.

Dearest Nick, we so miss and love you and hope you will soon decide to return to the social world. You have so much to offer, and I know you could find Someone who would recognize and appreciate it as I do. I wish you would consider the surgery offered by the VA that would make you whole again as when you left us. It breaks my heart thinking you will go much longer without hearing my voice or your father's voice or the music you loved and lived by. I had a message from your lieutenant remembering your friends who were lost and mentioning three more, but he said he would not list their names unless you wished . . .

Her letter continues but he stops reading at this point. His father and Mr. Fischer are moving around outside his cabin, poking the rotten window and door sills and measuring the missing panes. Through the swirly and cracked old glass both of them seem to be back on the other side of a line or membrane through which those who have crossed over cannot return.

He writes his father a note on the yellow pad. *YOU TAKING OFF?*

WE HAVE TO, his father writes. *BACK TO WORK.*

CATCH A RIDE? Nick writes.

His dad bursts into a smile of misunderstanding that he quickly corrects.

NOT HOME. TOWN. TOW THE DORY, ROW BACK.

He'd never darkened the door of the Ledgeport Public Library in his life, but now he needs to know what he's unearthed from the gravel bank, as if those bloodstained tools and bones could tell him what happened in the desert and where he's supposed to go from here.

He waits for his father and Mr. F to leave the shack, then reaches under the floor plank and carefully rewraps the carved point before securing it in the buttoned inside pocket of his camo jacket. He joins them on the beach and they launch the dory and attach a towing line. Even with the heavy load dragging behind, the twin outboards churn up the four miles in twenty minutes by the dashboard clock. The world only exists as green blips and masses on the radar screen, then they're at the Ledgeport Marina, tying up.

Mr. F jumps into his Land Rover and he's off to class. Then his old man starts up the van and opens the passenger door for him as if it's a personal school bus to take him home. He waves him off. That would be the end of a freedom he's just beginning to understand, that began with the freedom from speech and could free him from time eventually, but not yet. For now he just touches the barbed spearhead in his pocket, whose tips have a decent edge despite their centuries in the earth.

Anonymous as a body double, he pulls up the hoodie under his camo jacket and walks down his city's one downtown street, from the marina to the yellow brick library at the other end. Under the half-turned maple branches the season's over and the town would be quiet now even if he could hear. Kids back in school and parents at their jobs, not consciously aware of who gave their lives for the liberty to work and learn.

He checks out the yellow street box of *Ledgeport Weekly Heralds*. His own face is gone from page one and they're already on to the next week's edition. The headline reads BUDDHISTS RELEASE 58 LOBSTERS. "We have paid market price and liberated them back to their underwater homes," says spokesman Gupta Rinpoche. Time goes on; Radiohead says *You'd kill yourself for recognition. Kill yourself to never ever stop.*

His headline felt like an obituary; people stared at him like the walking dead. Now he's incognito with his Taliban beard growth, watch cap pulled low under the deployed hoodie, wraparound shades: If you can't see maybe you won't be seen. Invisibility is freedom's uniform. The downside is not knowing what may be coming up on him from behind; he turns around every five seconds like a fugitive, but he makes it into the library unobserved.

Inside, he removes hood and sunglasses but keeps the cap down almost to his eyebrows. He can breathe easier in a library knowing he's not missing any sounds. On the street his brain aches trying to imagine what he doesn't hear. No one's in here anyway but an ancient librarian who could be one of the old hookers from his grandfather's day. He's in the basement kids' section where the chairs and tables are like toys. A wallboard with a big map on it says *IRAQ: WHO CAN TELL US WHERE IT IS?*

The old librarian stands, pulls last week's newspaper from beneath her desk, then smiles and hands his picture to him along with a pen. It didn't take long to penetrate his disguise. She points to his likeness, makes motions for him to write something under the headline. He signs his name and rank and she mouths "Thank you" and he pulls the cap even lower over his ears. He once shaved his head like everyone else in the hooch, but no more razors. The less he's recognized the better. He doesn't want to be what he was in his prior phase, dog-spooked warrior sealed in his attic room. He lives elsewhere and he's finding a home and ancestry out there. This is a city of strangers he's passing through.

The librarian takes her pen back and hands him a pencil stub and a yellow post-it but he can't recall what Ms. Barron called them, so he writes, *INDIANS,* though he's not referring to reservations or high-stakes bingo but free sovereign giants from the edge of time. He scratches that out and writes, *EARLY. BEFORE INDIANS.* She writes, *NATIVE AMERICANS?*

That's what you're supposed to call them and they deserve it, they came before we did, but the Thanksgiving Indians would have been like immigrants compared to his.

She leads him back past the Iraq map to a side room with one barred, narrow, eye-level casement window looking straight out onto the sidewalk, very dangerous; the dumbest improvised explosive could spray the room with glass slivers and leave you blind.

MCLANE HISTORY COLLECTION, the sign says. The librarian pulls out a chair in front of a computer terminal, bends down to type the password, then turns the seat over to Nick and leaves. He scrolls down till he finds PREHISTORIC SITES, then something stops him and he opens another screen. He needs to watch something else first—the attack on America that has made him an alien in his native town. He googles "9/11" and runs the clip, the first time since his return. Looking as small as a heat-seeking unmanned drone, the 737 cruises toward the second tower, bloody uniformed corpses with their throats slashed surround the hijacker taking the pilot's seat, the high-amperage word of Allah searing his brain cells like the electric chair. In the twenty-fourth story of the North Tower, an office worker like his mom looks up from her terminal at the oncoming nose cone and sees through the plane's tinted windshield her last glimpse of a human face.

He stops the program and squeezes his eyes shut but can't control the images: Dupuy Williams laughing with his false tooth like a gold coin in a pussy, that's what Ramos said, then he'd say *Bunch of retards in Maine*, and he's right, this state is clueless about evil; you could walk in here with a land mine and the librarian would tell you to deposit it in the book drop. He can feel Ramos's arm over his shoulder, his voice saying *Mohamed, Maine, that's where this dude is from.*

He googles "Mohamed Atta" and what does it come up with but his Last Will and Testament. What could he leave to anyone, childless hadj fanatic that watched porn all night, then slaughtered an aircraft crew and waxed three thousand noncombatants in a religious trance. He hits PRINT and three pages shoot out, which he folds into his hip pocket for another time. That's not what he's here for, but he needs to read them and he'll take them home.

He looks at one of the big new plastic-wrapped hardbound books on the table and there they are, right on the cover, tools like the grooved knife blade and barbed point. The book's called *The Maritime Archaics* and it's filled with illustrations of what he's found. He searches "Maritime Archaic" and gets back "The Lost Red Paint People."

> *They are a mystery because a once great people, thought to be Native Americans that lived 6,000 years ago, completely vanished from the historical record. The red ochre was used to mark their burial grounds, and the grave goods were buried with the dead. They were thought to be a highly advanced people, because of their beautiful craftsmanship and carving tools. They were also an excellent seafaring people, because there is proof of them actually fishing for swordfish. They thrived all across their lands for a thousand years, then they disappeared.*

They passed by Amber in their seagoing dugouts and chose it for the red color of its soil. They glazed their bodies and all possessions with red hematite for the blood that joined them, blood of killed mammals and swordfish and finally their own, mixed with the ferrous capillaries of the earth that still leach out of the island like a shrapnel wound. Ice-water currents took them over the horizon in prehistoric weather, knowing no more of the universe than this island and the open sea. Their bluewater gamefish would have outweighed the hollowed-out boat and all the hunters aboard. In the last days they interred each other in pits of iron oxide because they could no longer continue in a shrunken world. They must be the people Ms. Barron had spoken of, each man the height of a center in the NBA. A stream bank on Amber Island is their last will and testament; they left no trace of themselves in any human line.

When he looks up from the monitor to the casement window, he can only see the legs and feet of people passing outside the library, workers' legs in jeans and coveralls plus a few pale tourist legs in shorts and sandals, once in a while a high-heeled professional woman back from her coffee break. Now a cop passes in short pants on a red mountain bike, so you can just see the lower half of his sidearm. A black Lab scents him behind the window and strains at its leash, trying to get past the security bars. He can't remember any trouble with dogs before. He used to love them. Now they unstring him like a seizure.

He feels a shadow that makes his neck hairs rise; someone's in the room.

He wheels around quick to the doorway and it's neither a dog nor the librarian but a girl in a blue sweatshirt with a black Nikon camera around her neck that could easily be an IED. Suicide bombers often pose as photojournalists; the C-4 in their lens barrel then shreds everything in the room.

You can tell this woman is not what she looks like. The sweatshirt is too big for her and could be a disguise covering anything. Sunni women hide their nitroglycerine vests under their burqas; who would know what their sex was after they're blown apart? She does not look like a hadji, but when the females are on a mission they are free to discard their head shawls because their deeds cover them with honor and they will soon be dead. Nor does she have the Arab coloration, but she could be a collaborator or convert like the Shoe Bomber, Richard Reid. Brainwashed American students provide themselves to al-Qaeda for such use.

She takes a seat in a leather armchair beside the entrance, effectively blocking passage; there's no other escape. It was careless and unprofessional to allow himself to enter a room with barred windows and a single door. He minimizes the Red Paint website so it won't betray him, but she's already seen the harpoon point left carelessly beside the keyboard and her eyes follow his motions as he buttons it back into the inside pocket.

He prepares to rush past her to the exit and leave, but she breaks into a smile with symmetrical ivory teeth that could be as false as everything else. He's watching every motion now for hostile intent. She draws a black headscarf from her backpack and uses it to conceal the camera while she inserts the fake film canister full of Semtex. Too late to move, he ducks behind the big monitor and prepares for oblivion, but for some reason it fails to detonate. She moves off. He breathes in to a count of four, holds for five, breathes out for six. Square breathing. Clears the sweat from his forehead and, after a few minutes, turns his eyes back to the Red Paint site.

The screen pictures the same spear-point style he has in his cargo pocket, with backward-pointing barbs on either edge. It was carved from a swordfish "rostrum," which must be the technical word. The spear point would have been the tip of a harpoon. They used its own weapon to impale it, and they carved their fishhooks from its inner bones. He first makes sure the girl has not returned, then takes out the harpoon point just for a second for comparison to the *Maritime Archaics* book, a life-size illustration basically the same length and pattern as his own. When he reads that it's six thousand years old the point seems to gain temperature and he slips it back into his pocket so it won't burn his hand. He can't tell anyone. They'd strip and desecrate Amber Island same as they looted the Baath museums in Iraq. These are his people; in their extinction they keep a strict code of silence, like his own.

Now the girl is back pointing the camera again, first at the ship model on the opposite wall, then cunningly swiveling to aim it at

Nick himself, and though he could not stop an explosion he puts up both hands instinctively to protect his face.

She lowers the camera, blushes bright red, and smiles.

The enemy are known to unveil themselves to distract their victims, then they explode. He could disarm her, but the devices are set to go off on impact, so he pockets the harpoon point, turns and springs out of his chair, past her and through the door, speedwalking by the librarian who now has a few kids around one of the low tables, not quite running because he doesn't want to attract attention. He strides a block and a half down a sidewalk ablaze with sunlight, puts his shades on, and turns to watch the explosion, but it doesn't happen. He invaded her homeland and disrespected her belief; he was the only target of her revenge.

He sits down on a black wrought-iron bench outside the bank where his mom once worked, next to a gray-haired homeless guy who's occupied this station as long as he can remember, vet of some other war, so far back in history he's no longer aging as time goes past. He watches the girl leave the library with her small purple backpack slung over one shoulder and the camera still around her neck. All over the legs of her combat pants are pockets that could conceal anything. She's going up to a small salmon-colored Japanese SUV with a kayak on top that's the same shade of purple as her pack. It's a clever operation. She looks like any student or hippie with the sandals and straight brown hair, small serious face possibly once attractive now warped and shadowed by her unswerving intent. Her body is mostly covered but still she'd be arrested on the Arab street. Using that kayak she could attach limpet mines to a ship's hull at the waterline, trigger them from a distance and paddle away as a US Navy vessel went to the bottom. Of course if the camera bomb had gone off, she would have perished too. She has the fanatical mouth and eyes of a street martyr who has weaponized her existence and could have smoked them both, along with the librarian and all the kids and books; he wouldn't have heard it even if it took down a skyscraper of yellow bricks.

He has the information he needs. The best course of action is to return to the dory and cast off. He knows what to call them now. The Red Paint People. Maritime Archaics. They put forth in primitive vessels without fear and they lacquered their corpses with the earth's blood so they would not bear the albino stain of death. They lived in a former world. He's heading back there as fast as he can row.

8

Julia Fletcher brakes and downshifts her little Sidekick for the long hill descending into Ledgeport. On her left, the ocean side of the road, there's a series of baronial old summer estates that nobody can afford to live in, so they're now luxury B&Bs. Beyond the parking lots full of Audis and BMWs, their close-shaven emerald lawns slope half a mile to the sea. Across the road rise the steep forested Ledgeport hills she used to climb with Will and their father; then at the top they'd look down on their own island set like a birthstone in the archipelago of Penobscot Bay.

Ledgeport's almost a hometown to her, much more than Boston, which was too grim and venerable to have any feeling for. Ledgeport was where her family stayed overnight before crossing to Amber the next day. The old Excelsior Hotel had decadent ocean-view suites plus a basement tavern where alcoholics could sleep over in a ten-dollar room, which is a kind of Maine socialism if you think of it. Ledgeport was where they'd shop in the morning for stove fuel and fishing lures, kids' marshmallows and parental whiskey, then they'd set off in the old *Hippopotamus* for a higher plane of existence that made school and Boston seem like the dark sites of Romania.

Her dad's architectural firm, Fletcher & Strauss, designed villas and high-rises for the plutocracy, but their own Amber vacations were spent in surplus wall tents with all meals prepared on a green Coleman camp stove under a canvas tarp. August was their housekeeper Rosina's annual vacation and Will and Julia found it amusing to watch their parents fuss and struggle over the gasoline burner, trying to fix dinner on their own. Her father had to live off the land to every possible extent. For supper there were black-enameled kettles of steamers and razor clams, for lunch, cold raw littlenecks with Tabasco sauce, and breakfast was planked mackerel taken at the dock from the schools that riffled through their little cove.

Their one-hole outhouse was hardly the grooming site for her civilized Back Bay mom, so every few days they'd steam over to Ledgeport for a night in the Excelsior where Camilla Fletcher could get a hot shower and fresh romaine. Then she'd peruse the Ledgeport shops and galleries while Julia and Will and Marston climbed Mount Amatuck for its summit view. Julia was the family infant, an afterthought, always one beat behind the conversation, one stage behind on the mountain trail. She was dogged if nothing else; she got up the mountain by imagining she was a little terrier following tongue out behind her owners, using her forepaws half the time on the steep parts, and when she reached them eventually at the peak, her dad and brother would applaud. Will would read Edna St. Vincent Millay's poem from the bronze plaque set in granite: ...*I saw three islands in a bay*, and her heart would race knowing their own Amber was one of them. Only later did she realize that was a death poem whose last lines could chill like an evil dream.

She and Will were inseparable island gangsters and co-conspirators though eight years apart. Her sister Nicole was different. She'd married and had children before Julia learned to speak. She was Aunt Julia by the age of four, big sister and role model, and when they came for Christmas her twin nieces, Brittany and Elaine, would dress her like one of their Spice Girl Barbies and serve concoctions from Julia Child. They're now both seniors at the London Culinary School. Nicole and Chad had a yacht business in St. Thomas which sailed into bankruptcy and now they're coming home, the whole family, home to commit such an atrocity she can't even say its name.

She's stalled on Main Street among late-summer tourist traffic outside Aaron's Drugstore where her father always stopped for the *New York Times*. Then, as if he'd forgotten, he'd turn around and ask if she'd like an ice-cream cone. The image engulfs her, blocking the day like an eclipse: her father, Marston Fletcher, in his Bermuda shorts and old Topsiders, his newspaper, discussing with old Aaron the Dow Jones or Operation Desert Storm. She used to call those grown-up subjects "adulteries," before she knew what the word meant. While Marston and Aaron went on, she'd try to lick off the jimmies individually with the sharp point of her tongue.

This is not possible, she says aloud, right in the orange car with all the windows open—Death, you can't keep him; you've had him a year now, it's time to give him back—till she's no longer a safe driver and has to pull into the first open diagonal space and slump over the steering wheel.

There's no reason for it, she thinks, shaking her head like a wet spaniel to clear the fog of anger and the blindness of tears. It's been almost a year and a half now and she should be over it, but she's not. It was months before she could bring herself out to Amber, though she knew that was where she'd find him when she was ready. Then this past summer she basically lived there. She kayaked the four miles in the flat water of sunrise with her camera in a Pelican case and pitched her tent on the ground between the two old decaying platforms where the green stove used to stand. Some of the locals must have come out there because under one of the platforms she found the foil wrappers of four condoms. It never bothered her that people used it, for duck hunting or copulation, though one would have preferred them to leave no trace.

Every day she woke up in their old campsite and thought of him, traced all their paths and activities as if he were still there hanging onto her hand, restraining her from running too far ahead; then he raced past her and out of sight. Guess what, I'm not returning: from now on, find your way alone.

Will showed up for a few days to escape his divorce proceedings with Lenore, mumbling "Never marry a lawyer." Then her roommate and everything else, Vira, spent a week that almost took her completely out of time. Vira skinny-dipped in the eutrophied quarry pool while Julia stole a photograph or two; they spent their nights in the steam heat of a double sleeping bag. Two girls: might he have disapproved? He would have loved Vira for her grace and spirit, her Såmi heritage, but now they're in different dimensions and can't meet.

One death was not enough for Marston Fletcher. He's getting a second one. His precious firstborn Nicole is plotting to develop their unspoiled island into a destination resort. Nicole and her husband Chad, who went bankrupt in the Caribbean, now want to try again in Maine. Ecofriendly, she says. How is it eco-anything if it deforests an island and paves their wild meadow for a landing strip? And how can her mom go along with it? And *finance* it?

It was her dad's silence and his sanctuary. His firm built half the infrastructure of the world, but he left no trace of himself on Amber Island. He respected every organism and growing plant, even the old quarry machinery that has stood rusting there since the Depression. He revered and cherished it as it was. How can they do this to him, his family and his survivors? The anger returns clawing like a wolverine, not just at them either but at him, her own father, for deserting her without warning or direction, leaving her to defend a whole island by herself. He'd laugh if he could see her. He'd pry her clutching arms off the steering wheel, pull her out through the driver's door, pick her up bodily and laugh at the foolishness of her anguish, the absurdity. Death is a part of nature, he would say, it's as natural as a leaf changing color and drifting to the ground. But Dad, it's not that. It's the *island*.

Amber's in trouble and you're not even around to help.

But he can't hear her, because the dead are protected from the future with its inevitability and pain. She sits in the driver's seat with her palms out like a Buddhist till anger and grief disentangle and she can think.

Work and love, that's what he always said, but what work is there after love's been abducted and its heart cut out? The news of his death came two weeks before her Hampshire graduation. She lost all interest in her senior photography project and reported to the Health Service where they gave her a Valium prescription. Back in her dorm room she put on the Waldstein sonata and swallowed the caplets in greedy little handfuls like the M&Ms he'd cache for her on the hiking trail. She woke up in The Hemlocks, this tasteful private Berkshires sanitarium in a room very like a college dorm except for the jail bars over the window so you can't jump out. Will called it the Joint, which was an understatement, because at least in prison they tell you what your crime was and who you are. The service went forward in her absence and her father was taken without her to an unknown site.

She inherited his old black Nikon F3 and began to work again on the asylum grounds. She shot in black and white, the monochromatics of the deceased. A kindly nurse brought her film into town on the way home and returned with tiny drugstore prints, but that was enough. She found a small seaside college whose MFA program would admit her without having finished her degree. It was in Maine, too, less than a hundred miles from Ledgeport, and when The Hemlocks finally released her, she enrolled.

Everyone in the program had long since gone digital and after she vacuumed the cobwebs and chased the spiders out of the enlarger, the darkroom was hers alone. Her thesis is to document Amber Island in its untouched splendor before they destroy it. If she fails to protect it in reality she can at least remember it with art. Vira says nothing beautiful can come from anger, but this project born of rage and helplessness will be dedicated to her dad. If it's good enough, if she's focused and devoted enough, it might find its way to him on the other side.

But today she's come to Ledgeport for another reason, an assignment for a class called Sound & Site. They're to make photographs that visually convey the sound quality of a given place. From the crystal-clear fall atmosphere, the assignment, and maybe being so close to Amber, she's acutely tuned in to everything she hears. A pair of unhelmeted, unmuffled motorcycles cruise down the main street side by side, old hippie riders with headbands and gray ponytails, elderly tattooed chicks on the back seat swapping biker gossip over the exhaust. They sound like the whole Hells Angels but it's all coming from two machines. A skateboarder perches an instant on the steps of the Catholic church next to the library, then rattles down the stone railing, bounces once on the last step, arcs right over the sidewalk into the street in a graceful pure curve that just misses a double-parked FedEx truck, then stops short at a bike cop, jumps off his board, and in a single motion swoops it up and into his backpack and walks away whistling.

Suddenly the street's so quiet a distant plane can be heard, and now seen, taking off from the antique airfield at Owls Head, a biplane from the early days of flight that sounds like a lawn mower and moves at bicycle speed through the clear air. Oh, the reason it's moving so slowly is a long yellow banner towing behind it, AEROBATIC SHOW SAT 10 AM, and you can hear the flap and crack of its fabric vibrating in the sky. It's what they saw all those summers from the island, the old planes doing their tricks like airborne circus dogs, climbing straight up, rolling over, flying upside down, Spad fighters closing in on each other in aerial combat, even once a skywriter spelling PEPSI in the azure sky. Her father loved them and would stop everything to look up with a boy's wonder. Though he had traveled to every airport on the planet, he was born of the Great Depression and flight still seemed a miracle to his eyes.

She stops at the old yellow-brick library where she used to visit the Children's Room on their weekly Ledgeport trips. Her mom would browse the shops and sip waterfront coffee while Julia hunched over one of the small round tables buried in Miss Frizzle or *Matilda*. A couple of senior citizens share the bench at the library entrance, numerous pigeons at their feet stabbing at peanut shells and pushing one another away with their soft aggressive coos. One's a bearded old warrior dressed for winter in an army coat, the other's a diminutive white-haired woman with a faraway look talking as if on a telephone but there's nothing in her hand and no one at the other end. Her skin looks like ancient parchment as if she could be a hundred. Her friends, her siblings, perhaps even her children must be mostly dead, and she's probably conversing with them now. She's saying "Francine, you have to deliver it yourself," and Julia completely understands; she's also been talking to the dead this morning. Nobody else wants to hear.

She sits unobtrusively on a low granite wall and takes three exposures of the invisible-phone lady, then one more of the flap and screech of a huge oatmeal-colored seagull scattering the pigeons to hog the peanuts for itself. It throws its beak into the air and yells a pathetic long mournful cry, not like a dominating bully but an overgrown bird-child in the world.

That finishes a thirty-six-exposure roll. She'll find a shaded alcove in the library to change film, and maybe an image or two of silence to bookend her Sound & Site series. She enters through the Children's Room with its downsized furniture, empty because it's a school day except for Miss Swazey, who's been here since Julia was first sounding out the letters of *Goodnight Moon*.

"Oh, I know *you*," she whispers. "You're Julia Fletcher. I'm so sorry about your father."

"He used to bring me all the way in here for story hour. We came by boat."

"He gave so much, in so many ways. He was a patron. His name is on the plaque upstairs. I was just looking at his catalog. I hadn't realized he has work all over the world. New York, London, Brazil, and that beautiful library at Pepperell, where you went to college."

"No, that was my sister, and my brother Will. I'm the black sheep."

"Oh, I'm so sorry. I just associate your whole family with Pepperell. That library is such a lovely building—modern, yet it fits right in with the colonial campus. You know, I shouldn't say this, but I always wished he'd have built something locally, so we'd have it to remember him by."

"I think he came here to get away from building," Julia replies, then ducks into the History room to sink into a leather armchair and change film. It's almost peaceful enough, among the old books and folios, to forget the doom facing Amber, as if it's no more than a footnote in the sweep of time. The only person in here's a guy her age, maybe a little older, buried in the public computer screen. He wears a torn camouflage jacket, black watch cap pulled down over his forehead, with intense black eyes and a dark beard just beginning to grow. He has sort of a trapped *Taxi Driver* look, like someone that doesn't want to be seen, so he could be a veteran like Travis Bickle. He's got some kind of object on the table that looks like a large stone feather or an antique comb, or maybe it's a fossil or artifact of some kind—probably looking up its value on the web.

She asks him if he minds her changing her film in there but he must be a library silence freak since he doesn't even pretend to hear, or answer. The sun's entering the window, so she gets the dark cloth out of her backpack to shade the film, threads it, and closes the camera. She checks the exposure on some objects around the room, then discreetly angles it back toward the non-speaking De Niro guy, for the visual soundprint of a library user: noiseless focus and concentration. He's so absorbed she hopes he won't notice the girl across the room taking his picture. He doesn't even flinch at the shutter click. She gets a couple of good shots and is about to squeeze off another, when he looks up, covers his face with his two hands, then immediately ducks behind the monitor.

"Sorry," she says, "I should have asked, but it's never quite candid if you do."

Without speaking, he pockets his treasure, jumps up, and flees the room. Maybe he stole the object he was trying to look up. She checks the book he left open by the computer and it's not an antiquities price list but *The Maritime Archaics: The Archaeology of Prehistoric Cultures*—so he could have been a scholar after all. You can't tell anything about someone from the way they dress.

On the way out of the library she pauses for one shot of the gaggle of noisy preschoolers that have just arrived with their moms for story hour, then scans up and down the street for him, feeling she should apologize now that they're out of the library and can speak. But he's disappeared, and as he fades from memory, the air reverberates with the departure horn of the Fox Islands ferry, a sound she recalls from so many summers as it blasted its way past Amber through the fog. She captures the clouds of gulls rising and circling at the sound, their screams somehow recalling her awesomely gorgeous Vira who has no classes till afternoon and may be still lounging in their room. When Julia pulled away from her early this morning it was like halving a D'Anjou pear with a knife blade; even now on this sidewalk in the glaring sun she feels Vira's tongue on the ridge of her spinal cord and has to put her left hand on a parking meter to stay upright.

After a minute she merges into the small crowd of pedestrians filing toward the ferry along with the line of loudly idling vehicles, refrigerated shellfish trucks, a convertible with two guys playing harmonica and guitar, an impatient diesel flatbed snorting black smoke, a pickup with four bewildered sheep huddled together in the back as if they were afraid of falling off. Their truck edges forward onto the ferry and with the jostle of the corrugated ramp one sheep begins squealing and the others pick it up with such lamentations it sounds like they're off to the slaughterhouse, which they may well be. This is an image she wants for waterfront sounds, and she frames the four animals bleating into the air, then zooms on one white woolly face with its mouth open and the sheer fright of a four-legged creature losing the stability of the ground. Their pitiful baas merge into the sound of her mom's voice on the phone last fall saying, "You have to see this through Nicole's eyes, darling—it will be your sister's chance for a fresh start." A curl of nausea rises in her like a red tide; she is a sheep at sea with the floor heaving under it, terrified without end.

9

She's in the college darkroom enlarging the test prints for her thesis while she listens to Ani DiFranco's "Evolve." Under the amber safelight an 8x10 image rises in the tray from prenatal darkness to the living surface: an extreme telephoto of a ravenous eaglet being fed a live crab by its parent, and for a moment she wishes for video because the crab was squirming with all eight legs as the sharp young beak tore through its underside.

In summer she'd lugged her tripod from the Nubble south of the boat cove all the way to the vacant and downfallen cabin at the far northern end, from the western ledges to the mossy and caterpillar-haunted spruce stands on the east. Chipping the soil away with an ancient track spike, she located the forgotten railroad that once hauled stone from the quarry to the loading dock. She traced the foundations of the house where the Italian quarrymen lived, gone almost completely back to nature beneath the matted grass and accumulated soil. All she could find to photograph was a rusted kitchen knife with a missing handle. It was like a world where humans suddenly realized the inappropriateness of their presence and withdrew. But not for good; they would be coming back with reinforcements.

She climbed a dead tree to photograph osprey nestlings and got dive-bombed by a furious parent. She ambushed one of the feral sheep for a formal portrait, caught four deer in the first light of a misty sunrise, recorded the spiderwebbed morning dew on the sensitive ferns and bunchberries, some kind of coyote or wild dog gnawing a porcupine carcass, a flock of gaunt turkeys fleeing into the impassable underbrush beside the quarry. Her father manicured every inch of the landscape for his clients, but on Amber he wouldn't cut even a shrub. She macroed the ferocious clawing of live open barnacles as the ebb exposed them, then the vaults of their closure in the sun. Under the boards of the old tent platform she surprised a colony of earthworms and centipedes, sow bugs and spotted newts that must have writhed and mated while her family slept in their cots above. In the huge interpenetration of all forms of life, visible and invisible, magnificent or repulsive, to destroy any one of them threatens them all.

The eagle print goes up on the drying wire; her next negative is the great gray owl. She went to Amber in deepest January, right after the first Christmas without her father, when Chad had revealed his plan. Her project was to record the visual beauty of the island while it still existed. She walked its whole length in the fierce unbroken purity of the drifted snow. Flights of snow buntings flashed their black-and-white wings against granite cliffs; razor-sharp sedge blades cast shadows on the frozen crust. The camera was her only weapon against complete destruction. In the old quarry, an enormous icicle hung from the suspended block that had been there since her father was in kindergarten. People had lived their whole life and died of old age with that rock poised there like the Last Judgment. All living things grow to full size and reach their peak and decease in their own fashion, and time is written in them; but the inorganic lives on forever without death or change. Her father grew up, conceived amazing buildings everywhere in the world, generated three kids, saved up enough to buy a whole island and amass a houseful of immortal paintings, then his heart stopped and gravity took him like a stone.

She reached the abandoned sheepherder's cabin on the north cove. A window was broken and the roof totally punctured by a tree limb so animals had found their way in, raccoon or porcupine scat everywhere and shreds from the old mattress along with pages of duck hunters' porn were all gathered into some kind of mammal nest. So many times Will had wanted to set the old place on fire but their dad hadn't let him: The cabin was part of Amber's nature and history, of his own generation, created like him in the Great Depression and heading toward decomposition at the same pace.

She cramponed her way seaward along the icy tideline in the shadow of the old-growth trees. Lens fully zoomed she shot a raft of eiders and the amazing face pattern of two harlequins riding an inlet's surge. When the winter light dimmed she turned back to meet Hallett Bunker in the cove, then suddenly stopped short and held herself motionless and inert. On a low branch was a giant bark-colored owl the size of a human child, staring straight down at her with immense yellow nocturnal eyes that took up its whole face. Its talons were sheathed in dark thick leg plumage and shifting from left to right as though about to leap off its perch and strike. She centered the owl in the focus screen; at the click of the shutter the eyes blinked horizontally and deep in its feathers the whole body shuddered as a green-and-beige power shit the size of a raw egg squirted onto the snow.

The owl will be the first image in her exhibit, beginning in January when the world seems dead until you take a deeper look.

Then the swish and slight breeze of the revolving darkroom door. No knock. No one else uses this facility. It has to be Vira, back from her research trip to Labrador. Julia feels more than hears her slipping her nylon jacket off in the close heat as she gropes from the entrance then emerges under the safelight like a photograph. She continues bathing the owl print in fixer while Vira crushes her soft chest against the small of her back, her teeth touching bare skin over the halter top.

"I am a vampire from the land of ice. I must have warm blood or I die."

"Dude, you don't want these hands on you. They've been in developer."

"You can develop me," Vira says.

"I like you the way you are."

"*Like?*"

"Adore, then." She turns to face Vira. "I wish I had gone with you to the North Pole. Everything's gotten worse since you left. Will thinks they've already hired some scab to start defoliating the trees, for a fucking airstrip to land the pieces of their hotel. The modules, that's his word. They've even asked Will to write a book for them, a history of the island for their customers. I'll have to talk to him on the way down. Can you imagine, paving the meadow where we used to camp? Why don't they scatter his ashes and pave them over too?"

"Julia, this is your family."

"I'd like to annul them all—Nicole, for thinking this up as a way to save her marriage, and my mom for permitting it, not to mention Will for selling out his talent to the dark side."

"Your mom would prefer a saved marriage to a saved island. And what is so evil about building a single house? It can't be all bad; didn't you say your daddy himself designed it? It will be world-famous and people will make pilgrimages to see it."

"That's just the point, Vira. The world owned him when he lived. Except on Amber. He has a right to rest in peace there as it was."

The owl print goes up on the drying wire beside the eaglet but she still doesn't want to touch Vira with her hypo hands, her apron splashed with Dektol and fixative. Bodies apart, lips kissing in the vermillion light, it almost submerges her island, but not quite.

"Vira, kissing won't change it."

"Hey, I'm not the one building the resort. I slept in a tent when I was out there, just like your father did."

"I'm going to try my mother one more time. They haven't broken ground or anything. She still has power of attorney and she can change her mind. I'm bringing Will. He's starting to look and talk like Dad, plus he's a man. Maybe she'll listen to him."

"Will has his book for them."

"Will doesn't need a resort to write a history of the island. He loves it and knows it. It will be a great book on its own. This is going to hurt her, you know. They'll need more money; she'll have to sell things from their collection."

"Oh," Vira says. "She must not sell them before I have seen them. Take me to meet her. I will persuade her to your side. Then I will view her museum."

"No, no, Vira. That would do just the opposite. If she knew about us, she'd annul *me*. One look at you and she'll think: *no grandchildren*. Which is another reason she favors Nicole and Chad; they're fruitful and they multiply. They have twins."

Vira leans over the darkroom sink to examine the drying prints in the dim russet light. Besides the owl and eaglet, the long stand of white birch on the east cliffs whose translucent bark caught the first photons of the morning sun; trees to be slaughtered for the tourist huts; the natural meadow that slopes to the boat landing, alive with brown-streaked savannah sparrows that jump like grasshoppers whenever you walk through, soon to become a highway for backhoes and bulldozers; the old quarry pond where Vira swam nude as a porpoise despite the gelatinous green surface; the sheepherder's cottage practically reabsorbed by nature with the shingles mossed over and falling through; the black-faced sheep still waiting for their owner's return.

Vira says, "If your family sees these images, they will understand."

"They won't. They'll want to hang them in their guest rooms like a motel."

She removes her owl from the enlarger and replaces it with one of the Sound & Site negatives from her Ledgeport trip: the library fugitive who fled from the history room. Vira's arms are around her waist as she shuts the safelight off, turns on the enlarger bulb. The man's face appears like a skull X-ray or hungry black ghost, dominated by the white dome of his watch cap.

"Who is this guy? Have you recidivated?"

"A man in the library," Julia says.

"Oh, was he cute? I cannot tell from his negative. He looks like a sonogram."

"He got angry when I pointed the lens at him. I got two shots, then he stood up and left."

"He could tell a girl who does not need males."

She puts the test strip under the lens and uncovers it for three, five, ten, twelve seconds, then into the Dektol and it's the ten-second gray she wants. She puts an 8x10 semi-matte under and presses the foot switch while Vira says, "I love watching you work."

"Watching? But you can't see."

"Feeling instead?" She fingers her hands into Julia's hair, over bare shoulders and under the damp apron in front.

"Hey, I'm too wet already," Julia says, but it's too late, she's had the foot switch down the whole time. "And look what you did."

"Process it," Vira says.

She turns the safelight on and slips the overexposed print into the Dektol and of course it turns immediately uniform gray, then all black. How long had she exposed it? A minute? An hour?

"There—nothing. A face without features, totally blank."

"It is not nothing. It is a face of the future, empty and unknown. Now I will go away and let you work. You know where to find me."

She swishes out the revolving door toward the lighted world, leaving Julia to hold onto the darkroom sink. Her eyes brim with dazzling scintillas as she recovers her balance one leg at a time. Then she makes the real twelve-second print of Mr. Maritime Archaic and hangs it next to the black square. He looks like a young transient guy who hangs out in libraries and lives in his clothes. Under his black brows, intense eyes try to burn a hole right through the computer screen. She can't imagine what he was searching for in the primeval world.

She'll wrap up the class assignment and get back to her thesis: to document every corner of Amber Island and every wild creature down to the nematodes. She has her winter pictures already from the visit when she saw the owl. She'll go to Boston and argue her case once more. If that fails, she'll make one visit in October, another in earliest spring before the ground thaws. Then derricks and steam shovels will arrive by barge, the boats will bring generators and cables, gas tanks and stoves for the twins' kitchen, chain saws in nesting season, helicopters landing materials on the paved airstrip: shock and awe of armed invasion, an invasion she will never see because once she's finished her MFA thesis she won't set foot on it again. Vira's family has property outside Helsinki in a society where they freely share their abundance and haven't molested another nation in a thousand years.

10

October sunlight streams through the large second-floor window like an invasion, and Camilla Fletcher closes the red damask curtains to hold it back. It's still a house in mourning. Each room has its own quality of silence: silence of Nicole, silence of Will, silence of Julia, and, darkening them all like an eclipse, the silence of her dear Marston, who took with him all the atmosphere or ether that conducts sound to the ear. She walks down the dim hallway turning on the brass picture lamps over their beloved paintings, one by one, and as they come to life she gets a flash of the sheer visual energy she always adored in him. He taught her to see; they saw together, and as she looks at each canvas with her own dubious vision it is brightened and intensified by his. Even when every atom of his physical being seems dissolved in the universe, she can find him here.

She lights up a small seascape by Marston's old friend Fairfield Porter, a gift of the artist just before he died. He's on a hilltop overlooking Penobscot Bay, and one of the islands is their own Amber—you can tell from the burnt-umber shoreline and the shape sloping from south to north. The cool sunrise colors bring it all back to her; she's there crawling out of her sleeping bag in the cold tent with its hard splintery floor, and Marston has already returned with a string of mackerel. Will and Julia are hungry children and she's trying to make breakfast on two sputtering gasoline burners and a campfire barely flickering in the fog.

And they're still hungry, she thinks: Will's driving from Maine for lunch today, and he's bringing Julia, her absentee daughter, who's boycotting her home and hasn't been back since December. It wasn't enough to lose her oldest companion, she's lost her youngest as well. The night she told Marston she was pregnant again at forty-four, he pulled out his Old Testament and read, *Shall a child be born unto him that is an hundred years old?* Then they became inseparable and she shivers to think that she almost lost them both.

Thank God Rosina will be here, not just to cook but to recall with her solid presence how it once was. But Julia will talk about Amber— why else would she cross her own picket line to visit her former home?

Decisions between children should be forbidden; they always end badly. Look at King Lear, look at Jacob and Esau, and doesn't some infant end up getting cut in two? He designed that stunning house for Amber in the very beginning, as a gift to her, then he changed his mind and consigned it to the cellar forever. Without a roof on the island except for the hornet-infested outhouse, people stopped going, even Will; it was just the two of them at the end, father and daughter in the mildewy wall tents, living on fish and mussels, fifty-five years between them and they bonded like warriors long after everyone else had given up.

Now Julia carries it on herself, the youngest and, in a way, most fragile, though she kayaks across the ship channel like an Eskimo— Inuit—with a boatload of camera gear, and stays the whole summer among man-eating insects in a mummy bag. She has his philosophy. She needs very little. Her one desire is to need even less.

Marston was the picture of health, straight-backed, somehow even taller than when she met him. Death seemed far over the horizon; then it was there, in their own home. It was Nicole who moved to Boston and spent a whole month with her helpless mom, took care of her like an invalid, and proposed an answer to everything. They would create something on Amber Island to commemorate Marston's life and work. They'd build the Amber house that he had designed their first summer there when she was pregnant with Will. It would unite the whole family in a common enterprise, and transform an unbearable loss into a new beginning. His vision would endure as an aesthetic seamark in Penobscot Bay. It was Chad's idea, Nicole said; he'd thought of it as soon as they got the news.

Nicole asked her mother's blessing and material help for this idea, and she acquiesced. It would be more than the Fletcher summer home, Nicole said. They'd also share it on a very select basis with paying guests who could appreciate living and dining on a private island in a Marston Fletcher design. During the off-season, they'd all live in Boston and bring life and spirit to Chestnut Street.

She's sure Julia will come to understand. She'd always loved the maquette of the Amber house that's been in the cellar all these years. She filled it with her dolls as a little girl. A glass tower shaped like a lighthouse, she wanted to shrink down like Alice and live inside. Now she'll be able to; her visit on this beautiful autumn day could be the start.

She illuminates Neil Welliver's rainbow trout on the stair landing and breathes deeply in and out until she's inhaling water, not air: a gill-breather weightlessly afloat. Then, next to it, Emil Nolde's single whitecap made of live salt water that makes one want to undress right in the corridor and wade into the emerald surf. She was always the last one in when they swam at the little beach on the west cove of the island, and the chill penetrated more each year till she stopped going. Then it was Marston and Julia, and now Julia alone, a population of one, if you don't count the young man clearing trees. Who can blame Nicole for wanting to people it? Nature is unborn without human beings; they give it meaning and intellectual purpose and, in Marston's case, beauty and order too. Coming upon one of his redwood-and-glass homes in a wild landscape can take your breath away.

Julia's right; if Marston were here there'd be no construction on Amber Island. They'd have just kept camping, father and daughter, because that's what he loved—the place itself, with its old shack, sand in the quahogs, planked fish.

But death changes everything. Without it we'd just go on and on.

She climbs to the third story where Marston's home studio takes up half the floor, with their bedroom at the other end. Over their headboard is Rockwell Kent's floating blue iceberg whose light comes from deep within, as if he used radium paint like the hands of an old watch. She opens the French door to a little alcove lined with his favorite books, Tolstoy and Balzac and Thomas Mann, where he'd get up and read quietly before his working day while she was dreaming away her life in the next room.

It was there that she found him that drizzling spring morning, not reading at all but sound asleep on the cold floor, his glasses beside him like a fallen bird, one wing extended. She took his head in both hands to slip a pillow underneath—she could barely lift it—and here was a scrape of blood on his cheek too. She swabbed at the cut with his plaid handkerchief, but it was already congealing and still he slept. She remembered what was done in these cases, when they didn't wake upon stimuli. She kissed his mouth and opened it by squeezing his cheeks with both hands and filled her lungs with air then exhaled it into him. Her lungs were tiny compared to his. She lifted her head and breathed in, then kissed and exhaled, but she couldn't fill him, like a child hopelessly blowing a huge balloon.

She reared back and struck his chest and imagined him with another woman so she could strike harder. Beat the shit out of you, she said, *beat shit, beat shit,* with no response. She leaned down with both hands on his chest and her ear over the heart but the respiration she heard, the pulse hammering in her eardrum, were just her own.

The bedroom phone was almost within arm's length and the

number was 911. But instead of the phone, her hand reached for a pillow so she could lay her own head beside his and press her lips against his neck, where the fine gray lower hairs meet the swell of the first vertebra, a spot she could nest in like a wren.

That was how Rosina found them after she let herself in to begin her usual cleaning day from the top down. She broke out laughing at first, thinking these two old coots attempting it on the floor, then she saw something and screamed and it was Rosina who picked up the receiver and explained to the dispatcher what she'd stumbled on.

For her lapse there was some unspoken judgment, for a while; but love was another thing far beyond that.

And it's Rosina now who rescues her from this reverie with a soft tapping on a pane of the French door.

"Mrs. Fletcher, it's twelve-fifteen. The bisque is done and I have *ensalada de pollo*. Are you gonna greet your long-lost daughter looking like that?"

There's already an autumn look outside and even in the sheltered courtyard the wind has been stripping the Japanese maple of its leaves. She chooses a dark navy, nearly black blouse with a small collar and adds the earth-colored sweater with caribou or reindeer on it—not a great match, but it was one Julia gave her from L.L.Bean. Just this morning the *Globe* had an article on the caribou herds of Lapland or Alaska, somewhere in the Arctic Circle, which once numbered in the millions but have now disappeared. This is what Julia cares about, the caribou and the walruses; the polar bears, of course—she had a sweet Steiff one from Schwarz's. At twenty-four you'd think she'd live for the future, she'd be buried in computers and cell phones with her generation. She's like the student who lay down in front of the tank, only

Julia's tank is the whole world; it won't stop as the Chinese one did.

She buttons her sweater up to the throat to conceal the mourning beneath, wraps the silk scarf over that; and, as she did the day they came for Marston, she follows Rosina down the stairs.

11

Julia leaves safe and beautiful Bar Harbor at seven a.m. The orange Sidekick blends perfectly with the raging October foliage along her route. She shortcuts to the River Road to avoid the strip malls and turns on the radio to *Morning Edition*. Students are fleeing schools in Iraq; females must wear the hijab or be expelled. Fourteen more US troops have been killed since Monday, nineteen Iraqis by a suicide bomb. She tunes away from the incomprehensible waste of it, this autumn morning with the earth on fire from sunlight: vermillion blueberry bushes, maple leaves bearing the whole spectrum of a burning flame.

She finds the alternative station and Bob Dylan's acidic sadness, he's in the rain in Juarez on the wrong side of the border fence, his gravity's failing, his negativities won't get him through. Back in her mom's time those nasal-depressive voices could stop a war. Their protest flowered and brought down the system, then *they* became the establishment and closed their ears.

She's heading south to Pepperell College to pick up her brother Will, poet-in-residence, then to the depths of Back Bay to save a defenseless island from the family scheme. It's not some piece of commercial real estate. Her dad valued its unbuilt wildness more than all the architecture in the world. She's glad Will's coming; he's much more eloquent. He was the one they bought the island for, to vaccinate him at birth with the sea's cadence and salt breath. In Africa, if they have to decide something, they bring the skulls of the ancestors to the table and let them speak. Will looks like Marston must have back in the sixties when her parents met. If anyone can successfully channel their lost father, it might be her brother.

She heads for the Dunkin' Donuts where they're supposed to meet, a bit late as usual, and there's Will's red Saab convertible, prizewinning writer rocking out behind the wheel. Before she even hears the music she knows it's the Talking Heads. *This ain't no party, this ain't no disco, this ain't no fooling around.* How Lenore could have left him, she'll never understand.

He spots his little sister and leaps out of the cockpit for a full-length brotherly hug but his unyielding male body feels strange as a horse to her, even though she's embraced it all her life. He's also vastly thinner than he was. The struggle with Lenore must be consuming him.

"Which car, Jules?"

"Duh."

They leave hers in the supermarket lot and head—top down— for I-95 with Will doing a breezy sixty, the air whirling around the windshield so she has to yell.

"So you've taken an apartment? Is Lenore still in the cottage? Do you even have the cottage anymore?"

"Lenore is not in the cottage. Lenore is living in Sackville, New Brunswick."

"What about Portland? You mean she's left the job with the big firm?"

"She left the big job and the big firm and the big country and the big loser."

"What do you hear from her?"

"Silence," Will says. "Silence of smoldering hell. Never divorce a lawyer. They'll remove your heart."

"That's okay—hearts are a lot of trouble. Anyway, you probably arranged it all subconsciously. Poets need total disorder, for their work."

"Need *what*?" Will shouts. He's now going seventy-five.

"*Disorder!*"

"Yes, we do! I can't get enough disorder. I need more. *An order is a great disorder.* Hey, the service area has a Starbucks. Let's order coffee!"

The featured flavor is Pumpkin Spice and she has one iced with skim. Will has the Tasmanian Bold. They hit the turnpike again, top down, wind howling around the headrests, lunatic driver karaoke-ing to "Burning Down the House." Lenore had been kind of a big sister for Julia. She visited three times at The Hemlocks, then said good-bye as if they weren't going to meet again.

"I can't believe Lenore was disloyal," she yells over the wind and song. "She was too busy. Also, she was obsessed with justice."

"For Lenore, justice was liberation from me."

"Why? What was your crime?"

"Same as everyone's crime: not being someone else."

"How could that be? You've always been someone else."

"Not else enough. But we're going to be there in an hour. What am I supposed to say?"

"You don't support Club Amber, or whatever they call it. Unless you do."

"Amber Retreats."

"She knows Dad would have hated it—you just have to remind her. She doesn't pay any attention to me. She'll listen to you."

"It's not for her, Jules. It's Nicole and Chad. Our sister needs an out, and Mom's willing to rescue her, and rescue herself at the same time. They've had a rough time in Charlotte Amalie."

"Why would Mom put Nicole's needs over Dad's and mine? Isn't being dead a rough time? I didn't know Nicole was committed to an institution."

"No one has gone as far as you did, Jules."

"Well, Dad went further. He went all the way."

"You were the one who took the full force of it. You lived out what we were all feeling. And you've come back intact—better than ever. You have a vision and a direction. You have to see it through Mom's eyes."

"Mom has her own eyes. I'm trying to see it through Dad's. I'm sorry about Chad and Nicole's business. Bankruptcy may be bad, but death is worse. If you're alive you have some power in the world and you can change it. The dead need representation."

"That may be, but Mom has her needs, too. It's not so great living there by herself. Do I want to move in with her? Do you? Nicole and Chad can run Amber Retreats in the summer, then spend the winter on Chestnut Street. They're willing to do that."

Even in a red convertible amid flaming foliage, it's as hopeless as the asylum. Will lowers David Byrne and pulls to the slow lane so they can hear.

"It makes me carsick when you say Amber Retreats," she says, "like it's a settled fact. It's not. It's a complete violation of his memory. He trusted her to preserve and care for that island, not to exploit it. And *Retreats*—it sounds like a monastery when it's really a country club."

"It will be all organic, Jules. Chemical-free. They'll have a greenhouse and a little farm, where the guests can harvest their own food."

"Come on, Will, that's such bullshit. They're totally taking advantage of her loneliness. I was counting on you to help. He's barely even dead and they're sticking a hotel on his island like it's a Monopoly game. People don't cease as if they'd never been. We are his family. We're as answerable to him as if he were alive—I feel that every minute. I don't have it in me to let him down."

"We're also responsible to the living," Will says.

"The living have voices; they can speak for themselves. He filled a thousand wetlands, building what he did, but he wanted to leave one place in nature the way it was."

Into the blue again, after the money's gone. The Talking Heads grow audible as they slow for the tollbooth. WELCOME TO NEW HAMPSHIRE:

LIVE FREE OR DIE.

"It's not celebrating his memory," she says. "It's monetizing it. The one place that would remember him for something besides development. Will, I can't even imagine my childhood out there without you in it. You and Dad, you'd head for the clam flats in old sneakers and I'd try to follow before I could even walk. I wanted so badly to join you. You led the way. And your book, *The Other Shore*. Amber is everywhere in those poems. Now it's in trouble and I'm hoping for some support."

She feels the empty rooflessness of the open car. Will's not with her; she's unaccompanied on this mission, except by a pale shadow who every day seems to grow further off.

"I'd like to be able to channel Lenore," she says out loud. "She's pretty confident. She just goes forward step by step with what she wants to say."

"Step by step over the corpses in her path."

"Women have to learn that, Will. Men have been doing it since the Stone Age."

"Jules, it's exactly what Mom's trying to do. It's one of the first historical rights of women, to dispose of their property in accordance with their own values, not necessarily the husband's. This is the first decision she's made on her own since she was twenty-one. Do you really want to be the ghost of King Hamlet trying to influence her from the grave?"

"I do. I do want to be his ghost. He has to be spoken for."

"You're being so adversarial, Jules. Maybe you *should* consider a legal career. Do you think there's really a right and a wrong in all this?"

"I don't know about right, Will, but there is a wrong. It's to privilege money over nature and to keep making that choice over and over till there's nothing left. We are so privileged to own this little particle of the Earth. *Own* is the wrong word; we're just the caretakers. Even if

Mom's decided, it's not too late—she could re-decide."

"Look, Jules, the bridge! The Mystical River."

Before she knows it they're on the down ramp for Storrow Drive and the encounter. She elevates her spine to its limit in the leather seat, straightens the beige cardigan Vira lent her for the occasion. It's true, she's dressed like an attorney with a case to plead; she represents an island that can't speak in its own defense, a father who due to an advanced medical condition is unable to appear.

They find a space right on Chestnut Street just a few doors up from their house, by a square of sidewalk where she once saw the word FUCK in red chalk inside a large red arrowed heart. She had a big brother so she'd heard that word on occasion, but to see it in print was as permanent as a tattoo; its dried-blood pigment and suctiony onomatopoeia have colored her block forever.

She stands at the bottom of the steep brownstone steps leading up to their front door, thinking this is where everything began. The street foliage is in its autumn glory, and yellow leaves strew the pots of geraniums Rosina puts out on every stair. She sees her mom first through the bay window, where she's been waiting on the window seat, then through the beveled-glass doorway, wearing the caribou sweater over a black garment for a house that has not yet recovered and maybe never will. Her own boycott may have added to the depressing gloom.

Will bounds up for a hug while Julia holds back, and though her mother buries her face in her son's collarbone, her eyes look over his shoulder to her lost ungrateful daughter, still standing on the third stair down. She seems so solitary and dispossessed that Julia gives in and puts both arms around her and feels how frail she's getting under the woolen sweater, like a great fluffy cat with a minimal body inside.

"Julia, darling, I gave up trying to call you 'cause you never answer. I thought you weren't coming home again, ever."

"It's grad school, Mom. They're serious and demanding. I basically live in the darkroom. But here I am."

"Dearest Julia, our youngest. *Although the last, not least*, Marston would always quote."

"I feel kind of least these days. I stopped for a rest last summer, and the family went on without me."

"We didn't. This is still your home. Rosina's making something delicious, as always. Will, even for a poet you're too pale and thin."

"A separated poet," Will adds. "They're the thinnest kind."

"Whoever thought we'd be one of Tolstoy's unhappy families? This was a house of light. It was never quiet for a moment. Now it's an old crypt with its one crepuscular old tenant."

She pulls them into the parlor and opens the half-closed curtains. Warm autumn light burnishes the rosewood piano and brick fireplace, and over the mantel, the centerpiece of the whole house, their red Katahdin, ablaze with fall blueberries, that brought the wonders of the north woods into their home.

Julia can't help but say, "I was so lucky to grow up with that."

"We were lucky to get it when we did. I like to think it made both of you what you are. Julia, your photos have that mystery. Nicole loves the one you gave her. I shouldn't say this, but she dreams of having some of your beautiful prints for the Retreat, the way Will's doing the book. She so much wants you to be part of it."

"Mom, there's not enough time in the universe for me to be part of this. I'm not their corporate illustrator. My project is an epitaph for the island. They're going to paper the walls with it?"

"I wonder if it's too early for a little something?" Will suggests, in loving imitation of their father's voice.

As if she'd heard Marston himself in the living room, Rosina steps through the pantry door bearing three glasses and a bottle of white Bordeaux. She puts it down by the three place settings and buries Julia in a heartfelt embrace that sinks her to the depths of another time.

"You are gone too long. Any more apart and I will not remember. We will have to be introduced. Mrs. Fletcher, you must not permit."

"Rosina, I'll take you with me."

"Oh no, not Maine. I have heard of that place; they are never warm. Same with Siberia."

The spring-hinged door closes behind her and she can just hear Vira:

You keep domestic servants?

Oh no, Vira, Rosina's practically family. We pay her social security; we don't have servants in America.

Will fills the glasses, which they raise and clink. "To Dad, and the family."

Her mom says, "To you and Julia, his dear children. Thank you for coming. He's more of a presence when we're together. Let's try to get through this phase. He wouldn't want to see us divided in this way."

The house feels like an immense vacant vault. The three of them with their three glasses barely make a dent in the emptiness. The low October sun, slanting down past the Japanese maple through the bay window, searches the dining room for something to illuminate. The walnut paneling looks like tar paper. The floor-to-ceiling shelves of matching hardbounds in the library look like fake inserts, rows of sham spines with no books inside. They wait in silence as Rosina passes and returns through the swinging door like someone from the spirit world.

"Mom, you're the one who's dividing us. You favored one of us over the other, like some patriarchy where the oldest child gets all the land. And you're dividing us from Dad. This was just what he didn't want to happen."

"Julia, darling, I was there when he designed the Amber house. He drew it by kerosene light in the canvas tent, as a gift to me, when we were expecting this character." She leans out of her chair to give Will a mother's kiss and nuzzle her cheek against his close-clipped beard, which at thirty already contains a scattering of whitish hairs.

"You should have stopped there, Mom."

"With the family forever incomplete?"

"I'm sorry, but it sounds like you want me not to exist. It doesn't matter if I'm the youngest or whatever. I should have had a totally equal voice in this decision."

"Dearest Julia, you were in The Hemlocks when this came up."

"They asked you for this when I was in the *hospital*? Dad hadn't been dead a month. They took advantage of my absence—they knew I'd never agree. They took advantage of his absence, too."

"It's his absence we're talking about," her mother says. "And something tangible of his, that could fill at least part of the space he left. It would be his own legacy for the island."

"But Amber was his sanctuary! His whole instinct was not to disturb it. You knew him while we were there; he barely allowed the outhouse. The only legacy he wanted was the legacy of restraint. You know, Mom, if you showed just a whisper of resistance I'm sure Nicole would reconsider. It's not too late."

At that moment Rosina reappears through the swinging pantry door with her steaming tortillas under a square of flowery embroidered cloth and one bowl of the lobster bisque which she sets before Camilla, still glaring at Julia for her estrangement.

"You are a rare little bird in this place. I'm going to get your autograph before you leave, so I can prove it to my grandkids. They're not going to believe."

"All I bring is trouble, Rosina. You wouldn't want me. I'm better off in Siberia."

"Trouble is better than nothing, young lady. I know 'cause I've seen them both. Trouble is life. Don't run away from it." She refills Will's empty wineglass but only to the halfway point, then lingers because she's part of the conversation now.

"It *is* late," her mom continues. "They've started on a small scale already. Out of nowhere appeared a reliable young man with a chain saw. He's a veteran of one of our Mideast follies, I'm not sure which. He's taken the old sheepherder's cabin in exchange for helping clear the land. Can you imagine? I'm not sure it even has a roof."

"Will, you said they were cutting some trees; you didn't say anyone was *living* there."

"He went out after Labor Day. I'm surprised you haven't run into him."

"Mom, I haven't been there. I'm taking four classes for my MFA. The closest I've come is Ledgeport, for an assignment. I looked over at Amber but I didn't go out."

"He's not just anyone. He's the grandson of Marston's old friend, Guido Colonna, one of the original stonecutters in the quarry days."

"I remember him," Will says. "Do you, Jules? He was a little kid, more your age than mine. His grandfather didn't walk well, and he leaned on him for support."

"It was a war wound," their mom says. "From the invasion of Sicily, if you can imagine, his native country. I had never seen a child so devoted. You see, the project is already doing some good!"

She reaches out with a heartbroken look and puts her hand over Julia's on the table.

"Can't you see, it's almost an omen—their first worker is someone whose family reached back to the quarry days. His mother wrote a short note to ask if he could live in the old cabin while he recovers. It sounds like shell shock. There's been such terrible damage from this war. If we can possibly help this young soldier to readjust, it would be worth the whole project. It could give him a sense of purpose, and, frankly, I hope for the same with Chad and Nicole."

"Chad went to Yale, Mom; he must have connections. He can rebuild his life without sacrificing a whole island. This is exactly what

Dad didn't want—to commercialize it. He loved you, he was proud of the house he thought up for you, he told me that, but it was out of the question. If he saw those bulldozers out there he would have driven them off the cliff. You know it meant everything to him. It wasn't negotiable. It was an absolute."

She knows now that it's doomed and hopeless, but she must get out there and record it before it's gone. She'll be in time for the last pigmentation of October when maples are gold and orange over the scarlet blueberries. With a red filter it will be even stronger in black and white.

She stands abruptly and excuses herself, then pushes through the pantry door to find Rosina, thank her and hug her, because if Chad's plan goes forward she will never darken this doorstep again.

Rosina gives her a heartfelt embrace enveloped by a cloud of scents that lead back to a time before she can remember. She's crying too. She's more intuitive than anyone and knows what this luncheon was for, and how it's turned out.

"Julia, I will miss you."

"More than anything," Julia says. "Take care."

She sweeps into the dining room and puts her hands on Will's shoulders from behind.

"I think I'll go back by bus. I just want to walk in the city a bit; it's been so long. I miss the pavement and the ambience. You should stay here a little while with Mom. You have so much to talk about."

"Come on, Julia," Will says. "We can work through it on the way."

It's too late for that. This is the worst outcome she could have imagined. She leaves the table and the dining room and pauses just for a second before the painting over the fireplace, as if art had the answers, but it doesn't. It's always autumn but there's no death to it and it doesn't change. She imagines her father at the piano, the way he would pause for a moment riveted on the score, then his fingers would strike the keys.

She gathers her coat and backpack from the hall closet and leaves, with Will of course right behind her, calling, half-running and reaching for her, but she strides up Chestnut past the red Saab and right over the sidewalk section that had the F-bomb and another which is being broken from beneath by a swelling root. She turns down Charles Street and blends into the crowd like any afternoon shopper. She takes the subway to South Station and sprints up the escalator to buy a ticket for a Concord Trailways that's already boarding passengers, not a minute to lose.

12

One windless morning Nick rowed the dory through thin peach-colored surface fog with a second roll of tar paper and four squares of cedar shingles to cover the scavenged and random planking of his roof. There followed a sundrenched mid-October week with a young all-brown eagle hovering above as if intentionally to provide shade for his bucket of roof nails and soundless hammering. He'd yell out like anyone when he misfired and smashed his thumb, but he had no idea what the sound was. The only other listener was the small sparrow that watched him and flew up every time he shouted, though it never budged for the sharp strike of tool steel on steel nail.

After the exterior and roof repairs, with the leftovers he built an enclosure for his outhouse bucket and a slant shed for the firewood he brings in daily from clearing oak and popple for Mrs. Fletcher. He removed from the Archaic gravesite three more worked and ochred tools including a honed slate gouge that could have hewn out one of their seagoing canoes. He took the tools home to his cabin to study the stone marks of their sides and edges as a common language spoken by men of the same craft or trade. His old man too hunts and works stone and his profession is to memorialize the departed, picking his material so carefully, as if, if you found a hard-enough granite, it could outlast death.

He slept for one night with the tools beside him on the scrubbed sheepherder's table then replaced them deep in the embankment where they belonged. He kept the six-barbed harpoon point that had been carved from the rostrum of the swordfish it was to kill, plus the bone hook for the lurking groundfeeders of that age. These objects he will need to remember the reality of their gravesite and the journey back to it in the end. He found two large mostly decomposed red-ochred bones, animal or human, then returned them immediately to the dignity of the earth. He sliced off a small corner from his photo of Dupuy Williams and included it with the bones before refilling the cavity with earth and shells. He logged up the windfall spruce that exposed the opening and made a woodpile of its trunk and limbs. Then for two days he hauled stones like a Neanderthal, shoveling and packing the loose gravelly sand, restoring six thousand years of layered accumulation to fill the cavity and cover the bones and tools. He transplanted a wall of ferns and seedlings to begin the work of reforestation so it would once again be concealed, leaving only one access point where a person could tunnel with spade and pry bar if they needed to add something to what was already there. That finished, he made with the Red Paint inhabitants a personal commitment not only to keep their secret but to join them if his life ever allowed him to earn his place. He has no idea how this could happen or if he would even recognize it when it did. But if he concentrates on every action with a warrior's discipline, it may reveal itself in time.

One morning, just after he'd finished returning the bones and tools to the gravel bank, he took a break to harvest some mussels off the northwest point when he felt the telltale ground-vibration of helicopter blades. First distant and watery like the Coast Guard looking for lost sailors, then closer and closer till the granite ledge shook and he threw himself facedown in a tide pool with his hands grasping raw barnacles, frigid seawater soaking his sweatshirt and pants. *Look like a dead body; they won't waste rounds on you.* He didn't look up till the tremors stopped and he knew it was out of the air and he could move.

He peeked over a sand ridge riddled with innumerable bird holes to see a red-and-white private chopper in the old pasture with a couple of men getting out. One of them was a pilot with a bald spot wearing a leather flight jacket and the other a light-haired civilian with aviator sunglasses, a mustache, and a blue necktie blowing in the rising breeze. As caretaker he ought to guard against intruders and he wished he hadn't left his rifle in the cabin, but when these guys saw him they waved and strode over, then they were shaking hands and moving their lips in speech. He pointed to both ears and shook his head to signal that he couldn't hear.

The necktie guy stared at him a moment then smiled and mouthed something to the pilot, took out a pen, and wrote on a large manila envelope, *CHAD DORMANT*. He pointed to himself, then to the pilot. *ROLF*.

Nick wrote *NICK COLONNA* with the feeling that he was signing a check or contract.

Chad underlined the last name with a glance at Rolf the pilot, then he opened the envelope which had GIS maps of the island overlaid with the next areas they wanted cleared.

YOU GOT YOUR SAW, YOUR FUEL?

YES, he wrote.

Chad put his arm on Nick's shoulder and the three of them walked back past their aircraft to the high point where the largest clearing was indicated on the map. He'd already removed the larger spruce and deciduous trees; now Chad made brush-clipper motions with his fingers, which climaxed in a mime of piled vegetation, then the motions of spraying accelerant and throwing a lit match. On the map that area had a tall circular building labeled AMBER HOUSE.

They walked down to look out on the sheltered south cove with Chad and Rolf mouthing words, then Chad pointed out a smaller flat spot which was mostly a tangle of juniper roots and blueberry leaves growing bright red in the fall sun. *The roots will be a bear to get out* with the chain saw sparking against rock, but nothing's impossible. The GIS map said CREW, which must have meant future quarters for the work staff, which has to include Nick if he's going to protect the site. They're not going to want him on this island if he's not part of the plan.

They turned back and clambered over bare ledges and salt meadows between the future Amber house and the tall southeast spruce stand that would have sheltered the first people from ocean storms.

Chad led them along the line between clearing and forest till they stood over the twenty-foot granite cliffs facing the ocean on the eastern side. A shoreline so exposed that only the gnarled and stunted forms of the jack pines can hang on with their roots fingering every rock crack for purchase against the wind. The zone was marked BUNGALOWS on the GIS overlay and Chad indicated with a sweep of his left hand that all trees on the immediate shore were to be cut and burned. The bungalow area covered a strip maybe one hundred meters along the shore, with eight small separate units blocked in, spaced fifteen meters apart. Chad was indicating with his fingers that he wanted the individual cottage footprints cleared and trees left standing in between. It was getting close to a sensitive area; a hundred meters northward lay the Maritime Archaics whose sleep was not to be violated at any cost. One of the lines marked WALKWAYS would funnel pedestrians dangerously close to the burial ground. Nick borrowed a pen to divert the path westward so he wouldn't have to chain-saw the thickets around the Red Paint site. He may look like a loyal resort custodian, but his real job is force protection of an extended family and safeguarding what they will never know.

OK? he wrote, then added *FOLLOWS OLD RR TRACK.* Chad looked at the steep-sided ravine cut and nodded yes, writing *THANKS* next to the *OK.* A couple of silent pen strokes saved a sovereign people from the dishonor of exhumation and display.

They picked their way through a field overgrown with eye-level beech and popple saplings. Nick blazed tree bark with quick Ka-Bar strokes marking the trail he'd clear, detouring well around the Archaics but ultimately leading to the quarry where the overlay said POOL. Chad spoke to the pilot then spread his arms wide as if to breast-stroke the air, and squared his hands off to indicate a swimming pool made from the old quarry, though who knows how rich tourists were supposed to swim in that septic tank, especially with a three-ton granite block over their heads. But Chad pointed to the crane's base footings and made cutting motions as if he expected Nick to saw through the steel girders with the Husqvarna. *To be removed*, he scrawled.

They walked back toward the chopper, past Nonno Guido's old dorm site which still had four or five apple trees riddled with pecker-holes, left from the old farming days even before the quarry. A couple of the feral sheep crossed their path hurrying toward their thicket, and Chad made a throat-slitting sign on his own neck and wrote on the envelope, *You have a gun?*

Nick nods; but nothing will happen to the sheep, as they're in his perimeter of care.

Chad led the way to the flat clear area of the meadow where he and Brenda Campion had swallowed each other live in the blue tent. On the GIS overlay this was marked TENNIS/HELIPAD, so they'll be taking the net down when the aircraft arrive with guests. The pilot and Chad paced off the length of a tennis court, swung their air rackets, then shook hands with Nick, and headed for the helicopter. When it took off he dove hard for the ground and stayed down till the last beat, which he couldn't distinguish from the pulse of his own heart.

When he got up he worked his way back to the Maritime Archaic site and sat by its hidden entryway, smoked a Camel, and renewed his covenant with the community deep inside.

Now as on every morning before sunrise he lies on his plank bed with eyes open in the remaining dark, visualizing an existence in the cool red earth, which would stop up the ear and eye cavities till silence and blindness become the same. It would be absolutely nothing to use the .30-30 for an act he wouldn't even hear, but whenever that thought comes he gets a voice. *What the fuck you do that for? Chill, man—you can't put yourself in the ground. Somebody else do that for you, jus' how it is.* Somebody that could be trusted with a testament of instructions, who could locate the place and seal him in there forever and never speak of it even to his own family, who like innocent vultures will be hovering at the end.

That can come later. For now his mission is 24/7 security for these people who don't know how close they have come to exposure and violation. Chad is a force of nature and no way is anyone going to stop his development, but Nick knows how to defend a boundary if he can keep living here and stay alive. Already he's been able to divert the proposed walkways away from the site; it's just a stream bank, almost unnoticeable with the tree removed. The only creatures that go in there are the wild sheep, four-legged survivors whose days could be numbered as the regime tightens its grip.

❖

He wasn't much worried about what food he threw in his duffel when he'd come in September—a few canned things, bag of rice. From that point on he would live off the land and sea. Once meals were something his mother or the mess cooks gave him; in the short time he lived alone he'd buy beef jerky and pizza at the 7-Eleven. But on the island he's day by day putting more time and care into his menu as if expecting some important visitor, though the only one at the old sheepherder's table is himself.

He's asked his dad to cut off the mainland food connection, even the strawberry pies. The sea has endless abundance and it will provide. The blue heron showed him the thickest mussel beds. Schools of mackerel riffle his little cove at mid-tide when the ledge uncovers, and one time he handlined a huge striped bass that towed the dory a hundred meters into the fog before going limp on the other end. He fried the bass in Crisco with a prayer of thanks to Nonno Guido for first showing him how to gut a fish. He's like two people: a cook who splits hardwood small enough for his woodstove, cleans mackerel, shucks mussels and rock crabs for their nuggets of precious meat; and a Ramadan hadji who's starved from his weeklong fast.

He has his .410 bird gun and his .30-30, a clam hoe, the heavy handline and a saltwater baitcast reel which has already caught two dozen mackerel on its four-gang lure, plus the striper snagged in the deepwater currents off the cliffs. He would love to try out the large bone fishhook from the gravesite but anything six thousand years old should be exempt from service, though he has honed it as sharp as the day it was carved. Using his mom's foraging book he's gathered beach peas and Irish moss and the iodine-colored dulse that adds the flavor of dark salt blood. With his long-handled mesh net he pries stones in the tidal cove for blue crabs with Popeye foreclaws and delicious whorled snails that yield up their inmost flesh at the first touch of steam. One day he shot and plucked two black ducks, cleaned and skewered them that evening over the open flame.

This morning he dozes till first light, then starts the stove with pine knots and kerosene. He got a rabbit just after sunset with the shotgun, skinned it by lamplight as his dad had showed him and locked it outside in the cooler against raccoons. Now he severs the small joints with his Ka-Bar as he puts it piece by piece in the cast-iron skillet: the small layers of fat over the muscles melt down on contact to provide a natural frying oil. Wild food must be cooked in its own liquids, he's finding out.

He's not alone this morning as he stands on the cabin porch with his toothbrush and watches a guy anchor a beat-up aluminum workboat near the clam flats of his little cove. He feels territorial for a moment and pulls the .410 off its wall nails, breaking the barrel in plain view of the clamdigger, but the guy just waves as if he can't see that it's a gun. Well, the intertidal zone belongs to the people, as it should, and when the urge passes he puts the gun in the cabin and waves back. The guy's got gray in his beard and Nick doesn't recognize him, but there are unlimited shellfish out where he's harvesting so he's welcome to them as long as he doesn't bring his friends.

He's been fishing and reading Henry D for the last two days. This morning it's back to his chain-saw work so he'll have something for Chad the Man when the chopper returns. Freedom is over, but hard obedient labor might keep him in residence, hearing or not, if he can listen to the other senses, which are sharpening in the absence of sound. He feels like the insect in Henry's old plank table, buried for sixty years and just starting to come alive. He shoulders the sheathed chain saw like a rifle and picks up the two-gallon gas can on the other side, leaving his armament behind. If it's decent he'll row to Lime Key to gang-hook mackerel from the dory and peel mussels off the low-tide shore.

After a few steps down the path, though, he circles back to move the harpoon point from his work table to the ammo box concealed under the floorboards. Not that he thinks the guy will try entering, but if anyone saw it, even a vagrant worm digger, it would have to be explained. Nick pictures him forking his rusty clam rake into the Red Paint site.

He lugs the chain saw through the red-spruce stand south of his cabin, which he does not have orders to cut, then the sixty-foot trees thin and break open and the trail climbs to the central highland with its view over the ship channel to the Ledgeport hills. They'll level and pave the landing pad. They'll build their resort. In the infinity of time things come and go like the palaces of Saddam. The Red Paint People have slept here for sixty centuries while the land broiled like the Arab desert and froze under year-round ice. Whatever Chad builds will get washed into the current when the real storms come, tsunamis and radioactive cyclones over the drowned land. The great warming will return as it has over and over, then it will freeze again; glaciers will form and recede over the sleepers in that bank like the cold tide. He'll be among them if it takes his entire life.

His first project is to clear the walkway as he himself re-drew the plan, detouring the foot traffic safely around the Archaic site. The hardwoods are in their intense peak coloration, blaze orange and red and sunlight gold among the unchanging conifers. Although he's ex-military and obeys orders without question, it's easier to bring down dark gloomy pines than to cut these maples in their autumn glory. He chokes the Husqvarna and blue smoke spurts from the exhaust so he knows it's running, but you can't start something properly without listening to the engine rev. It glides like a fruit knife through a six-inch beech that topples in silence. If a tree falls in the forest and a guy standing right next to it can't fucking hear it, does he even exist?

Just as he starts to log up the pieces for firewood, the wind shifts and the remaining beeches shudder as if every leaf were a raw nerve. Within a minute the sky goes black over the mountains, the air puckers with salt mist, a cold rain blows slantwise in from the northeast. He sheaths the saw blade and tightens his sweatshirt hood. By the time he's back at the cabin he's soaked to the bone, and after wiping the chain down, he throws some pine knots into the woodstove and strips his clothes off in the growing heat. He almost thought he'd be joined by the clamdigger but the aluminum skiff is nowhere to be seen, just the raw greenish-black sea beyond the breakwater ledge and a flock of gulls hovering pale as spirits over his little cove.

He's got a bucket of live mussels and two sea cucumbers, which he's never tried, some late rose hips from the rugosa around the old outhouse site, a bag of cattails, an onion and three potatoes from his dad's last visit, plus a dozen stalks of beach parsley. The mackerel from yesterday spent the night in the outside cooler; it's as moist and fresh as when he hauled it in. The colder the nights get, the more meat and fish he can store. Three cans of evaporated milk, a leftover drumstick of the rabbit to add some land energy, and he'll have a serious chowder in the galvanized bucket that once caught a roof leak but is now free for a higher cause.

Next to his plank bed is a green-and-white Wal-Mart duffel his mom sent out half stocked with clean, folded familiar clothing from his high-school days, half with brand-new heavier stuff for fall. He picks some old shorts and a Radiohead T-shirt carrying all the scents of the laundry room at home, even the lotion his mom uses on her hands. His sense of smell has grown keen as a bomb dog. His nose had blistered and grown numb in the Sandbox from the diesel and sewage stench, ammunition and blown-out oil wells, rancid street food and the odor of ever-present death. Now he can see with his nostrils like an animal. He can tell which side of the island he's on and where the wind is and if the sheep have been around the cabin or a distant tanker has navigated up the bay. At one point he pulled his watch cap down over his eyes and smelled his way from the cabin to the south cove pier, knowing where he was at every turn by scent: the path with its balsam and hint of wild garlic on the right and decaying beech leaves on the left, the stereophonic balance of salt sea and balsamic fir, the leftover creosote smells of the old dorm site, freshness of the wellspring and then the bleeding sap of his own clear-cutting, the pier's whispers of gasoline and chain metal and the rotting wooden traps of the old lobsterman that lived there once. One windless morning he returned to their old campsite and picked up the year-old scent of Brenda Campion in the meadow air. Even if something should blind him he could still survive.

Now as the pine-knot blaze steams the mussels open in one pot and the onions and beach peas simmer beside the slowly warming condensed milk, the aroma is like a chorus with each instrument adding its own flavor that can be inhaled and swallowed as he always wanted to do with music but never could. His new roof is holding against the strong heavy rain. He wipes the condensation off the window to look outside over the cove because he cannot perceive its hammering overhead. It drills bomb craters into the water's surface and the half-tide mudflats. It's more than ordinary rain: a hail of .30 caliber ice balls that riddle the surface like a Gatling gun and ricochet off the aluminum cooler and the red paint of the upturned dory's keel. The heron who usually fishes in all weather is out of sight.

He takes the six-barbed harpoon point out of the ammo box, places it on the bare tabletop which he has rubbed smooth with a flat beach stone the way they used to scour decks on the old ships. The point is a treasure and a connection, the only object he needs to possess. *The more you have of things*, Henry says, *the poorer you are.* He has two rifles, a shotgun, a chain saw, a shelter that withstands a storm so thick he can't see the dory anymore. He pulls the mussel pot back from the burner, cracks open the hinged window to replace the oxygen sucked into the chimney by the stove.

He's read Henry's book through twice, wondering what foodstuffs kept him alive. No tea, coffee, butter, milk, or meat. He fished for pickerel, he tasted the woodchuck, he foraged some berries; otherwise it was beans. *One looks, and one does not see; one listens, and one does not hear; one eats, and one does not know the savor of food.* In the desert

Nick lived on MREs but he might as well have been eating dog shit; he didn't taste it and he didn't care.

He pulls a silvery-blue mussel from the boiling pot. It's steamed open, yellow and black inside, the softened hinge barely hanging onto its shell. He fingers it and for a moment flashes on Brenda in the sky-blue tent: this salty portion, boiled in seawater, now body temperature in the palm of his hand. He slurps and holds it in his mouth to grind fine sandy bits between his teeth, lets it slip warmly down tongue and throat. She loved it when he went down on her. She'd clamp his head with both legs so he couldn't stop. With his dish towel he clears steam from the window like a memory; outside, the hail's smaller now, pea-sized but still peppering the overturned dory like a firing squad.

Then he clears the pane and looks again. Through the slant hail and wet sweeping fog an upright shape walks toward him entirely concealed in a sky-blue burqa with only the eyes showing and a humped back like a deformed freak out of a dream. His first thought is, They've fucking come for him, either Dupuy or Ramos or some Ba'athist zombie has crossed from the other side. From the brace of guns against the back wall he instantly picks the shotgun which will spray lead even if his aim is bad. He'll stand his ground at the threshold but he won't go out there. He prays with tight silent lips that the apparition will walk on past and disappear into the hail and mist and beyond recollection when the weather clears, but the burqa keeps coming along the footpath through the downpour and he knows in five seconds it's going to be either them or him.

There's nothing but a cracked wooden turn-latch to keep the door closed which will explode open in an instant and he wishes the fuck he'd done more about security. Three miles of deepwater channel is not an obstacle if the time has come. He stands before his door with the gun pointed at chest height waiting for the breakthrough but it doesn't happen. He circles to look out the window toward the front door but the hail's even worse and the panes are thick with condensation so he can't see. The steam from the mussel pot is turning black as the last drops of seawater must be drying up.

Keeping the .410 trained on the door planks, he edges to clear a windowpane with his palm and jumps back when he sees a human hand against the same glass trying to wipe it from the outside. Why aren't they entering? Why aren't they forcing their way through? Finally he feels the door and it pulses like something's striking the other side. He turns the latch and swings it open the way they were trained, pushes the shotgun barrel right up against the burqa with the rainwater sluicing down off the roof over its hood. One hand goes up and the other pulls the head cover off and it's not a black ghost or Arab but a pale wet human female with gold earrings and her mouth open trying to speak through a deluge of hail and rain. He's seen that face before, over and over: She has been sent every night to kill him in his dreams.

She sees the gun and spins around fast back into the storm but trips and collapses to a kneeling position on the rain-soaked path. It would be an easy shot but she's down and kneels there on all fours unable to rise because of her deformity, one leg under the burqa while the other sticks out and her foot's bare, with a micro tattoo over the ankle bone. He leans the gun inside on the door frame, pulls his hat and wet camo jacket off the peg, and walks out to help her up. She takes the hand offered and rises slowly due to the reverse curvature of her spine, but lets go the minute she stands up and heads back along the woods path in the unceasing hail. He turns her around by her shoulders and basically marches her inside like a detainee. He seats her on his sleeping bag spread out on the plank bed. Water is streaming not only off her rainwear but out of her eyes and nose like a drowned body and her whole face seems to overflow onto the bed and floor.

He has a jar of instant coffee and some Lipton's tea bags from his mother's last shipment, but the first thing is to help remove the burqa which is flooding water onto the bed. She's all tangled up in it but he can stand over her and lift up the fabric by the hood, though it's hard to get it over her shoulder hump. Then she frees the wet nylon by raising her weight a little from the sleeping bag and it slides free. With the burqa gone, it appears the hump is not part of her body but a maroon-colored daypack with a small tripod strapped to the side, the kind snipers use to steady their muzzle sight.

He hangs the wet garment near the stove on a wall peg and by the time he turns around she's got a fake camera out so he moves for the closest weapon, the carbine, since she's blocking the shotgun from use by sitting there. He points the .30-30 toward her feet but does not raise it. She's got both hands in the air, one with the camera in it. As he was trained, he motions with the carbine for her to lay the camera on the bed, which she does, though it could be on a clicking timer and he wouldn't know. Even though she's disarmed he keeps the gun in his right hand while reaching into the food crate for the box of tea. She nods and moves her mouth as if trying to talk and smile, though she also seems pale and shaken and despite the nylon covering, her jeans and sweatshirt are soaked through.

The face is familiar not just from the dreams but from the library where he researched the Maritime Archaics. She had the same device, the hollowed-out camera packed with C-4 explosive, one of the commonest IEDs. He escaped just before she could detonate it in the public library.

Without putting the shotgun down he steps over to the bed to pick it up by the neck strap, not wanting to touch the device itself, slowly and carefully, with the cool concentration of a sapper. At first she tries to keep him away from it but at the slightest movement of the gun barrel she withdraws her hand. He goes to open the door and neutralize it by throwing it in the rain, but he's stopped by her look of terror and lowers it gingerly to the table beside the harpoon point.

With the device on the other side of the room from her, he leans the carbine next to the shotgun on the back wall, throws in three more small pine knots to goose the fire, and measures out two cups of fresh water for the pot. She's shaking all over now, hugging herself while the chill blues her cheeks. He opens the Wal-Mart duffel and puts it in her lap. She looks directly at him, the way captive insurgents try to bridge the language barrier with their eyes, then touches the back of his hand with her fingertips, all the time moving her mouth. He would signal his handicap, but why reveal weakness to an adversary who will at any minute stop trembling and recover strength?

The water's sending up a cloud of steam; he pours out two cups and when he turns back she's foraging in the bag, looking up and forming words that may be asking for privacy in the one-room hut. He slips her damp poncho over his head and starts to step outside, then turns back to pick up both guns and shelter them under the loose blue nylon, same way the hadjis carried them under their prayer robes. He walks out into a deluge which is no longer hail but huge globular tropical raindrops the size of paintballs. He hunches his body forward to protect the weapons and to feel on his back the intensity of the rainfall he cannot hear.

When he returns and leans the rifle and shotgun in their corner, she's in a blue Red Sox jacket and khaki Dockers that bag around her ankles and reach the floor. Her feet are completely hidden except the toe tips as she stretches above the stove to hang her wet sweatshirt from his dulse-drying line. She's not moving her mouth anymore, just quiet and close-lipped as she sits back down with the tea in a Del Monte can. He throws his remaining beach peas with eight ounces of pearl onions in the galvanized bucket and sits at the table with his Ka-Bar to shuck the mussels. The shells go one by one into an old chain-oil carton, eyes keeping watch on her all the time. Her hair is the color of a fallen leaf. She shakes it a few times like a wet Lab, reaches for

The Portable Thoreau under the window and smiles with the uniform even teeth that marked the kids in the AP class. She remembers what her mother said about shell shock. Maybe he can't hear her because of the downpour on the roof. On the table where the book was is also the notepad his father brought. His last words are GAS. SAW OIL. KEROSENE. CAMELS. GRASS WHIP. MACHETE.

He rips off the lower half and writes, WHO ARE YOU?

She writes her name in a fast rounded print, not the expected cursive, and then points at him and draws a question mark.

CARETAKER. He starts to write his name, Nicolas Colonna, but his training kicks in and he stops. Give nothing away during interrogation if you can help it.

OH, RIGHT. MY MOM MENTIONED YOU. SO, YOU'RE PROTECTING THE ISLAND FROM ME.

He turns his back on her to tend the stove, pours the condensed milk and drained beach peas into what's left of the mussel broth. He opens the central ring of the front burner to expose the main dish for a few minutes to the open coals.

This makes twice they have sent her after him. He evaded her the first time in the library, but now escape is prevented by the violent storm outside the door. They chose this weather knowing he'd be forced to take her in, which he was; even an animal couldn't have been left outside. She must be hungry but there's no decent bowl to serve her, only the stew cans he uses for himself, though his mother did send four spoons wrapped in a rubber band. She was a grizzly about manners and on Sundays wrapped each cloth napkin in a silver ring.

He drains out the seawater from the vegetables, throws in a handful of rockweed for an ocean flavor, and pours half the stew into that can, using his spoon to divide the peas and mussels equally. One time they brought an insurgent into the base who was so hungry his face was stretched over the bones like a skull. He had been on the run from a roadside explosion and he was heading for prison, or worse—that is, if he ever got there, since just looking at him the guys were thumbing their sidearms and M-16s. Yet they opened an MRE for him and when he scarfed it down they gave him another, and someone gave him a Red Bull and an Almond Joy. Hunger is a language everyone understands.

He shuffles the table over to the girl in the Red Sox jacket, puts the stew cans on it, and slips out two of his mother's spoons. She's shaking her head, though, and trying to communicate something in words, with her eyes enlarged and liquid, as if she's absorbed so much water in the storm that it overflows.

He downs a spoonful of the delicious stew the way you'd show an infant what to do with food. She stares at the barbed point in the center of the table between their two meals, reaches out almost to touch it, then draws back, takes the pad and writes, YOU WERE IN THE LIBRARY. I HAVE YOUR PHOTOGRAPH. I REMEMBER YOUR GRANDFATHER. WHY WON'T YOU TALK TO ME?

She's not going to eat till she gets an answer. He takes the pad, draws a cartoon ear in a circle, then a diagonal line through it. She nods understanding, then writes:

HOW? ALWAYS?

COMBAT.

Now she knows. Under the glare of hostile inquiry, he has broken. Failed his unit and companion in revealing as much as he has.

She studies the contents of her stew can for a moment with spoon upheld, as if looking for something moving or still alive. She had been wearing makeup or eye darkener, possibly a disguise, but the rainwater has slurred it on her face, making her look like a soldier in nighttime ops. He takes another bite, including a mussel chewed slow to show they're nontoxic, and finally she dives the spoon in, finds a couple of beach peas and then a mussel that she swallows whole, and another.

Among the raw shellfish there was one oyster left at the bottom of the hod and he retrieves it and puts the Ka-Bar in its slit and bangs it once on the table top to split it open. He hands it to her on the half shell as a dessert and she swallows it raw without hesitation, like someone who's done it many times before.

They don't have anything to drink but the lukewarm tea, so he empties the two cups and opens the new bottle of Jim Beam that came with the last visit from his dad. Almost a week and he hasn't broken the seal. Henry D's like the hadjis on that point: *Water is the only drink for a wise man.* He pours one for himself and offers it to the visitor, who sips lightly but steadily and drains it off.

Thank you, she mouths, white upper teeth touched by her small red tongue. It's not just lips that you read, it's the whole mouth. You see the word being formed inside, then it sounds clearly in the ear of the mind.

He takes the pad and writes, How did you get here?

Kayak, she writes. South cove.

First time?

~~100th~~ 1,000th time.

Who are you? What is your mission here?

She prints, Julia Fletcher. This is my father's island. Have to take photos before it's too late.

She could be lying; how could you know? It would be the obvious cover for this operation. How can you tell what's inside of anything, under the surface? You can't trust any language written or spoken. Evans said human speech got invented so that people could lie. Nick thought he was free of words but they've followed him even here.

He writes, Chad your old man?

No. My father died. Marston Fletcher. Last May, the 22nd. Chad is my brother-in-law.

Husband's sister, Nick writes.

SISTER'S HUSBAND. HIS DEVELOPMENT. CLUB ~~MED~~. CLUB AMBER.

AMBER RETREATS LLC, he corrects her. He knows the name; they're his employer.

She writes, SAME DIFFERENCE, then pours a half refill of the Jim Beam.

Outside, the rain and fog have abated so he can see the cove behind her. The blue heron returns with its huge wingspread and settles on its rock. The waterfall off the roof has slowed to a light curtain of separate drops. For some reason the girl is crying, a tear or two already discoloring the yellow pad.

DAD WANTED IT FOREVER WILD.

MOTHER?

RESORT. SISTER RESORT, BROTHER RESORT.

BROTHER-IN-LAW?

REAL BROTHER, TOO.

OUTGUNNED, he writes. OPTIONS?

PHOTOGRAPHS, TO REMEMBER WHAT IT WAS. SUMMER, FALL, WINTER. THEN NOT COME BACK.

WHERE?

END OF THE EARTH.

Her forehead and cheeks red from exposure and sadness, she hunches over the yellow pad with the pencil he sharpens with the bayonet. The moisture of her face makes it look transparent though it could still be a mask over what's beneath. Half the broth is still in her can and she didn't touch her rockweed or dulse, but it looks like all the mussels and peas are gone, she ate the oyster, and the whiskey cup's empty—a good thing if she's going to head out through the ongoing rain and paddle a kayak four miles to the mainland.

He does nothing to stop her when she reaches to put the camera back in its yellow case, just steps aside as she reclaims her poncho from the drying wire. Then she pauses and laughs, touches her own shoulders, surprised that she's still wearing his shirt and pants.

He grabs pad and pencil and writes, YOURS. KEEP THEM.

She writes, TRADE?

YOU CAN COME BACK FOR THEM.

AND GET SHOT?

SORRY ABOUT THAT.

OK—DOING YOUR JOB, I GUESS.

She rises to take her spoon and stew can to the dish basin on the stove, then writes THANKS. When she turns the latch and opens the door to leave, the cold air passes right through his T-shirt to the skin. He puts a hand on her shoulder to stay her and purses his lips to form the word *Wait*. He takes out the wooden ammo box and offers her the carved bone fishhook with its red glazing half worn off by sixty centuries. TAKE IT. DON'T SHOW IT TO ANYONE. YOU ALONE.

She hesitates, then picks it up, turns it around in visible respect for its antiquity and lethal sharpness, then writes, WHERE DID YOU GET THIS?

HERE. THIS ISLAND.

WHERE? I'VE NEVER SEEN ANYTHING LIKE THIS.

So he was right; he is the first to grope back through the sediment of time to find these things. The tree had to come down, then the Labor Day monsoon that sluiced the vertical bank into the streambed. He poises the pencil and starts to answer, then presses the point down till it breaks and the word he writes makes no impression on the page. The moment for that may come, but not just now.

She takes a damp flowery red bandana from her daypack and wraps the hook over and over, then puts it in a zippered compartment in the pack. She takes out the camera and asks permission with her face. This time it's okay, even if the thing goes off.

He stands by the stove and she moves to the far corner for enough distance. He tries for a thousand-yard stare but the room's only twelve feet across. Outside it's clearing by the minute; the interior floods with brightening daylight from the half-open door. He stands still without smiling, one hand on the empty ammo box. Her finger presses the shutter button and he closes his eyes for death. He's ready; he may not have done all he intended, but they're expecting him. Then he looks again and she's frowning, shaking her head. She takes another, eyes open, then she puts the Nikon in its case along with her folded poncho in the pack.

She writes one more thing on the yellow pad.

COMBAT WHERE?

OPERATION IRAQI FREEDOM.

She nods, straps the daypack on, pauses for a second before turning away out the open door. She knows now not even to try speaking to him. He held her at gunpoint, then gave her food and clothing and shelter from aerial bombardment. Out of an unknown impulse he broke all discipline and risked everything to give her a token from another world. They scared each other like two animals meeting on a path, then they sat for a meal harvested from the land and sea. Her father's just dead and the children are gathered for the inheritance; like lean desert scavengers they draw in close.

She came with an adversary's stealth and a landowner's confidence and stood there defiant with a shotgun trained right at her chest. She arrived here alone and self-reliant till assaulted by ice balls from the stratosphere. The resort is destined to go forward and she knows it. Anyone that arrives with a pilot named Rolf on a helipad, one girl's not going to deviate his plan. Chad's a bull colonel driving his Stryker over in-laws and mute caretakers in his path.

Julia Fletcher.

He could join her in protest, then they'd fire him and he'd lose the power to guard his people, who are not this hailstorm succubus but the ochre-hued sleepers in the gravel bank. Out of blind impulse he gave her the fossil hook, but if she was sent to distract him she did not succeed.

By now the storm's stopped and his visitor has walked the wet pathway all the way to the woods' edge. He watches her shrink and vanish among the tree shadows, just a vertical blue shape among rain-blackened spruce trunks, then she's gone. Overhead the clouds are disintegrating and sunlight floods down in white-hot patches over the bay.

He turns back to scrub the cookware out with seawater and a wire brush, no longer thinking of Juan Ramos or Brenda Campion but another kind of ghost, barefoot and walking ahead of him in time.

13

At one a.m. he stands for a moment on the public pier, glancing back once at the snow-covered Ledgeport waterfront, all streets festooned with multicolored lights. The towering municipal Christmas tree is topped by the blazing star that has more than once blinded the hadjis in the Babylonian night. One day, if we lose vigilance, they'll come to avenge Saddam and harness their tanks to that tree and pull it down. The work lamps of the docked ferry illuminate the few wintering vessels, including his own dory patiently waiting at the one remaining float. Lights shimmer and reflect off the surface, beneath them the water absolutely black and still. His green-and-white duffel's full of supplies and wrapped gifts from spending Christmas Eve at his parents' house, an inexcusable weakness and mistake, but at least he's out of there on a flood tide with the island ahead of him in the dark. Not a breath of wind on the harbor surface.

Off to the eastward a faint glow brightens the horizon from the unrisen moon. A kid might have walked here once after a game or party just to watch as the lighthouse's circling beam sweeps the harbor and darkens and sweeps again; it's in his own memory but it was someone else. Time circles back to a place which is no longer there, nor the people contained by it. That life ended in an unsurvivable explosion with his remains picked at by jackals in the street.

Thanksgiving he'd made the right decision and stayed on the island despite all efforts to extradite him to New Mexico to see the baby. He wasn't going. The clamdigger Merton Alley, who has no known family on Earth, showed up Thanksgiving morning with a 20-gauge shotgun and a half-gallon of Fireball Whisky. Merton isn't much at writing but he made his acquaintance with the Sandbox back in Desert Storm, so they have an understanding that needs no words.

They followed wild turkey tracks through the first snow till they found six hens in a harem circle around a big tom. They didn't need the male, so Merton dropped a stout little hen with the 20-gauge while the other birds rocketed into the woods. Turkeys stalk around on their long legs like human beings; it's a joke when they try to take off, then they're out of sight.

Nick plucked and spitted her over the uncovered stove fire while Merton boiled up all kinds of shellfish out of his clam hod, not just mussels and quahogs but whelks, snails, oysters, razorfish, anything that digs in the tidal mud like he does, Merton will eat it. He lives on the bottom like a bloodworm with no attachments and the only thing going for him is he's alive. Steamed clams and whiskey and turkey with baked crabapples from the old farmstead; they ate like a couple of Pilgrims at Plymouth Rock.

Christmas has been a different story. His father came out with Mr. F on a windy Saturday with a letter from his mom begging him to come home for the holiday. Angela was coming with Rebecca and you'd have thought she was bringing the Christ Child Himself. He surrendered and despite Hallett Bunker's offer to taxi him, he rowed the dory the morning of the 24th in a snowy nor'easter that blew him across the ship channel and all he had to do was keep the boat straight with his oars.

He first hit the Ledgeport Savings Bank, then Planet Toys for a soft, large-eyed green octopus and a pink blanket, as it was a girl. He also got ammo for both guns, chain oil, Camels, a flashlight plus batteries, a case of canned goods, a hundred pounds of organic sheep feed, five gallons of kerosene for the long winter nights, and stowed them all in the dory for the return trip. If the cove ices in there won't be any supply runs for a while.

Brenda Campion showed up briefly in a tinselly green velvet cleavage dress like a tree ornament, immediately picked up little Rebecca, and rocked her with her eyes closed; it made him wonder if she was pregnant now herself. It was a scene he'd envisioned day and night in the desert but her image has since been superimposed by a sky-colored poncho, wet with rain. Brenda hung on to Nick's little niece and her stuffed octopus while his mother huddled with Angela in the kitchen, his sister crying in a way that said the child is wonderful but already the marriage isn't right. Toward the end of the evening his mother wrote PLEASE DON'T GO BACK TO THE ISLAND—BUT IF YOU HAVE TO, CAN THE BABY USE YOUR ROOM FOR A WHILE? ANGELA'S GOING TO SPEND SOME TIME WITH US.

Earlier, after Brenda had cheek-kissed him good-bye and walked off toward an idling Dodge pickup, his mother had pulled him aside and written, I THINK SHE STILL MISSES YOU! Then she added, AND DR. BORQUE DOES TOO! HE SAID HE WOULD STOP BY TOMORROW. CAN YOU IMAGINE? HE MUST BE ANXIOUS TO SEE YOU.

A VA house call on Christmas morning; the next step is a locked corridor and you're involuntarily committed with no way out. Time to cut his ties with the mainland again, starting at midnight. He slapped and hugged his old boss Mark Davis, work buddies Travis and Roger, and his dad and mom and little Rebecca and Angela, who never stopped crying, even though it was Christmas Eve. He hugged his dad who suddenly looked like a grandfather, as if Rebecca had brought him the present of old age. He'd arrived with a few Christmas gifts and a change of clothes he didn't even use; he left with the Wal-Mart bag slung over his shoulder, containing a fresh bottle of Jim Beam, a goose-down sleeping bag, and a pair of thermal boots from L.L.Bean. Wearing a brand-new Cabela's Thinsulate stalking coat from his mom, he shouldered his pack like a camouflage Santa to head down the snowy hill.

He chips through the thin rime of ice on the dory seat with his Ka-Bar and pulls off from all mainland connections with his seaward oar. The small luminous compass on the stern thwart gives a true bearing amid the confusion of Christmas and harbor lights, village and home and family that would have encaged him like a ferret if he'd stayed the night. Now 25 December 0100, with a sense of new birth perhaps from his niece Rebecca, he watches the town tree diminish and become just one of many points of light, then the stars start to outshine the streetlights till finally there are only stars. As his eyes open and adjust he can look up to the great overhead space track of the Milky Way, center the transom under the Sword of Orion and darken the compass to row by starlight till the moon takes over and lights him home.

One time in the desert he was hanging outside the hooch with Dupuy and Evans after some shit had come in and it was quiet again and they stood speechless, listening for more. The Arab sky was so clogged with road dust and diesel fumes that only one star shined through and Evans said this was where the Three Wise Kings came from, the Magi, right here, can you believe it? Fucking Arabs were princes and scholars at that time. Then Dupuy said they ain't looking so wise anymore, we got them with shock and awe. Evans said the Arabs were the smartest fucking people on Earth; they invented numbers and arithmetic and predicted eclipses of the sun. They followed a supernova from here to Israel and knelt down and submitted their wealth and kingdoms to a kid that was less than a week old. Moby said yes sir, and they just submitted again, to a bunch of motherfuckers with M-16s.

He thinks of his mother and Brenda and Angela clustered around the newborn like the livestock at the Nativity. He was no different. Besides the green octopus, he'd brought a whistle of birch wood that he'd carved with his Ka-Bar, which he could blow through for Rebecca but he couldn't hear.

After he's past the breakwater lighthouse, every oar stroke in the sky-black water stirs phosphorescent plankton into a whirlpool of light, more stars under the surface than there are above. Sky and water reflect each other as the dory's wake mirrors the contrail of a high-altitude aircraft, maybe troops bound for the desert, maybe their bodies flying home. Dupuy Williams believed Jesus was a black man. His own Texas preacher told him that. Evans would say, "In your dreams, man; he would have looked like a hadji though." All that shit happened in the desert, the Ten Commandments, the stable and the animals, the kings from the Orient, a guy nailed to a cross, Arab or African, it didn't matter, Mohammed and all his women like the hen turkeys around the old uncle Tom.

One time at the checkpoint a beat-up old Nissan pickup didn't even slow down. They shot for the tires but hit the gas tank and the driver ran into the desert, his clothes on fire like a human torch. Now on Christmas Eve the running flame and black gasoline smoke appear as a mirage over the unlit water behind him, so he rows faster to get away and the steam of his own breath blends with the pillar of fire behind him from the burning man.

When he turns to see forward the island lies before him, its mild snowy surface like an old silver photograph. So it was when they paddled home late from the swordfish grounds, their catch silvered from starlight in the hull. The slow tidal heave pushes a layer of sea ice against the breakwater rocks of the north cove. Henry D says the frozen pond made a noise like artillery in the night; saltwater ice could go off like a hydrogen bomb and he'd never know. He runs the dory hard onshore and it almost self-propels up the slope of iced beach stones each individually illuminated by the risen moon.

Behind his cabin is the silhouette of a woodshed that's doubled in size since he added the sheepfold to the other side. The sheep had been coming closer and closer as the ground froze, cropping the salt-sprayed grasses between the cabin and the red spruce woods. No shepherd has used this structure for at least thirty years, but it's as if they remembered who once cared for their ancestors over the winter and they've come back. He rounds the woodshed corner to where he's roofed over a simple three-sided enclosure that they cluster together in for warmth. Every day he carries a contractor bag and a grass whip along with the chain saw, returns from his clear-cutting with a load of winter spartina over his shoulder so they can snack during the night. By touch he counts their invisible faces as they crowd around and tongue the fingers of his gloves. Sometimes there's five or six, sometimes as many as ten, the oldest one ragged enough to be a survivor from the original fire. Others are smaller, still clinging and dependent. They couple and multiply out here not even knowing they're cut off from their own kind. Merton's always pointing the carbine at them but Nick lifts it out of his hands, turns it, and touches the barrel to the center of Merton's chest. The sheep are family; he'd eat ten fucking clamdiggers before they came to any harm.

He kneels between two of them with each hand deep in the gritty warmth of their neck wool: slow soundless inhalations and the pulse of their living skin. He could half imagine spending the night out here amid warm bodies, but his legs cramp from kneeling on the cold ground and he stands upright.

This night, or morning, really, the twenty-fifth Christmas since his own birth, he leaves the sheepfold and stomps his boots on the packed snow before slinging the duffel inside. A drink of water would be good after the long row, but his two-gallon container is frozen solid and won't thaw till morning when he cranks the stove. The Jim Beam, however, is like drinking antifreeze. They must have invented alcohol during the Ice Age; nothing else would have gotten them through. It stays liquid and keeps the blood from crystallizing in the night. It warms him enough to get the lamp started and zip into the new sleeping bag to watch the moon-shadows morph and progress along the cabin wall.

Thinking of Rebecca, he remembers what Evans said once in the hooch: If the Virgin had given birth to a daughter we'd all be better off. He imagines a thirty-three-year-old woman crucified over the altar of St. Joseph's Catholic Church, bleeding from sword cuts and naked except for the loincloth, but he's not sure that would improve the world. Then he's in a Bradley with Evans and Juan Ramos and they're looking for Dupuy who knows a military secret and they have to bring him in. It's arctic winter in the desert and there's all these human corpses frozen in the permafrost. They find one alive and moving but instead of Dupuy it's the visitor Julia, just sleeping in the desert snow. Evans and Ramos wake her up to arrest her and the last thing he hears is her voice streaming through the cabin window like the sun.

He can't see anything through the iced-up glass but the blood orange of winter dawn. The stove's gone out and the top of the Beam bottle's lying on the table by the harpoon point, which he must have brought out to examine, he can't even remember. The whiskey's a third gone and he'll have to ration it now till Merton brings another, though it will be a while before Merton or anyone else can get in here. He was lucky to leave when he did. Last night he could barely crunch through the sea ice to reach the landing, now scraping a windowpane with his Ka-Bar reveals a sheet on the whole cove that's been rising and expanding with the tide. Iced in. Two crows are strutting around on the glazed surface and glancing at each other like it's a miracle—look, we can walk out here, just like the waterfowl. Henry might have consumed nothing but water but he didn't live on a Maine island where you have to use an icepick to get a drink.

He throws some kerosene and a match on the half-charred stove wood and it flares right up, then he puts the water jug to thaw on the upper shelf and carefully places the barbed point back in the ammo box. The Red Paint community will be snowbound and sealed with cold, out of danger till March or April when the choppers will start landing materials and the island begins its new life as a destination.

A few more pine knots and the air around the stovepipe starts to shimmer and mirage from the flue heat. He puts the new boots on and steps outside with the rest of the salt grass in the contractor bag along with some new organic feed. Through the vapor cloud of his breath the whole cove appears frozen solid. Behind that, a layer of sea smoke bleaches the air over the ship channel. The visible world is a huge white one-dimensional curtain, except for two crow-shaped openings to the complete darkness beyond.

Not wanting to have breakfast before the animals eat, he carries the bag around the woodshed corner, but they're not there. Their footprints lead up the path through the snow to the spruce woods, round little sheep turds frozen solid as ball bearings on the icy floor. He follows their scat trail thinking to find at least one or two of them, then a huge shape rises suddenly from the wood's edge: the brown eagle with a red stain on its yellow beak. It keeps hovering low and close. Its shadow darkens the snow like an eclipse, its pinions black fingers in the cold dense air.

He sees a depression and discoloration in the path, as if someone spent a rough night there. His heart pounds with the image of Julia camping fifty yards off in zero weather unable to come in, knocking and knocking and not being heard. But there are sheep droppings under the skim of frost, and the snowpack reddens when he scrapes at it. A trail of congealed blood drops leads toward the old-growth spruce around the eagle nest. He comes upon the lamb at the field's edge, its throat torn and its belly of entrails exposed like an operating room. The snow's fanned and leveled all around as if a chopper had landed there. He's thinking the eagle might have come down and killed it, then he sees the half-covered paw prints all around. Coyote. He thought he saw one once, when he was clearing the number-four bungalow site closest to the south woods. It was a shadow of a canine shape just lightly visible among thick trunks, low-slung, slinking phantom-like at the periphery of vision. Armed with the Husqvarna, he hunkered into the grass and waited, but it didn't show. He figured he'd hallucinated, started the saw again and carried it idling till the cabin was in sight.

The paw prints in the snow are not a hallucination. It could have been one or two animals, maybe just one, a loner like himself, that must have scattered the sheep from their shelter while he was gone, then taken the slowest or smallest one. This happens when your commitment softens just for a moment, one evening spent hanging with kids and women, and an animal under your protection is dragged through the snow by its broken neck. But it could also have been while he was in his bed, it could have been yapping and howling every night behind the cabin, closer and closer, he'd never know, nor hear the bleats and hoofbeats when it struck the sheepfold. How can he guard anything, the way he is? He couldn't protect his own even when he could hear.

By its hind legs he starts dragging the stiff carcass over the frozen surface toward the cabin, but it seems thoughtless. Even an animal corpse must be respected; death makes no distinctions as to rank or privilege. He bends down and scoops it up like a child you'd find in the street or forest and carry home. It was the smallest of them and not much heavier than Rebecca with its liquids drained off and so much of the midsection chewed away. He carries the sheep home like a human being. Tears glaciate on his cheeks and around his eyes till he can hardly see. His mother's voice is crying *That's your brand-new coat,* but the frozen intestines aren't leaving any marks, nor the congealed blood from the ripped throat. He puts it down on the icy pathway a hundred feet from the cabin, close enough for a decent shot, hopefully far enough so it won't sense his presence when it returns.

He throws some more wood in the stove to keep the water jug thawing, then with the blade of the chain-saw tool he pries one plank from the small boarded-up back window so he can observe the dead sheep out in the graying air. A few large flakes parachute slowly down to whitewash the torn stained wool. Black crows and ravens arrive and jostle in a loose circle around the kill. Every once in a while one makes a half-flight over and rips at the wound's edge, then startles back. The eagle perches on a high limb looking down, wise enough to respect the new opening in the cabin wall.

He takes the .30-30 from its peeled wooden pegs, fills the magazine, and levers a round into the chamber. For once he wishes for a scope sight so he could leave the bait closer to the woods. But if the coyote came all the way to a sheepfold thick with the scent of man, it must be starving and will return. He rests the barrel on the window plank and sights in on a thick-beaked raven on the lamb's shoulder that's pulling at the neck wound without much effect. He leans the rifle and pours out some water to boil for coffee and oatmeal, then places on the stove grate a slice each of his mom's Christmas fruitcake and Angela's sourdough bread. When he returns to his gun port the ravens and crows are scattered and it's the young eagle standing guard over the carcass. He wonders if the eagle would defend it against a coyote or give it up, and whether he's even going to see it or if it only returns by night, and if it does, with the late moonrise will there be light enough to see?

He spends the rest of the dull windless morning dragging deadwood like a beaver through softly falling snow, to pile up a fourth wall for the sheepfold. They'll be protected on all sides except for a small opening, which might let them defend themselves better at the entranceway.

By midday the snow has cleared and the sea smoke lifted. A green supertanker slowly passes south to north in the ship channel. They suck petroleum from the sweltering desert where people have never seen a winter day. They ship it eight thousand miles to the furnaces of these little Maine houses whose lights are beginning to turn on one by one after their Christmas dinners, far above them the military caskets headed to Dover, Delaware, right over the oil-transit lanes.

He squeezes his eyes shut and sees the World Trade Center as if it's on a video screen, Americans dropping like snowflakes from their office windows and the pilot Mohamed Atta incinerated in the tower's heart. Back inside he finds the pilot's Last Will and Testament among the papers from the Ledgeport library and pins it with the point of his Ka-Bar to the cabin wall.

Let each one of you sharpen his blade, so the one he butchers will be glad. If Allah gives you a victim's throat to slit, then carry out this sacrifice. The flight attendant opens the cockpit door, a box cutter at her throat, then at the throat of a United Airlines captain as if he were an unclean animal, a human pig strapped to the killing chair, the lamb's neck opened by coyote fangs. He moves without fear in the determination and surety of his revenge.

Off to the north, all that's left of the supertanker is a faint stern lamp surrounded by the bright yellow tugboat lights. He carries the last wood load for his sheepfold wall and heads to the gun port with his loaded rifle at hand. He has not lit the kerosene lamp or refueled the stove, keeping the darkest possible profile. The opening is less than a foot square but admits such a cold draft that his hands will tremble and ruin his aim. He slices a spare work glove with his Ka-Bar so only his trigger finger will be exposed. He must have been ten or eleven, not long after Nonno Guido died, when his dad first taught him to use a rifle, to steady himself by closing all chambers of his mind but one, to fire on the top of the breath cycle, between the slow beats of a controlled disciplined heart. He and his dad would return with two carcasses in the pickup which they would paunch and scrape out at the hunting camp. He came to do more of the knife work each year, from the first cut under the breastbone to the pile of organs and entrails that steamed in the cold air of the skinning yard.

The sheep's silhouette is barely distinguishable as an inanimate mound in the early dusk, then it seems to change slightly, to rise out of itself and take canine form as if it had contained the coyote within it: gaunt skeletal body, wolf-shaped ears, long snout that bends to feed at the lamb's nape as he lines the foresight in the rear notch and lowers the barrel till it's right at the shoulder. If he had the M-16 he'd forget about precision and just rake the snowyard, but with this one he gets one chance, then it'll be in the woods before he can lever another round.

He counts breaths: two slow and steady while the coyote pulls at the lamb's crystallized windpipe, then on the top of the third between heartbeats a smooth cool squeeze and it recoils hard and silent on his right shoulder as the muzzle flame lights the air like a photo strobe. In that blinded moment he sees the unblinking Arab sky through the top opening of the Humvee and Dupuy Williams up there spraying the street backhand with mini Mr. Goodbars and red Tootsie Pops.

His eyes adjust back but he can't see the coyote. It's gone back to the woods, or if he hit it it's howling on the ground. You can't aim if you know you're not going to hear the report. He steps outside with the rifle on point for a wounded animal and his breath white and visible in the clearing air. Soon as he steps behind the cabin he sees the thing writhing and trying to get away from the carcass as if the dead sheep has a grip on it and won't let go. It's up on its forelegs but the hindquarters stay bound to the ice; it must have taken the hollow-point in its lower spine. In the veiled twilight he stands halfway between cabin and coyote and levels the .30-30 at its skull, for once wanting his eardrums back to hear its helpless and trapped yowling before finishing it off. He's in no hurry. Leashed to its victim by the spine shot, it's a windup toy animal spinning its wheeled base in a single spot. It chose the smallest and weakest of the flock, then bit through the throat fleece unprotected by the deaf-mute in the shepherd's house.

At close range he pumps one more into the upper neck just under the left ear. It dies in spasms and he puts another a bit higher, at the base of the skull. A bullet for Ramos, a bullet for Dupuy. He takes the Ka-Bar from his belt sheath and, lifting the coyote by the ear, he decapitates it in a couple of strokes made easy by the rifle's previous work. He lobs the head underhand in the direction of the spruce trees so in the morning the eagle can gnaw through the eye and throat cavities to its frozen brain. The body he hauls by the hind legs, not looking back to see the trail or if any more coyotes skulk in the tree shadows. Just as he's dragging it past the vacant sheepfold, a break in the cloud ceiling fills with uncountable stars, then swallows them up again.

He lays the animal on his overturned dory and brings a kerosene lantern to light his work. He grasps the neck opening and deploys his Ka-Bar under the sternum till the tip stops at the spine. He draws the blade toward him through the underhide to the long sheathed pecker and the two balls still swarming with future coyotes to the end of time. With both hands he spreads the belly open and peers in, as if he could find in its steaming depth the source of a hatred that goes beyond the scattered flock and the killed lamb.

He slices away the coyote's organs along the spine, hoists it up vertically, and pulls down the windpipe to release the heart. Intestines and viscera fall vaporous on the snow. Using his Ka-Bar he cuts the skin and fur away from the left haunch and hind leg and severs it at the joint. Only now does he let himself fully imagine the shrieks of its victim torn from its panicked flock and overpowered in the night.

He stands there holding the coyote leg like a spent sidearm and lets his own heart feel the gravity of the last twenty-four hours: Angela and her separation, the fatherless infant Rebecca, his mother unable to talk with him, and Brenda like some random female that he never knew, while his room now belongs to the new child. They could be putting her to bed now after a holiday heavy with gifts she doesn't understand. They could be gathered at his window with starlight on the snowy rooftops and the blind ocean beyond them where their lost brother's butchering a predator of the night.

He brings in the lantern and the coyote haunch and throws some pine scraps in the fire. With the chain sharpener he puts a new edge on the Ka-Bar, having first sliced it with kerosene to get the stomach contents off. The stove grates are red-hot by the time he's cubed some small filets from the hindquarters and two strips of purplish sinewy coyote meat from the scrawn of the upper thigh. He scoops a fistful of lard from the Crisco can and throws in cayenne pepper and oregano from the spice set that was one of his mom's presents. His parents hung small red stockings on the mantel over the gas log for their estranged and wounded children and a huge one for their granddaughter that she could have lived in like a sleeping bag. But if his mother could watch what he's about to do, she'd never again cook for him or sit at the same table.

He's eaten bear steak at his uncle's camp and venison every fall for years, but the smell of the coyote meat has a livery tang that he's never sensed anywhere on earth. It crosses his mind to take this meal on the floor on his hands and knees because he is no longer human but one animal eating another. It is not rocket science to be the night watchman of a remnant flock, but he failed it just as he fucked up his mission as Vehicle Commander of a routine street patrol. He came to this island either to remember or forget. Now he is starving after a day without food and before him is an entree of concentrated loathing and reprisal.

He toasts three pieces of sourdough on the hot grates while he pours a shot, then when the meat's cooked he dribbles the coyote gravy over the bread and puts the charred haunch on it and slices it thin with the Ka-Bar so it will be tender enough to eat. It doesn't taste like the wilderness but like the hot skewered *shashlik* they ate on the Arab street. It was the bitter and gristly smell all around them when they'd leave the wire for the night patrol. There was the one crack from Dupuy's carbine in the Humvee turret, then there was nothing. He hears the voice in his ears now—*You eatin' dog meat* and he says out loud in the cabin *It ain't dog, Moby, it's a wild animal,* rasping out of his throat in meaninglessness and pain, but if there's no one to hear him he's not there.

14

Julia wakes at the first sign of sunlight through the gap where the curtain doesn't reach the sill. One clock's on Newfoundland time and the other's on DST, so she doesn't know what time it is, or, for a moment, who else is burrowed under the huge goose-down winter quilt. In her dream she was married to a blond farmer in Scandinavia with a couple of offspring that might have been some kind of domestic animals, because she was walking on all fours into a pasture to nurse them in the open air. She shakes her head to clear the dream threads, then stands to look at the quilt in the dull light. It seems so much like a big moth cocoon that she laughs out loud and Vira's head pops out: the pupa or whatever it is, in the moment of birth.

"You weren't supposed to wake me."

"How could I help it? You looked so larval. Go back to sleep. I'll see you sometime." She can't resist the impulse to bend down and submerse her own head deep in the comforter where it's still night. She finds not a cold sleeper but a warm wakeful Sámi mouth and she knows she's not leaving for another half-hour, at least.

The last thing she packs for this trip to Amber is the rust-stained bone fishhook to be restored to its rightful home. She sits on the edge of their bed and unfolds the red bandana to show Vira for the last time.

"It is preserved and buried with red ochre," Vira says. "I told you, I have seen it in the Sámi museum, the same exact. It was a circumpolar culture. I am originated from those people, they are the Sámi too. Take care; it is extremely old."

"It must be. It's guarded with a shotgun. And he swore me to secrecy."

"It is also a barbed hook. Do not be caught." A warm arm slips from the covers.

"I'm caught already," Julia says. It takes all her strength to detach herself and stand up or she'll be there another hour.

Beware the caretaker is the last phrase she hears going out the door.

The light is still low and dawnlike when she loads her gear and maroon daypack into the Sidekick. She tries to continue her mood with music, turns on the radio, but it's tuned to Amy Goodman on the Mexican coal miners caught underground for days, some already dead, some still clinging to life. She shivers to think of the complete darkness, the unbreathable methane, the bodies beside her who could be corpses or half-alive. The mine owners raised profit margins by cheating on safety, Amy says. And now it's Noam Chomsky asking which is the true Failed State? Not Somalia, not Bosnia or Chechnya or North Korea or Kyrgyzstan, but the USA. Capitalism stalks blind as a cavefish even in her own house: She is the youngest of a failing family in a failed world. She fingers the radio for the classical station just to recover, if she still can, dawn's amniotic bliss.

She gets a banana and coffee at the Irving Big Stop and continues past the bare lawns and mudfields, shuttered tourist motels, naked leafless trees of a defiled nation that has done nothing to deserve the warm grope and embrace of spring. It's past the solstice but the Maine landscape's still stark and raw, people's yards are sheer half-thawed mud with riding toys and old bikes where they left them when the snow arrived. She has a 9:30 departure from Ledgeport with Hallett Bunker, whose lobsterboat ferry has transported them to Amber Island ever since they sold their boat. She's running late but Hallett will understand. Her cartop rack is empty; she's not taking *Ms. Silkie*, her intrepid kayak, because this isn't a pleasure trip.

Will says the construction crews have been out there since the first of March and she wants at least one last glimpse of the island before it's totally defaced. After this trip she'll never again lay eyes on the place that means more to her than anywhere else in the world.

She is bringing camera and tripod to finish the missing link in her thesis, this undefinable season when winter loosens its grip and things secretly happen under the desolate surface: tentative phoebe nests, swelling alder buds, pussy willows whose name brings a blush and smile to Vira's face. Once this shoot's processed she'll have her June exhibit, graduation, and her requiem to the U.S. as she becomes a Scandinavian citizen with a future unknown as a brand-new tongue.

She pulls up and parks at the Ledgeport waterfront with its marina and Coast Guard station, bright red and green navigational buoys stacked on its wharf, and beyond that, almost blinding her, the spill of spring sunlight on the open sea. Hallett Bunker is patiently waiting in the deep cockpit of the *Alice B.*, surrounded by four yellow chain saws, several surveyors' transits, a portable Onan generator, and three wooden boxes of dynamite, on their way to demolish a defenseless island. If her father were here this cargo of explosives would never be allowed to leave the dock. Every hour he spent on Amber he was conserving it.

She throws her daypack and Pelican case among the oil and fuel containers in the crowded cubby, gives Hallett a two-armed squeeze around his yellow slicker, the way she did back in the day, then pulls away sharply, remembering his collaboration in the resort. He is allegedly a lifelong friend but when the time comes he'll ferry the clientele.

A few minutes at full roaring throttle leaving no space for speech, then they're beyond the breakwater lighthouse steaming straight into a sharp northerly wind from the cold land, with Amber's distinct shape and color appearing dead ahead. In summer she'd be sitting up on the bow for the salt spray but she's now huddled behind the windshield as close as she can get to the red-hot exhaust stack that rises up through the cabin top. They're just passing the green bell buoy whose clangor can be heard even over the diesel roar, when Hallett throttles down so they can talk.

"Going out to meet your sister?" he yells.

"*What?*"

He thinks she can't hear and yells even louder. "Your sister. You're running behind her. She went out at sunrise with the construction crew."

"*Nicole?*"

"You've got another? I thought I knew all of you."

"No, I just thought she was still in the Caribbean."

"Mr. Dormant ain't here yet, but Nicole come out this morning. She's wearing Grundéns raingear, same as this. She stayed the night in town."

"I had no idea."

"Family ought to keep in touch—you two could've gone out on the same trip."

Hallett throttles up again so the spray drenches the windshield and he has to steer peering into the radar screen.

Julia spins around to look back at the harbor dissolving in their wake. She could ask Hallett to turn back, say she's changed her mind, forgotten something. She gropes for her cell to text Vira, who'll be in advanced bio class, ask WTF to do. She can imagine the quick response: *KEEP GOING—IT WAS MEANT TO HAPPEN.*

Everything's predestined for Vira. She has her tarot read by her friend Alexa, then just settles into the outcome and it all happens as foretold. What will she think if Julia shows up tonight with no photos, having run away in fear from her own family?

She turns from her thoughts of jumping overboard to stand beside Hallett as they near the island. She's already straightening her hair under her sweatshirt hood for a more professional demeanor to greet this big sister who left home before she could even talk.

Spray covers the windshield now as the bow turns straight into the wind's eye. It's not till they come under the lee of Amber that she beholds her father's island covered with neon-citrus backhoes and graders like a post-life planet populated by machines. There's a construction barge alongside the dock float and a two-lane eroded mudslide leading uphill from the little south cove. An orange hydraulic derrick stands dinosaur-like on the hilltop and beside it what looks like a cement mixer for a foundation that will outlast the granite ledge.

A nausea deeper than seasickness brings up the banana along with an impulse to dive over the stern so the propeller could liquefy her like a blender.

Hallett throttles down as they approach closer and observes, "That's going up like the Empire State Building. They're moving warp speed with the leveling and the foundations. They paved the helipad. They'll fly the prefab sections from the Owls Head airport suspended beneath the chopper and right into place without ever touching ground. They brought one of them out there already, just to test the flight. Modules, they call them. They fit right into each other like a Lego set. You'll be having your grand opening by July. Shock and awe, that's what George Plummer says. He's the foreman. You figuring on a career out there with the rest of them? Can't beat a family business, everyone pulling in the same direction."

"This is my sister's project," Julia says. "I have other plans."

Their little cove is like the scene of an amphibious invasion. The grassy path she walked down barefoot and hauled her kayak up among wild rugosas now looks like the D-Day beachhead in *Saving Private Ryan*. The bush that last year held a delicate wren's nest has been bulldozed into the mud, along with the cluster of fringed trilliums that welcomed their arrival every spring. The diesel generator and rumbling cement mixer bury all other sounds.

She's come too late; she didn't think it would be this far gone. Or did she have to see the destruction to know it's real?

Hallett says, "They barged a big flatbed trailer the other day, got a derrick on it to pull the old crane out of the quarry pond."

"What about the standing one?"

"That'll go next. You don't want that stone dropping into the swimming pool. It's a wonder that hasn't killed someone in all these years. I guess nobody would've swum in that place anyway, but a little chlorine and it'll be crystal clear."

She starts lugging her camera and tripod up the slope with Hallett behind her, a heavy man audibly panting from the climb. The full horror is revealed at the top of the dock path. Up at the highest point they've clear-cut the hardwoods and alder thickets where the phoebes and yellowthroats lived. They've already poured the octagonal foundation slab; she had no idea it would be so big. Two guys in watch caps and gray sweatshirts are removing the wooden forms and another is capping the foundation rim with cut granite flagstones that appear to be right from the old quarry. The bearded one looks familiar. She realizes it's the caretaker that trained his rifle on her chest. When he turns to glimpse Julia, his deep-set eyes widen and one hand goes to his forehead in a military salute, an improvement anyway on their first encounter. He can't pull a gun with that many witnesses around.

Hallett says, "That guy's a disabled vet who doesn't hear or speak but he's the best worker on the island. George set him up with a Blackberry. That's all he needs. When they have a job for him, they just type it in. The Blackberry vibrates in his pocket. The crew's got their own sign language already. He's the local hero—got ambushed over in Iraq, lost his eardrums, then spent the whole goddamn winter out here living off the land, not hearing a thing. Guy's got a sixth sense, though. You try sneaking up behind him, he knows where you are before you do."

"I met him," Julia says. "He pointed a gun at me."

Hallett laughs. "Guess he takes his job to heart. I might be jumpy too if I couldn't hear."

"It wasn't necessary. I was unarmed."

"They bring the war home with them, those guys. One of them drove his pickup into a tree last week—on his way to the VA in Chamberlain, but he never made it. Another one holed himself up with a private arsenal till the State Police had to take him out. They used to call it shell shock, then it was Vietnam syndrome, now it's PTSD."

She knows that term from The Hemlocks. It was one of the reductive labels they used to file you into a little compartment so they could sell you a pill. That's why he went out to Amber; she totally understands. She's been there too.

"He was very secretive," she says. "My mother said he's a descendent of Guido Colonna, but he never told me his name."

"That's true. His name is Nick. Nick Colonna. His old man's father worked the quarry here before the War."

"Yes, my mom mentioned that. I remember him. He came out when I was a little kid. He walked with a cane. Dad said he was wounded in World War Two."

"It gives Nick a connection to this place—which is a good thing. Half the battle's won if you know where you are."

On the high meadow where they'd camped all those summers there's the fresh black asphalt of the landing strip with its lime-green wind sock and the neon-orange target circle in the center, outlined by a grid of white lines for its use as a tennis court. Beside it stands one of the house panels diagonally braced upright against the wind.

It's an awesome structural element, like everything her father did. It's slightly rectangular, maybe twenty feet long and ten high. The blue-tinted glass must have some reflective element to block sunlight, or maybe it's tuned to the colors of the sea; it returns her image clear as a silvered mirror. The frame of dark redwood is rounded at the window corners for a gentler effect than his usual hard edge.

"There's going to be eight of those segments on each floor," Hallett says. "And four high, like a tower of visibility over the tree line, all hardwood floors with a spiral stairway inside like a lighthouse and Mrs. Fletcher's apartment at the top. Your dad would be very proud of that design. Shame he can't be here when it's done. The best things we do, we don't always get to see how they turn out."

There's also a gigantic hole dug out of the earth to the left of the cove path, with heaps of fresh earth mounded all around. It could be the burial pit for a full-grown elephant.

"Hallett, what's that enormous cavity? Is that for another foundation?"

"That's for the septic system. It's gotta be on the opposite side and downhill from the well."

"It's huge. They've dug up the whole hillside. It used to be covered with daylilies and wild roses."

"It's coastal, so the code's very strict. I guess you didn't worry much about septic when it was just the family."

"We had a privy that was there from the quarry days. Dad didn't want human traces on the island."

"First thing we took down," Hallett says. "You can't have your kind of guests dressing for dinner in an outhouse."

She can't take her eyes off the septic pit, remembering the exact windblown shadbushes that grew there. Whole flights of cedar waxwings would cover them in September.

"This is a nightmare, Hallett. I don't even recognize it. It's like seeing someone you love on an operating table with their heart opened up."

"They stitch them up, you know. Healed and better than new. Wait till you come back this summer, everything in place and landscaped, you won't believe it. Oh, and there's your sister, just like I told you!"

She spots a female shape up near the old wellhead, along with a guy in a hard hat, both looking at blueprints on the helipad. In the grim ravaged Anselm Kiefer landscape, Nicole's a standout in her bright fisherman's slicker and baseball cap with her silvery-blond ponytail sticking through. She's looking in their direction, curious about another woman on the island. When she recognizes who it is, she hands the plans over and clambers to meet her baby sister over the lacerated ground.

"Julia, Julia! When Hallett said you were coming I couldn't believe it. We thought we'd never see you again, now here you are."

Despite her tropical zip code and yellow oilskin, Nicole's as pale as a librarian. Melanoma is one thing, but the heart needs sunlight and she can feel anxiety or tension even in the folds of her sisterly yellow hug. Will says she takes Valium or Xanax, he wasn't sure, which was another thing they feed you at The Hemlocks, so she feels a bond. It's hard to despise someone who may not be inherently evil but just blinded or coerced by domestic love. Plus Nicole's the closest of all to their father with her tall figure and the cast of her features and visible character of the eyes.

"I didn't know you'd be here," Julia says. "I came for a few pictures, but I'm too late. Or maybe Hallett took me to the wrong island. I can't believe this is Amber—or used to be Amber. Now it's a shithole. Sorry, but that septic cavity is gross."

"I know. You couldn't have come at a worse time. But the septic will be sustainable for thirty guests! No more outhouses. Just close your eyes and fast-forward to summer and imagine it when it's finished. That was Dad's gift—he could envision in total detail something that wasn't there."

"Nicole, if Dad were here he'd be closing his eyes and envisioning what it *was*. It's like a bombed-out village after a civil war. People come home to it but there's nothing left."

"I'm sorry, I never thought you'd let yourself see it in this state. It's such a shambles. But look at these drawings. Dad did them himself. They're beautiful! I have to remind myself there's a lot of chaos before creation. It will come back, and better than before."

"Something will come back, maybe, but it won't be the place he loved."

"Oh, Julia, sweetheart, it *will*. It might be changed but it will still be Amber. The house will be such a constant remembrance of Dad, totally organic and sustainable. People will leave with a new respect for the environment."

She stops and looks directly into the face of this older sister with her empty fists clenched in exasperation.

"Nicole, how can you say that? How can you respect the environment if it isn't there? I started to count the organisms that have been destroyed and I had to quit. It's like the Sixth Extinction. The trilliums are gone forever; you can't replace them—their underground root systems are torn up. There was a killdeer nest on that meadow. They're going to come back and find their homes gone. I feel like Dad's going to appear like Hamlet's father and ask how I could have let this happen. How can I answer? I'm glad he's not here to see it. It would break his heart."

Nicole looks down at the ground at her feet, which has been corrugated by a bulldozer tread.

"Julia, I hate it that this is driving us apart. It would be unbearable to Dad. It should bring us together as a family. That's what he would have wanted. I didn't grow up here like you and Will did, but I'd like to be part of the island, too."

Julia's about to say you can be part of the island without wrecking it, but now a hard-hatted man approaches with a professional smile and inquisitive narrowed eyes looking out past a trim black-and-gray beard that might have been uncut and radical back in the day.

Nicole says, "George Plummer, my sister Julia."

"The notorious environmentalist," he says. "Young lady, you would not believe how righteous this is going to be. We have a desalinator that will make water directly from the sea. We got solar coming in for the roof, we got a wind turbine with a thousand amp hour battery bank. All underground cabling between buildings. You're not going to see a wire when we're done."

"I'm not going to see it 'cause I won't here. I've been invited to live in Finland. I'm leaving right after graduation."

Nicole looks shocked. "Finland. It's so far away."

"Far from where? Nicole, this country is unlivable. This island was a sanctuary—it's where Dad came for quiet and inspiration—but not anymore."

A diesel truck roar drowns out the generator as the flatbed trailer emerges from the quarry path snorting exhaust smoke and carrying the wet algae-covered girders of the sunken crane. Off in the distance she can see the transport barge crossing the ship channel to pick it up. Nicole's unable to make herself heard for a whole minute while the load passes, solid red rust dripping with green pond water like Vira when she came up naked from her quarry swim.

"Come on, Julia, let's go to the old quarry. They're just about to dismantle the other crane. You should be happy! We're removing all traces of the industrial past. Chad plans to repurpose that hanging block as a poolside bar, to honor the old stoneworkers and the granite trade."

"Nicole, you can't honor laborers with a cocktail bar. It's like a monument to inequality. Dad wanted to reference a lighthouse that saved the lives of working men at sea. He wasn't thinking of Trump Tower. I look at you and you look so much like Dad, more than any of us. I squint my eyes and I see him standing on this exact spot in his yellow coat. Then you talk about this island like a developer and the spell is broken and I have to ask, who am I even speaking to? Is this even your own vision for Amber, or is it Chad's?"

"Jules, when you've been married for twenty-three years, a vision's not his or hers. The word *you* has no singular anymore. The word *I* doesn't even exist."

"And that's supposed to be love?"

"It's love in the beginning, then it goes past that and there's no word for it. This is our vision for Amber, as a couple, and I think Mom shares it."

"Well, you can't say Mom and Dad have the same vision. One of them's dead."

She's looking over their former camping meadow as she says this, squeezing her eyes to blur the black airstrip and imagine the two wall tents and the tall architect grilling a pan of mackerel over the Coleman stove.

Nicole comes closer and rests her head on Julia's shoulder for a moment, enough to feel the heat and moisture of her face through her light sweatshirt, then straightens up to her full height, a couple of inches taller, so as always Julia must look up.

"I'm sorry. I know you didn't expect me here. I don't want you to think of our project as just greed and exploitation. I hoped Amber might be big enough to accommodate both our dreams."

"It's not, Nicole. It's a tiny and fragile place. It can't accommodate any dreams—it just has to be itself. We were so lucky. We had the most amazing inheritance in the world, and a father who honored it as it was. All it takes is one year and it's as fucked up as everything else."

"Sweetheart, his whole work was to create beauty from a bare landscape with nothing there. It gets disrupted, then it gets transformed. To build the Amber house for Mom, in Dad's memory, it's not a demolition—it's an act of love."

Behind Nicole's yellow raincoat, a green backhoe raises its five-fingered bucket to cut into the wellspring that supplies the only freshwater on the island. Nicole has to shout over the diesel sound.

"George is diverting the spring so it will flow toward the new buildings instead of the quarry. It's our big water project. Chad calls it the TVA."

They step over the rivulet which is about to have its flow reversed against the law of gravity, following a new walkway slashed out of prime warbler habitat that curves around the sheep thicket to the quarry.

"We looked for arrowheads here," Nicole remembers. "Dad and I, when we first came. Mom was pregnant that year with Will."

"We looked for them too," Julia responds.

She's not divulging that her daypack holds a carefully wrapped bone fishhook from Amber's own prehistoric heart, and she's hoping the caretaker will show her where it came from, so the last thing she'll ever do on this island will be to put it back.

Meanwhile an orange derrick truck saying ROBERT PRENTISS & SONS has maneuvered onto the granite shelf to support the old quarry crane as it comes down. The great stone is missing that has hung suspended all these years, its looped cable dangling like an empty noose. Three men in welding helmets are cutting away the crane's base where it's bolted into the granite ledge. When they cut through the fourth and final leg, she feels it like an amputation.

"It's painful, Nicole. It's been here since before Dad was born."

"It wasn't exactly nature," Nicole says. "It was an industrial relic. It was a menace. You should have heard the insurance guy when he saw it. 'No one comes anywhere near this place with that thing there.' "

Julia takes a few steps away from her sister and checks her cell. It's already noon and she hasn't taken a single photograph. She'll work till she's stopped by darkness, then call Hallett to rescue her from this tar pit of havoc and desecration. She shouts to Nicole over the din, gesturing toward her camera.

"Nicole, I'm losing my best light. I have to find some spots that are still unspoiled, if there are any, so I can finish my work. Then I'll say good-bye to the island. I'm leaving right after graduation. I'll miss Amber more than anything in my life, but after this visit I won't be coming back."

She ignores her sister's shocked expression and tightens her daypack straps. Words are so pointless and impossible. Hot winds drive people from inside and out till it's impossible to blame them for what they do.

The early spring day has colored and brightened until even the construction machinery looks toylike and innocuous. She hikes northward in bright unfamiliar sunlight along the vague ruts leading to the old cabin and the protected woods. All last summer the two huge-winged eagles governed the upper branches. They were male and female but you would have to anatomize them to tell them apart. Their one feathery nestling grew to a golden-brown raptor that dwarfed its parents as they hovered and taught it how to fly.

She leaves the footpath to bushwhack toward the aerie perched over the wild northeast point. There are no eagles in sight. She completely identifies. With all the earthshaking upheaval they've relocated to a better place.

In the most deeply shaded spot she photographs the last lingering skim of ice over a tiny standing pool with air bubbles trapped beneath like live amoebas trying to escape. She finds fresh glistening scat from the wonder sheep that manage to scrape through winter without the humans that were supposed to care for them. Their trail leads westward through a forest of dead spruce limbs interleaved like locked turnstiles in the subway. Then it comes out right behind the caretaker's cabin and leads to a rough shelter overflowing with firewood and a roofed-over space full of fleece scraps and droppings that must be their new home. He's fed and tamed them so they've lost their wildness and grown codependent again on man. Their fate is the same as Amber's. They'll never survive what's coming. They have a couple more months to fatten up, then they'll be on the locavore menu in curry and tajine. If sheep had wings they would flee this place like the eagles and not return.

She hears the crack of a twig and stomping footsteps and feels for a moment like a trespasser till she remembers who she is. She checks the zippered pocket of her daypack for the fishhook to be returned. She thought they'd meet at his worksite, not at the cabin where he drew the gun, but she's not afraid. Despite the rifle and chain saw, he is another of the wounded and he has a bond with this island like her own. His complicity in Chad's project is the price of remaining here.

He's wearing jeans and a camo hoodie and carries two plastic water jugs and no gun. This time he actually smiles, and his eyes seem to have lost their hostile stare. He puts the jugs down, throws up a hand with V-ed fingers to show his peaceable intent. He gestures with open palms at the sheepfold, indicating he doesn't know where they are, then beckons her in.

He's got a line of mackerel on the wire that runs from wall to wall over the rusted cookstove. It smells like the lair of a hunter-gatherer: dried fish and raw human mixed with the woodstove's creosote and a woolly aroma as if the sheep also have moved in. He slides a Blackberry out of his shirt pocket, which in this decrepit old shelter looks like an object that's landed on this planet from outer space. He's got two chairs at the table now, so she takes one and pulls the wrapped hook out of the daypack pocket to return it.

Then he scares and stupefies her by saying in audible language, "*Yours.*" He looks as shocked by the utterance as she is.

She instinctively responds, "You speak! Can you hear now, too?"

He puts his hand on her mouth gently to stop her from talking, then repeats on the Blackberry, *YOURS.* He purses his lips together and shakes his head like a bearded young monk who has broken his vow of silence.

She texts, *I DON'T WANT IT. IF IT BELONGS TO THIS ISLAND, LET'S PUT IT BACK.*

He pulls two cups off his shelf and sets his bottle of Jim Beam and a tea bag on either side of them. She points to the whiskey. Her hands are still shaky from the Nicole encounter and with the sun lowering and no heat in the cabin, she's also cold.

Before pouring, he brings out the small wooden box, which now has snapshots of a couple of soldiers taped to it—one African-American guy with a huge smile, one brown-skinned with shades and a mustache.

WHO ARE THEY? she texts.

NOT HERE. GONE.

WHERE?

DEAD.

I'M SO SORRY. She chokes up and for a moment has to cover her eyes. In sympathy she touches the back of his hand and feels the tendons move as he responds. Then she watches his face as he types but it does not break.

NOT YOUR FAULT. MINE.

He takes out another antiquity from the box, a spearhead or weapon with six separate barbs, the same timeworn russet bone color as the fishhook, maybe the red ochre that Vira described in the Sámi museum. It looks like what he tried to conceal from her in the library. He arrived on this island and stumbled upon a secret her whole family couldn't discover in all their years; it may be that somehow these soldiers showed the way.

When she picks up her cup for a sip, he clicks with his own and his gesture includes his two companions as well as the former inhabitants of Amber Island who left these tokens of their existence and moved on. He thumbs on the Blackberry, *1ST PEOPLE. THEY WERE HERE, 6,000 YEARS AGO.*

She grabs the Blackberry and thumbs back, *WHERE WERE THEY? WE*

NEVER FOUND. He wouldn't tell her before, but maybe now.

He leans back with his cup and just stares at her, as if she's supposed to read the answer in his face. He's an intense-looking guy anyway, but more so now with the dark inward-gazing eyes, restless dark hair now raggedly grown out, black beard like some Taliban zealot or Che Guevara anarchist from the movies. He's a collaborator but he's also grandfathered with his legacy from the quarry days. No one before him survived a winter alone on Amber. He has to be part of her thesis. He's part of its nature even as he works to despoil it.

She takes the Nikon out and points to it while silently mouthing the question, *OK to take a picture?* He nods. She widens the lens and backs as far as she can into a corner, so she can expand the context, including the line of stiff mackerel and the wooden bone chest with the two soldiers on it. She zooms a bit to bring the background closer and takes just one shot, the only subject she's known who does not flinch when the shutter clicks.

Outside the window, the light appears darker and lower and the shadows have lengthened inside the cabin. She hears the soft hoofprints and brief bleats of the sheep flock, no longer wild, who must return here in late afternoon. He hands her an article that's been folded and unfolded so many times the creases erase half the words. *The Red Paint Culture.* She skims it while he sips and waits. *They thrived all across their lands for a thousand years, then they disappeared.* One summer when she was ten or eleven her dad took her to an archaeological dig on one of the Fox Islands where he knew someone. Mosquito-plagued students were chipping away in square excavations crisscrossed with a network of strings and pegs. They had stone weapons and arrowheads and the professor said there were human bones but they weren't allowed to be seen. But now, touching the barbed point as well as the bone hook she kept all winter in Bar Harbor, remembering a red-stained artifact in her father's hand, there's the chill of contact and slight radioactive fear as if she were handling time itself. They had no photography back then, no written tongue or any protection from the hungry future. Each moment streaked through them like a neutrino and was gone.

He scrolls back to THEY WERE HERE then deletes ~~WERE~~ and writes ARE. ON AMBER. U DIDN'T KNOW?

No.

He writes, FOR UR EYES ONLY. CONFIRM?

She texts, BUT WHERE? I KNOW AMBER, BUT NOT THIS.

He picks up his pencil as if his urgency demanded a more-human form. The brown, sun-weathered fingers bear down on the point as if he wants to gouge the words permanently into the yellow pad. AGREE TO ONLY YOU? He's not trusting his own voice even though it works, because he can't hear it.

He stops to sharpen his pencil with the bayonet double-strapped over his calf. She can see why he wants to keep this under wraps, an unknown time layer of this island where the quarrymen blasted and harvested granite for fifty years and no one ever guessed. It would be confiscated by the State if the archaeologists came. It would be like the Fox Islands excavations; they'd julienne Amber's entire surface with their grid of pits.

He delicately sharpens the harpoon point while he waits, using the bayonet as a precision instrument. Tiny particles accumulate under his hand like dust. It seems disrespectful to disturb an antiquity with a modern tool, though he's not touching the red part, just the very tips of the pointed barbs. She focuses for a minute on the tendons of his hand at such a sensitive operation, the fingers that make us human, like those that must have carved it in the first place, on this island, how many light-years ago. She writes OK on the yellow pad, very lightly, to avoid breaking its whittled point.

He rewraps the fishhook in a fabric that looks like an old mattress, then stands and puts on his camouflage jacket and watch cap, grabs a small collapsible spade from the corner, and offers his hand to pull her up from her chair and out the door. They pass the shelter with three formerly feral sheep in there chewing on a pile of cut grass in the stall corner, tame as a petting zoo. In the other corner she spots an empty burlap sack saying ORGANIC FEED, and stops for a picture of the sheep from behind, then crosses past the woodpile to get their faces from a better angle. Her spine briefly shivers when she sees a deer's skin nailed to a tree in back of the cabin, its forelegs pinned to the protruding branches like a crucifix.

As they approach the spruce grove behind his cabin, she points to the high limbs where the eagles perched, stops to text *EAGLES?* in the Blackberry, and he texts *GONE*. It's April already and they should be upgrading the nest and vocalizing with their lyrical mating calls. Eagles won't live and reproduce in a construction zone. She imagines them, like herself, looking down for the last time on their wasted homeland before they emigrate.

They turn sharp left from the main path and follow the newly cleared walkway toward the quarry. On the other side of their old camping meadow the backhoe is gouging the water pipe trench, and by the quarry itself the three welders are removing their helmets, turning away from the remnants of the fallen crane. She looks at her cell phone. Quarter of three. The crew boat arrives in fifteen minutes. The welders pick up their lunch pails, stow their equipment in the truck cab, and drive back over a mudway that once was a meadow path. They smile and wave to the caretaker as they pass.

It's weird to let this complete stranger lead her across terrain once as familiar as her own skin. It's now an alien landscape and she needs a guide. They skirt close to the quarry pond then head diagonally southeast on one of the pathways cut through fresh alder stumps still hemorrhaging their golden sap. It's strewn with wood shavings to smother the lady's-slippers and bunchberries that once carpeted the ground. Nick points to the eutrophic green biomass in the quarry pond and punches the Blackberry: *SWIM POOL*. She can just imagine the white lounge chairs on the granite ledge, the slap of tennis balls on the helipad, her nieces Brittany and Elaine serving hors d'oeuvres from the cocktail bar.

She squeezes her eyes closed, wishing her father were alive. Nothing in his philosophy would permit this massacre and these extinctions, the paving of their meadow for a landing strip, the lifeless uterus of an abandoned eagle nest.

They come to the dense cedar and raspberry thicket with its tunnelled sheep path too low for a human being. As a kid she'd scootch down and follow this route to the oldest and hugest tree on the island, which was brought down in an October windstorm the year her father died. When she came to photograph it last summer she found a pair of catbirds nesting in the upturned roots that mewed at her so fiercely she'd backed away.

Her guide hunkers on hands and knees, so she follows for fifty feet in a prehuman crouch and they emerge at the old stream bank where the blowdown was. Now the fallen spruce is entirely gone, there's just the detritus of bark and sawdust where last year its giant trunk lay at full length. Her whole life it had stood alone there as the tallest, most ancient thing on the island with a long shallow rhizome that fingered its way down the embankment and groped for nutrients in the dried-up stream.

She takes the Blackberry from his belt sheath and texts *WHERE IS THE TREE?*

CUT. BURNED, he thumbs. He must have logged it into firewood. The tree probably heated his home and food through the whole winter. All that's left is the hacked-off root stumps leading into the soil and the broad exposed crater now cunningly filled and replanted as if nothing were ever there.

With a few quick spadefuls Nick makes a small horizontal tunnel halfway down the bank where the tree was. He reaches his arm in to its full extent and seems to spend a while feeling around in there, then pulls out a long sandy blade-like artifact with the same eroded-red pigmentation the bone fishhook had. It resembles a greenish stone knife with a horizontal cross engraved in the handle and stained with red. It must be from the same site as the hook.

CEMETERY, he texts.

"They're in there?" she asks out loud, then catches herself and texts IN THERE?

YES.

HOW DID YOU KNOW?

FOLLOWED SHEEP PATH.

It comes together like the last piece of a puzzle. The downfall of that tree exposed a prehistoric vestige like the one on Fox Island that had long since been covered by layers of material time and a web of roots. Just this past summer she walked right up to the huge upturned divot with its mewing catbirds without ever envisioning what might be beneath the surface; yet this guy dug his hand into the soil till it made contact with a buried world. How did he know? She'd looked right at it but she was blind. She belonged to this island more than anyone but still her preparation was incomplete.

WHY SHOW ME? she texts when it comes to life. DO YOU KNOW WHO I AM?

ISLAND IS YOURS AND THEIRS, NOT CHAD'S.

He points out with his foot a bluish, ice-colored ovular stone half-buried at the foot of the bank, a landmark that maybe he placed there, maybe always existed. Then he takes from his sweatshirt pocket the barbed fishhook in its mattress wrap and carefully reburies it, right at eye level, directly above the blue stone and deep in the gravel bank. He seems totally independent in the camo and combat boots, like an individual without a species, but he's also open and vulnerable on another side, approaching this stranger to share what his silence can't contain.

Now he's texting into his Blackberry, ONE MORE THING.

WHAT?

WHEN THE TIME COMES, BURIAL HERE.

WHAT? MORE OBJECTS?

NO. ME.

YOU? ON AMBER?

HERE IN THIS SAND. U CAN ARRANGE. NO ONE ELSE.

SEE YOU IN 50 YEARS, she texts.

50. 100. WHATEVER IT TAKES.

UM, NOT SURE IT'S LEGAL.

His answer shows on the Blackberry. HIGHER LAWS.

It is the strangest request anyone's made of her, if she understands him correctly. How can he even expect her to outlive him? He may be a year or two older than she is, twenty-six at the most. But he's in a hundred times better physical shape from boot camp and bodily labor and living out here in total self-reliance. Hearing or not, he is an armed combat veteran trained in survival skills and if January out here couldn't kill him, nothing can. He has a soldier's purpose, to protect these people from molestation by Chad or anyone. He can't go anywhere as long as the resort is here. He'll live to be one hundred, while she'll be beside Vira in some Finnish graveyard where it never thaws.

She checks to see if he's teasing; his head's cocked a little to one side, like someone with a proposition, but no sign of a smile or irony. He's sharply focused on her with inaccessible dark brown eyes that must see and hear at the same time. Even though he's breathing beside her he suddenly seems as dead as her father: two ghosts out of a misty Japanese movie with a task for someone in the living world. He wants Amber Island for his final resting place, after he's finished his tour of duty, here in the gravel bank with the Archaics. They'd have to move the whole culture aside to fit him in.

She texts, *WHY?*

HOME.

He's right. He has a place here and an essential job plus a classified mission unknown to anyone. He's returned from the war where he must have done or seen something that drove him to a speck of land restive with prehistoric dreams. More than this island's so-called owners he has a right to call it home.

IF U REMEMBER, he texts. *IF U CAN. IF U ARE HERE.*

She grabs the Blackberry and thumbs, *NOTHING CAN KEEP ME HERE. U WILL COME BACK. SOMETIME. I CAN WAIT.*

The two of them huddle over the tiny screen in the ravine's lengthening shadow and poke at it so intensely it seems like a single hand with four thumbs. She came out to take some final photographs and say a quiet farewell, and now she's arranging an underground funeral rite. Maybe he saw something like Abu Ghraib, or was even in it, those gruesome photographs with the storage batteries and barking dogs.

She writes, *YOU SHOULD HAVE KNOWN MY FATHER. HE LOVED THIS ISLAND TOO.*

He stops texting to pull the camo hood up against the cold. Julia's just wearing the nylon shell and she can see the wind shivering the jack-pine needles across the ravine, but she doesn't feel it.

Then he writes, *RETREAT HIS PLAN?*

HE DREW AMBER HOUSE, NOT RESORT. HE DID NOT BUILD IT.

HE ISN'T HERE.

HE IS, she texts. Then uppercase. *HE IS.*

Her shoulders fold together from chill and sadness, and she instinctively tips her head in his direction, against the loose fringe of his camouflage hood. He pushes the *m* key of the Blackberry and lets it stay and repeat *mmmm* across the screen. Death is all around her in the damp of the sea-wind and her father's serrated absence, the violation of the island and this guy who wants a Stone Age burial in the sand.

He turns his head so the hood partially opens and she lets her face nestle into its fleece interior. They are each holding the Blackberry with one hand, their thumbs touching each other across the screen. She looks down expecting him to text something but what would it be? He turns his head and nuzzles for warmth in the hollow of her neck just under her ear, his lips actually making contact, and she can feel the little hairs of her ear cavity tilt toward his touch like fronds. The back-and-forth brush of his nose makes a storm wind in its inner spiral and she wonders what it's like for him there with no sound at all, or can he hear the blood pulsing as she does? He's keeping a steady pressure on her neck so she can feel the surge of her own artery underneath, his hand starting to pull the Blackberry away; but she can't do it, she can't go where he wants her to. Every place that's awake and interested at this moment is already occupied and colonized by another being. She's like a packed train or subway in which every occupant is Vira and the electric door won't open 'cause there's no room.

All this time sharing the Blackberry they've been kind of huddled together by the camouflaged sandbank where he deposited the tools. When the old spruce was here, it was where she used to come and hide from her family when she needed to be alone. She never suspected what slept beneath her under the ground; not even when it lay uprooted in front of her did she have eyes to see. Now she stands up and he stands with her, staying face-to-face as she hands his Blackberry back. She pulls him forward with both hands in his kangaroo pocket, lifts up her face for a kiss on the bearded mouth, lips open to question on both sides. Alibis swirl through her mind. Hallett's engine broke down, she lost track of time photographing the island, she's staying in Ledgeport with Nicole, uncountable creative possibilities of the untrue. Then she imagines Vira in the same situation and the air suddenly feels frigid and she shivers and gently draws away. She takes her hands out of his pocket and draws her mouth from its warm nest in the woolly beard. She finds the smallest finger of his left hand, squeezes it for a moment as a way of saying good-bye, then lets it go.

He taps, SOMEONE ELSE? on the Blackberry and she taps, YES. There may have to be a little cover-up, but not the big one.

She turns around and leaves him crouched in the shadow of the Archaic site, then heads back along a different route, walking away not as a quadruped but as an upright human up over the gravel rise and toward the shore, where beyond the short shield of jack pìnes the clear-cut begins for one of the guest bungalows, then another and another, joined by the broad walkway and its pavement of cedar chips.

She flips open her cell and punches in Hallett's number.

"I'm so sorry. Time got away from me. Can you still come?"

"You think I don't know you?" Hallett says. "Be at the float. I'm halfway there already."

She would like to hike back though the calamity of this island with her eyes closed but an animal sound surprises her, more an indignant snort than the usual *baa* you expect from a sheep. Two of them stand on one side of the woodchip path, not looking goaty and wild as they used to, but like fat farm animals from the feed they've been noshing at the caretaker's shack. Then it's the lime-green backhoe and blue plastic water hose, the helipad and the forklifts and the eight-sided slab foundation with its network of floor grooves and vertical copper and plastic pipes, its two cement mixers awaiting the next day's work, the coils of electric cable, stacks of blue piping, the gross septic cavity, the shed-shaped metal utility building already in place across the mud row from the future hotel. Beside the shed, the long blades of the wind turbine rest on their sawhorses like three quills from an albatross long extinct. Through the window she can make out the massive stacked black cells of the battery bank, the stainless-steel commercial-sized refrigerator, a desktop Mac on a filing cabinet hooked to a storage battery. In the open doorway, three white toilets face each other with their lids open as if deep in conversation, disconnected from everything and unplumbed.

Then she sees the note tacked to the shed door.

> *JULIA, MY BOAT IS LEAVING. I TRIED TO CALL YOU BUT NO*
> *SERVICE. WE CAN'T BE SO OUT OF TOUCH. I'M STILL 340-228-*
> *2822. I LEFT FEELING WRETCHED AFTER SEEING IT THROUGH YOUR*
> *EYES. I AM SO SORRY. WHEN YOU NEXT COME IT WILL BE AMBER*
> *AGAIN, I PROMISE.*
>
> *XOXO,*
> *YOUR SISTER NICOLE*

By the time she's digested her sister's note and its subtext, she spots the *Alice B.* and sprints for the pier so he won't have to tie up and come in search. The sun's setting over the Ledgeport hills as they cross the ship channel, Hallett not even looking out the windshield, just gazing at the radar like a video game. Behind them the island is at its most painfully beautiful, with the deepening spring sealight playing off the russet shore, all scars obliterated by distance, construction machinery reduced to neon pastel shapes like innocent Tonka toys.

Vira's in bed already when she gets back, but wide awake, wrapped in the Lapland reindeer quilt with steaming and honeyed ginseng herbal tea. Julia stopped in the Irving Big Stop for coffee and yogurt and for a profound facewash with an alcohol-tinctured abrasive cloth that cost $2.95 for just one. There remains a peripheral scent, though, that must be coming from her hair, and the first thing Vira does is draw back and say, "Whew, where have you been?"

"I was in the sheepfold. I guess I must have come too close. Those so-called wild sheep are tame now and they're pretty cute. One of them was almost a lamb. I couldn't help but nuzzle it."

"So let me nuzzle you," Vira says, and she chews above Julia's ears and forehead, takes bites and mouthfuls of her tainted hair, then fluffs up a backrest of three or four pillows and pulls her under the quilt with its shamanic patterns of black and green. "So you shot how many rolls today?"

"Two, maybe. Nicole took half my time."

"And the sheepish caretaker. Or wolfish. He had his weapon out, or was it concealed?"

"Oh Vira, it was horrible. My project is over. There's nothing left to document. The island's in ruins. Even if you turn the lens away from the damage, it's in the atmosphere. The light was everything out there and now it's gone."

"How could they take light away?"

"The tower. It's not even built yet and it's casting a shadow over the whole place. It's not just the caretaker. There must have been ten machines and twenty workmen out there, some of them taking down the old crane, and the hanging rock's not there anymore."

"For the swimmers," Vira says, "that may be a positive. They will be happy without that over their heads."

"How could I take pictures out there? The eagles have disappeared. They won't ever be back. It's much worse than I expected. You know the field where we camped? How it sloped down toward the shore on the sunset side? They've leveled it for an airstrip. Helistrip. Hell strip. With a target and a wind sock. Which Will says will be a tennis court when the buildings are done."

"People like tennis," Vira says.

"Sadist. You have no empathy. They have bulldozers, forklifts, backhoes. A bottomless septic pit. I shouldn't have gone there and I won't ever again. I must have thought, if I saw it, if I was there, somehow it could be disappeared—I don't know, as if it had never happened. But then you would have to turn back time. Which can't be done."

"Which can be very easily done," Vira quotes. "Just take it on Highway Sixty-One."

There's no stopping the tears now as she buries her face in Vira's short blond frizzly hair, drops down to gnaw through the hollow of her collarbone, but there's now a barrier and she can't. The whole day's narrative mutely floods out and soaks the neckline of the flannel nightshirt.

Vira says, "You've driven a long way. Details can wait."

She opens the top two buttons and Julia slips inside.

15

Camilla is here in the Amber house finally after all these years, bare and unfinished but structurally complete, spare and pristine with its tall central spiral staircase and unscuffed hardwood floors; and all around the supernatural clarity of the glass, whose solarized tint makes it absolutely invisible without glare or substance, as if you could walk through it into the other world. Nicole has stepped out and deliberately left her alone in the glorious light-struck space of vast windows that impart the whole seacoast morning to the unfurnished room. To the south, the blinding glaze of the June sun on the whitecapped Atlantic; to the east a deep coniferous shadow like the pines in her little Hopper roadscape whose vacuums of mystery forever lead you in.

The black wrought-iron stairway recalls Marston's early sketches of their island home, done by lamplight that first summer in the canvas tent. They had just climbed the Matinicus lighthouse with its rickety ladder circling upward toward the revolving light, and he hoped that spiral would center and bind the family like a twist of DNA. Night after night she'd wake up at the cry of a night heron or gust of wind and he'd be awake, working by the yellow flame. If Julia could have been there to see his love and excitement, she'd realize what a tribute his children have given him, this tower that's both a lookout to the open horizon and a shelter from infinity. Of all of them her youngest suffered the loss most deeply, distilling a whole family's grief into a single heart. She lost her boundaries from it. She wandered in search of him through a place where no one alive should have to go.

She stands barefoot on the fresh-laid floor that smells of milled birch and varnish, recalling all the brand-new interiors Marston would proudly lead her through, the west wall still looking out on bulldozers, backhoes, and the vertical white post supporting the turbine blades. Chad walks among them in a yellow hard hat, a tan corduroy sport coat, and one of the Yale neckties that set off his eyes like flakes of the blue sea. Time hasn't touched him, his smile still almost adolescent under the blond mustache. Nicole follows behind him, then Brittany with her red headband and glint of reflected sunlight from her navel jewel. Belly button for Brittany, nostril for Elaine; finally she can tell her granddaughters apart without having to ask.

Now, with her family working in harmony with a common purpose, Nicole looks more buoyant than she has in years. She's withdrawing from all those prescriptions that even in the tropics turned her skin to parchment, the pale shadow of Chad's ruddy health, as if he'd been draining her at night. She has made her father's spirit visible in the Amber house and everything around it, bright goldfinches and needly hummingbirds, smells of balsam and wild roses through the drifting fog. Nicole was the firstborn; she knew him from the beginning, when the past still lay distantly ahead.

The young man passing outside the window with a flagstone under his right arm like a textbook is Nicolas Colonna, invisibly wounded. Of all their laborers he's the one most closely engaged with the construction, as if he were Marston's personal representative. Nick is the kind of workman her husband so admired, centered in the present and single-mindedly concentrating on his task. He laid the low circular granite bench surrounding the open hearth and faced the foundation with stonework that could have been quarried by his grandfather. He came to Amber as a child almost as young as Julia, and he stayed by old Guido's side as faithfully as a service animal, man and boy caning their way slowly over the ruins of the workers' housing and the covered well. She has to bite her tongue to keep from trying to talk with him, as if his memory could restore an earlier time.

The main door opens and Nicole comes in. She brings a graceful little glass-topped cocktail table with a small rug to protect the floor, then goes back to the cook shed and returns with a vase of early rugosas from the little cove. The effect of that singular still life is stunning in the room's austerity.

"Mom, you're just standing there. Are you all right?"

"I'm letting myself occupy this space for a moment, after all these years. It's so spare and eloquent as it is: the bare floor, the hearth circle, the staircase. It makes me remember him, that's all."

"I know, Mom. I stood here the same way, yesterday. There's so much of his presence in this room." She sits on the circular granite hearth bench and takes Camilla's hand to draw her down beside her.

"The open fireplace wasn't in Marston's drawings, but it's perfect. I love how it echoes the building shape. I can just imagine a chilly Maine evening and an after-dinner conversation around the fire."

"The fire circle was Nick Colonna's idea completely. He designed it and offered to build it and Chad agreed. Before the war Nick's work was installing chimneys and fireplaces. He's a good woodworker, but stone is his calling and his legacy. Look at the joining of these bench slabs—no mortar or anything, yet they're as solid as if they were a single piece."

"It's beautifully constructed. I wish Julia were here to see."

"I knew that's what you were thinking about. She came out unannounced at the worst time, back in April. It was the island from hell, the clear-cuts, the construction, the machinery ruts, everything torn up. I never expected her but there she was, with her camera and tripod."

"I wish she could come again, after they've done the landscaping. Look, the grass is already coming in. Life is miraculous, the way it triumphs over all we subject it to."

"We're planning a housewarming, Mom, just a family moment before it all begins. We have to try out all the systems on ourselves before we can host anyone. There'll be state inspections, board of health, before money can be accepted and we can start repaying you for all you've done. We'll clean up the site and if Julia comes she'll see the Amber house in its true setting. The tiger lilies will be out. Look out through this window—we've surrounded the foundation with gladiolus bulbs! Martha Colonna brought them when she came. We'll have it on the Fourth. We can watch fireworks and remember the old celebrations."

"We'll have sweet corn and lobsters, the way we used to every year."

"Oh my God, remember the totally black lobsters from the open coals?"

"He wouldn't have had them any other way. I can still see him bending over the embers with the tongs, his face glowing from the heat."

"Mom, his face was glowing from the lobsters. They were on fire."

"They were delicious. You could prepare them right here, actually, on the hearth. But I'm not sure how you plan to use it without a chimney."

"They're making a copper fire hood that will taper right up through the rooms for some warmth upstairs. You see that opening in the ceiling? It will go all the way up, through your room and through the roof."

"We never had heat in the wall tents," Camilla recalls.

"You didn't care, Mom, in those days. You sprang out of bed and dove into the freezing sea."

"I did not. Your father would get up before dawn and feel around for his fishing gear and I'd procrastinate all morning, waiting for it to warm up before I swam. Though *warm* is probably too strong a word."

"Cold nights were necessary, or it wouldn't have been Maine. I remember those mornings. Our breath would steam. I'd sleep with only my nose out of the sleeping bag like a seal. But for guests, who won't be, you know, Aleuts or anything—"

"Primarily from the temperate zones. Your guests will be very grateful for the fire."

"I don't know how you survived it, and with little kids. I never felt right bringing the girls, because of the ticks and mosquitoes. But Chad's planning to spray."

"Oh dear, Marston never allowed any persecution of the insects. They were a vital link in the food chain."

"So were we, Mom. They carried our blood back to their children in the swamp. We'd have to pay people to stay here if they had to follow Dad's lifestyle."

"I can just hear Julia bringing up *Silent Spring*."

"Mom, I know Julia will change. She came out of a nightmare and found her direction and now she's about to get her degree. I know when she actually sees it she'll understand. But come on, the top floor was designed with you in mind, and you haven't even climbed the stairs."

Camilla follows her daughter up the black spiral staircase to the first landing, where three doorways open into the sundrenched suites. The bare birch floors sweep out from the central core to the glass walls, projecting the whole room into the air as if it could take flight.

"Let's not walk on the two middle levels," Nicole says. "They're all sanded and Nick's coming to varnish today. He finished yours yesterday so it's okay to walk on it. Today he's going to work his way down. He's a perfectionist, and of course undistractable, though God knows the twins try to get his attention. He has that military discipline, and he rarely stops."

"We're so lucky to have found him."

"It wasn't luck, Mom, it was you. And Martha Colonna, who reached out to you in the fall. You'll see the job he did on the topmost room. There's no limit to the time he puts in. And he's not even hourly. He'll keep going till sunset and he can't see anymore, hours after the crew boat leaves. He's done all this in exchange for the old cabin, which he should own several times over for all his work. Chad's even suggested we might give him some small holding on the island, eventually, for his own use."

Camilla turns to look down upon the pristine finished floor and Nick's elegant amber-tinted hearth. "I understand why he's so intent on creating things, in answer to the waste and destruction he must have seen."

Nicole offers a hand to her from a higher stair, and she allows herself to be drawn upward by this capable young woman, her father's child, so intent on bringing his vision into the world.

"I was pregnant with Will when I went up inside the Matinicus lighthouse. It was even more precipitous. I was like a cow trying to make the climb."

She's a little bit dizzy even on this one, but with Nicole's help she makes it to the topmost step, where the black iron joins the new varnished floor, a huge open room containing an architect's drafting table and, against the far opposite window like a hallucination, a baby grand, its legs on three scraps of carpeting to protect the floor.

"That can't be a piano!"

"Well, it's not a cow."

"How did you get it here? They couldn't have brought it up that staircase. It's like a piano suspended in space."

"It *was* suspended in space. It was the last helicopter load before the roof went on."

She hesitates on the top step, unwilling to let go the steadying iron rail.

"And do you recognize his drafting table? We got it from the firm."

"It's hard even to think of this as a room. The walls seem non-existent."

"Chad calls it an aerie."

"He should. I feel more like a hovering bird than a human being. An aerie with a piano!"

"I came up one day after they brought it and Nick was seated at the keyboard. Not making a sound. I ducked back down. I don't think he saw me."

"It was his own island for all those months, before everyone came."

"It's the only time I ever see him stop and rest. He'll climb to the top of the stairway and just look out. Maybe he's thinking about the war."

"I can't imagine it," Camilla says. "Having to hold that much inside."

The sheer glass wall gives her a touch of acrophobia as she crosses the space from stair to window, then reaches the drafting table and steadies herself against it with both hands. On it they've placed his architectural sketches of the Amber house, still bearing the smudges of kerosene soot and driftwood fire. One of them's signed, *For Camilla—*.

She peers down over the drafting table to the roof of the metal utility shed. Its gridded solar panels conceal the disorder of plumbing and laundry, gas line and septic, as our own skin conceals the pumps, sacs, organs, labyrinths of tubing that deliver us into this life and keep us going. The wind turbine, even higher than she is, is just beginning to spin around and orient itself to the late-morning southerly like a small aircraft turning and taxiing to the wind. Beyond that, in the whitecapped ship channel whose emerald color denotes its extreme depth, a bright orange tanker steams seaward past the Ledgeport hills.

The only interruption of the top floor's open octagonal space is a white-walled wedge whose paneled door implies a bathroom.

"Facilities?" Camilla asks. "May I peek?"

"The plumbers haven't made their big visit yet. But we're thinking that wall space would be perfect for the right painting. You should choose one and we'll bring it up."

"It should be one of Fairfield's," Camilla suggests. "The one that includes our island as a distant speck, the yellow sunset. It will be almost like a mirror."

"Let's go down. I hear Lanie and Brit outside; maybe we can lure them in. They're so excited. This gave them the boost they needed to finish up at school."

Descending the spiral steps is trickier than going up. As soon as she reaches the ground floor, Brittany breezes in with a smile and hug, then Elaine, with two wire chairs for the small round table.

"Oh Grandma," Brittany says, "we'll need all your recipes, and Rosina's, too!"

"They're not very vegetarian. Your grandfather was an omnivore."

"That's okay. We'll just make them with wild game. Nick's going to supply us."

"We've drafted him into the food chain," Lanie adds.

The twins whisk back to the annex, leaving their mom to trim and rearrange the rugosas in the cut-glass vase.

"How easily we forget," Camilla says. "Our tents were right on this spot, but I have to concentrate to remember them."

"I haven't forgotten, Mom. Remember the fuel can we washed our hair with? We're lucky we didn't go up in smoke. We all smelled of kerosene. But Dad was so delighted with everything. He'd be up frying a string of mackerel on the Coleman stove, and we'd still be in our sleeping bags."

Elaine brings a cold and sweating bottle of white wine.

"An organic Riesling, Grandma, just for you, on this awesome day. Someday we may even have grapes here, and produce our own. Can you imagine—Amber House Wines. Grandpa must have been a connoisseur, when you look at his wine cellar. And, when they finish the wiring, our whites are going to be chilled by the wind. Aunt Julia will so approve!"

"So, you, Grandma," Brittany adds, "must convince her to give up her majorly uncool boycott and come to the housewarming."

"She won't be persuaded," Camilla warns.

"We'll do what we can, Mom. But she has another option. Vira, her roommate, has invited her to Finland right after they graduate. So they might not even be in the country for the Fourth."

"The roommate whom I have yet to meet," Camilla says.

"I haven't either, but Will says they're very close."

There's a polite knock on the stained-glass entry door and Nick Colonna comes in, carrying two gallons of floor varnish with rags and brushes, Camilla forgets herself and starts to say something to him, but her daughter touches her hand. Without even turning around to look, he puts one of the cans down and carries the other up the spiral stair, then disappears into one of the second-floor suites. Even so, Nicole still leans across the small table and lowers her voice instinctively.

"Nick's become quite the superhero for the girls. I love the idea of providing game for the table. If it's wild it's automatically organic, isn't it? He and a friend shot a wild turkey for Thanksgiving, can you believe it? Turkeys out here?"

"We never had them before."

"We have them now. Nick has a lobster license, too, just for a dozen traps, but that should keep us supplied. He's also harvested some native plants. Have you heard of lamb's quarters?"

"Not the sheep!"

"No, Mom, it's a vegetable."

"I've never tasted them. Marston's dream was to live off the land."

"People are trying pre-agricultural diets—that's supposedly what we evolved to eat. The girls are planning a Pleistocene option on the menu, what our guests would have had if they'd been foragers here in the Ice Age. Brit says Nick eats raccoons and squirrels, too, though I'm not sure the guests want to go that far."

"Will there be any other options, I hope?"

"You'll see, Mom, when you come and occupy the topmost room. We're putting a boardwalk through that little swamp, so the guests can gather some of this food themselves, cattails and frogs and wild rice. Shellfish—and sea urchin roe for our own sushi. You wouldn't think they'd vacation at this level to squish around barefoot up to their knees in mud, but Chad thinks they will. An 'authentic experience ' he says."

They hear movement above them, then resonance of footsteps on the iron stairs as Nick returns for the second can, picks it up, and reascends two steps at a time. Nicole leans even closer and whispers, "I think Brit may have developed a little crush. She summons Nick on his Blackberry to show her where to find the edible plants. She seems intrigued that he's a soldier. It makes me realize, outside of Nick I don't know a single veteran from this time. Our friends' children simply don't serve."

"We had a houseful of soldiers," Camilla remembers, "when I was growing up. They'd gather for beer and poker and I'd be jealous of how close they were. They were so proud. They'd saved the country from the unthinkable."

"Chad has a lot of respect for Nick. You've seen them texting back and forth. He consults Nick before just about anyone, and there's a trust there, too, which doesn't come easily to Chad after what he went through with the yacht business. He'll try to make year-round work for him, caretaking and maintenance. If you can imagine anyone wintering here alone."

"But he did. I wouldn't have thought it possible, the solitude day after day, unable to leave when it's iced in."

"He seems to have found his place here. He hasn't been on the mainland since December."

Chad recrosses the window in his hard hat heading for the annex, by himself this time.

"Sweetheart, can't you get that man to stop work for a minute and join us for a glass?"

"Maybe later, after the workmen go, but not for a glass. Chad's pretty disciplined about alcohol these days. We owe you so much, Mom, for helping us out with everything." She pauses as if there were some further confidence, but Brittany appears at the doorway with a dish of tiny strawberries, the tenderest shade of red.

"Grandma, they're from the island! Nick found them. They're just buds, really, but I wanted to show you."

"Oh I remember! We had strawberry feasts in our time. You two would have loved them."

"I feel so lucky that we knew Grandpa," Brittany says. "I like to feel we're doing all this for him."

"He'd be proud of you two," Camilla says. "But now sit down with us—you've been working all afternoon."

"I would," Brit says. "But I'm going upstairs to bring Nick some water. He has two floors to finish and the day's getting hot. He doesn't take a lunch break like the other guys. He works as if there's a deadline, which I guess there is, since it all has to be ready by the Fourth." She bounds up two steps at a time with the Poland Springs bottle. The blue trace of a butterfly ankle tattoo flashes on the spiral stairs, recalling the spring Julia came home with hers. They need to mark themselves, this generation, as if afraid of forgetting who they are.

When Brittany comes down she has exchanged the Poland Springs bottle for an empty varnish can, with a smile that Camilla remembers from Nicole when a man was around. She wonders if she'd looked that way herself, a young intern in an architectural firm in the summer of—when would it have been—1963? A cup of coffee spilled on a blueprint; like a servant she rushed over, sacrificed her own ironed handkerchief to wipe it up. The most trivial moment, but all this is what it unfurled into, this house, these children and grandchildren, and it will again, there's no stopping it, though people are lost in the night or left behind.

Now Chad comes in the door removing his yellow hard hat to reveal the genteelly rumpled sun-bleached hair whose gray filaments seem less like time and age than a transient change of season.

"Chad, sit with us for a minute," Camilla says.

"I have a quick kitchen errand," Nicole says. "So, Chad, don't leave Mom alone till I come back."

Camilla reaches over the small table to take her son-in-law's hand in gratitude for realizing Marston's vision and for bringing her daughter home.

"Chad, I must admit I wasn't certain this could be done. It's the first of his homes that he didn't personally oversee. But you've made it happen."

"He oversaw it. There hasn't been a day I didn't feel Marston looking on. But we'll have to work on Julia. She sees all this with a different eye."

"The eye of her generation, idealistic and defiant, as we all once were."

"Except us," Chad laughs. "We graduated into the Reagan years. Peace through prosperity. But the world has changed, and will change again. Julia's protest is to leave the country. In time, her love of Amber will bring her back."

Nicole returns with a quick kiss for both mother and husband.

"I have to kidnap this attractive stranger. Remember, the electricians are leaving and they won't be back for a week. Mom, Hallett's coming for you in half an hour. In the morning he'll pick you up at the Excelsior and drive you to the plane. Climb up again and look out at the ocean from your bedroom, then we'll get ourselves together and head down to meet the boat."

On the third level Camilla pauses for a glance at Nick finishing his work, facing away from her, varnishing expertly backward away from the glass walls, so he'll end up at the door. Marston so envied artisans, their work contained entirely in the moment, yet crafted to last forever.

She's alone in the tower and the deepening light as the June sun lowers toward the distant hills. A white gull beats past the glass wall at the same altitude, not floating recreationally but focused on some destination to the north, as it passes between the wind turbine and the highest room. Despite the glass barrier she feels the draft of the gull's passage and with it a lightness, a happiness, from the whole day, maybe helped by the cold Riesling and this dizzying elevation from the earth, like a gray-plumaged seabird aloft on its own wings.

On her way down, she looks in on Nick's progress but finds the floor all lustrous fresh finish and the room empty. She sees him working in another suite, the one facing the stand of tall conifers that even at this height block out the Fox Islands to the east. This time he turns and looks up, rests the brush over the top of the varnish can, and looks right at her as if about to speak. She carefully mouths to him, *The floor is lovely.* He acknowledges with a single nod, then returns to work.

16

It's night in the desert and the ground shakes from deep shuddering explosions in the sky. They're burying Saddam Hussein in a sandbank graveyard but the body is still alive and he's twitching and moving so they can't stuff him in. Then Evans says "Shit, it's not even Saddam, it's one of his fucking doubles. Every corpse in the sandbank is a double; no one they've killed is really dead. All this time Julia Fletcher has been standing beside them and under her burqa he can see the outline of an M-16. She ignores Evans but takes Nick's hand gently by the smallest finger and says, "Soldier, it's almost time."

He starts up awake and checks the Blackberry in his pocket which says 1:00 a.m. It was set to vibrate at 1:15 but 0100 is better. He's had only an hour of sleep so he's glad Julia's still in the room with him, telling him what to do in a rested, well-organized way, but at the same time firm and decisive which makes her soft-spoken directions easy to obey. She has been close by and her words have guided his tasks and movements for every waking moment of the last two days. He'd like to kiss her or at least touch her hand but in the complete darkness he can't tell what corner her voice is coming from; it could even be coming from someplace above the roof. In the darkness he can just make out the white rectangles of the sliced-out pages taped and tacked to every wall surface, so the whole cabin has become the inside of a book. He's nailed up the sections Mr. Fischer had highlighted and added pages marked as important on his own. Some sentences he's committed to memory without even trying, though in school he couldn't memorize a word. *Every man is tasked to make his life, even in its details, worthy of the contemplation of his most elevated and critical hour.* That was a hard one, not because he didn't get it, but because how does a man know when that hour has arrived? You could have missed it; it could be now, and you're missing it even as you read. *If you have built castles in the air, your work need not be lost.*

He also nailed up pages from the Red Paint printout and Mr. F's start-up sequence and the small-game recipes and the Last Will and Testament of Mohamed Atta. He's like an animal living in a cave of words, every one known by heart so he can read them without light. *Then when the time is upon you, slay the idolaters wherever you find them.* The Pilot. He prepared his mission with a discipline that no American can even approach, we are such slackers and fobbits, asleep in our beds when the strong and attentive are wide awake. The most elevated and critical hour. Who knows if we would ever be able to rise to his level of purpose and concentration.

He hears the voice clearly, but now spoken in the intonation of his mom when she first sent him off to the Ash Street school. *Tighten your shoes well, wear socks so that your feet will be solidly in your shoes.* Though it's midsummer, he wears the insulated boots he opened under the Christmas tree. *Strap the Ka-Bar to your left leg as always. You won't need anything else. Wear the sweatshirt I left there the time I came in out of the hail and rain. Put the harpoon point in your pocket and button it so it can't fall out. Don't take the Blackberry; you won't be needing it. Hurry, it's almost the earliest sunrise of the year.*

Not quite completely obedient, he does sneak the Blackberry into his sweatshirt pocket along with the harpoon point, each barb sharpened with the Ka-Bar to a critical edge. They'll understand, putting their own instrument to this use. The Blackberry contains the one photo he captured of her face when they were communicating with it back in April, plus another as she was walking away from the Red Paint site, with the camera bag over her left shoulder, after a kiss that left long-term radiation on his lips as if they were glossed with a uranium round. It's the second picture he chooses to keep on the screen, showing only her back, because she has left the country to protest her family's disrespect, not just for the island, but her dead father who walked to the old quarry with Nonno Guido. Nick has personally dedicated his labor to the memory of those two men, in teamwork with the rest of the building crew, to prepare for the Fourth of July gathering this day when her tall gray-haired mother comes to the tower room.

She's now speaking in fluent Arabic. *The time for playing is over,* she says, *and the serious time is upon us.* The words are the Pilot's but the voice is hers.

He never thought they'd finish it on time. For two weeks straight it's been urgent and top priority for every guy on the island and even if they'd come out as backhoe operators and brush cutters, they dropped everything else to focus on the final preparation of the house. He completed the stonework and joinery with his most professional level of craft and concentration. He worked in the moment of time without consideration of past and future, though beneath the artisanal surface this day grew blindly inside him like a spore.

Bacon's Appliance had sent a crew of electricians to wire the control panel for the exterior lighting that would give the tower the look of a beacon in the night. When they finally turned it on at ten p.m., the Amber house lit up like an industrial power plant that could not only have been seen by a passing vessel but by an observer on the moon. They had hoisted Mrs. Fletcher's queen-sized bed up the slender fire escape piece by piece, but the mattress wouldn't fit the half-height emergency exit so they brought it down and finally corkscrewed it up the winding stair. Dressers, window seats, sinks, toilets, Persian throw rugs, a crated oil painting with three guys easing it up the spiral: worth more than the whole island, someone said. They took apart, carried up, and reassembled a barge load of furniture while plumbers flared and sweated the bath fixtures and the electricians installed lighting inside and out. They used the Motorolas on everyone's belt to coordinate efforts but kept Nick in constant touch with short texts on the Blackberry. *TOWER OF BABEL*, Chad texted him once, but he knew firsthand. He'd been to the site of it less than a year ago: Hillah, Iraq, where men were splintered into different languages so they could never again collaborate. Silence would also have been one of its severed tongues.

It was after sunset before they finally finished and hid all the construction vehicles behind a screen of trees to look natural when Mrs. Fletcher came. Chad had drenched the grounds with insecticide and with the complete absence of mosquitoes they'd worked shirtless all day and evening in the July heat. When they were done and Chad closed the battery circuit the crew cheered like twelve sunburned mimes with their mouths open and George Plummer pulled three cases of cold beer from the wind-powered fridge. One of the twin female cooks, whose name he still doesn't know, stood there beside him with the amber-colored gem in her navel catching the light as if her body had been wired into the circuit. She had been hitting on him all evening whenever they passed each other and her likeness to Julia Fletcher almost got him, but the Pilot spoke sharply to him like a military command. *Purify your soul from all unclean things.* He stood up and walked her to the cook shed where her sister hung huge pots and cleavers from the ceiling in the blaze of electric light.

Now at 0117 he knows even in the cabin's darkness that preparations are complete. The bone hook she kept all winter was re-buried deep in the gravel bank. He's taking only the barbed point and the Ka-Bar strapped to his left calf under his cargo pants. He fills the kerosene lantern that can go eighteen hours if it's dim enough, turns it down to a bare glow and leaves it burning on the upper stove shelf.

It will stay lit till it runs dry. On the table in the opposite corner he leaves a page from Henry's book, impaled with his jackknife to the stone-scrubbed wood. *It is easier to deal with the real possessor of a thing than with the temporary guardian of it.* He knows who the real possessors are; they were the first to purchase it with their blood, and their bones are woven into its soil and glacial sand. The original people and the Tuscan stoneworkers and the father who kept it from invasion and the girl who is the living inheritor: a circle that might be opened to admit another.

He starts tearing pages off the wall, crumpling them into the woodstove, but there's only time to insert a few. Outside, the smoke plume from his chimney rises against the glow from the still-lighted tower. The moon's still hidden behind clouds, but over the sleeping town and hills the sky is a black curtain with a hundred thousand bullet holes letting the light through. Instinctively he checks the sheepfold but it's been empty since the Amber house went up. They've either hidden themselves deep in the dense northeast woods or made the night crossing to a better home. He hasn't seen them and no one in the crew has texted anything about sheep. He picks and feels his way to the beached dory, then starts back at the rush and shadow of huge wings just over his head. In its unsleeping hunger the blue heron fishes both day and night.

The full tide makes it easy to slide the keel down the sloping beach. Though no one should be up at this hour, he's careful to minimize sound and movement. After the celebration the work crew returned to the mainland on the construction barge, leaving the family up late to complete Mrs. Fletcher's accommodations in the piano room. He steps over the transom then poles away with one oar through the clutching rockweed. He's just floating free when a red flare arcs up high over the horizon from somewhere on the mainland shore. His body instinctively hunches for the explosion as it bursts into a shower of flaming petals that dissipate down to the invisible sea. Somebody up early or late has set off the first rocket for the birthday of an exceptional nation, conceived in armed combat and many times tested and strengthened by its wars. He casts off and eases the oars between their wooden pins, then starts for the mainland in long low strokes which should be soundless although each is a whirlpool of bioluminescence mirroring the sky.

Facing backward he can see the lamp in his own cabin window as if someone's still seated there looking over his possessions or reading late. Any night owl passing by, any woman seeking him out by flashlight or starlight, might think him home and awake; but he's not in, he's pulling hard now past the jetty through slack water, not slanting southward for the Ledgeport breakwater but directly west across to the nearest point on the mainland, two and a half miles as the crow flies, which he has given himself forty-five minutes to row. When he pulls out beyond the tree line he sees the blaze of light that makes him think of Cape Canaveral or a missile launch. Every bulb is still on, on all four stories, so it appears as a column of white fire. This was a remote island that had known nothing but the gas lamps of his grandfather's day and before that, the sprucewood blazes where the first inhabitants grilled their oceanic fish. Facing backward and rowing away from it in the clear night air, it looks like a nuclear furnace that would incinerate anything inside.

Then in an instant it goes dark. Their work must be done so Chad shut the generator off. They'll find their way to the bunkhouse with flashlights to sleep for a few hours before they go down to meet Julia's mother at the pier. He rests his oars just for a moment to listen for the voice that has been dictating every action step by step, the details of woodwork and masonry, then the rituals of preparation and the things to carry and the time to leave. Her silence now is a hundred times quieter than deafness, the silence of absolute zero without the confident words that have come to direct his work. But only for a moment. Now she is here again, as if on the water nearby or in the mist of the air. *You were looking to the battle before you engaged in it, and now you see it with your own two eyes.* She speaks a desert language with the rasp of a street Arab, but Nick hears in his auditory center and understands. *Know the plan well from all angles and expect full response to the action and the resistance of the Enemy.*

To the northward a set of red and green running lights appears, so high off the surface it must be an empty supertanker bound for the oil fields. Tailwinded by the midnight ebb, the tanker's going to be making five times his speed and on this course will grind him under the surface without registering on any instrument. It's not the time or place yet for oblivion. He has to row the heavy dory across the shipping lane before the intercept and he knows because of its constant bearing it is going to be close. Almost in prayer he asks his shoulder and back and arm muscles to pull harder by the promise that if they succeed, that level will never be asked of them again.

Faster than he imagined, the tanker is on top of him, the distance more vertical than horizontal. Now he can make out the superstructure towering high aloft as he pulls past its centerline with the dory's keel shuddering from the vibration and the starlit bow wave approaching him like a surf line. He closes and strains his eyes to bring even their tiny sinews into the effort and then it's behind him, he's facing the side of it and reading the name *Exxon Qatar* illuminated by the deck lights and already its first wake lifts up the dory's stern like the arm of God. He's over that one when the next catches and pitchpoles him and the stem buries in cold black water but then comes up. He's taken half a foot into the bilges but the following wave hasn't the same strength and just pushes him, and the next, so he's coasting down them and the tanker's a ghost castle throbbing south into the gloom.

It's hard rowing so much ballast so he stops to bail out but then spots a night cloud in the east whose underside already has a purple glow. It's not time for light or anything like it. He rows with his eyes closed because he doesn't want to see, blinking only once every five strokes to stay straight, and suddenly there's a huge colorless cone-shaped buoy looming beside him that he almost hit, then the swells shorten and steepen to mark the shallows. He feels more than sees land rising to the north of him, then some kind of outcrop to the south, a felt channel through blind ledges that could be called luck or could be allowed him because his intent is singular and clear. No voices direct him now because there are no decisions. Everything is given or not given. The dory lifts with a low beach wave and when it comes down, the strakes on the right side scrape and bounce off but he pulls harder hoping the flood tide will carry him high onshore. The bow strikes a ledge and he rows hard but the blades entangle in rocks and seaweed so he stands in the cold ankle-deep bilge water and poles forward till the oar breaks off, then shoves with the other and the boat heaves on a final wave push and jams dead.

He steps onto the kelp-strewn barnacled rock and keeps the good oar to balance himself up the dark shore. He'd like to release the dory but he stabs at its prow with the oar and it won't budge. All its life it's been tethered and subject to human command; the coming tide will float it and in the freedom of sunrise it will find its way.

He picks his course upward as the rocks dry off and become pebbles and finally sand and he's on a night beach somewhere north of Ledgeport, shadows of big shorefront estates above him and beyond them a semi's red running lights passing on Route 1. She made it clear: It's not the estates you need but a random ordinary Maine house with kids' bikes lying around outside. He's on some kind of boat landing now as the beach slants upward to an asphalt ramp and a single incandescent lamppost on the highway corner. The way it is on this coast: palaces on the shore side of Route 1, hardscrabble poverty on the other.

He crosses over to the poor side and for time's sake jogs southward toward Ledgeport before spotting an orange streetlight over the green sign for Dyer Lane, for the first time knowing where he is. His coworker at Davis Stonecraft, Roger Leblanc, used to live in a trailer on this street. There are fishermen here, too, and any other Wednesday there'd already be pickups warming up next to lighted kitchens, guys awake and dressed at 0300 with coffee, checking the weather report. Today, though, is a national holiday and their boats will come into use much later for family picnics, then the community fireworks at night. *How much time have we wasted in our lives.*

He enters a yard and almost trips over a half-deflated children's wading pool beneath a stack of yellow wire traps strewn with Day-Glo green lobster buoys under a dim mercury light. He imagines a guard dog and draws back with a sweat of fear. It would be on his throat and he'd never hear it. Then a man's voice he's never heard, and it's old and Southern, not Dupuy but Dupuy's dad maybe, big-bellied heavyweight who's never run from anything in his life. *Fear is a great worship*, the voice says.

He unsnaps the Ka-Bar sheath and walks past the pool and lobster traps directly toward the dim yard light where the dog would lurk, because that's where the bike was in the dream and it is there, old ragged-ass Schwinn on the far side of the trap pile just lying where the kid left it, not even propped against the traps, nose down, pedal and rear wheel in the air.

If the dog's coming out it will be now, as he bends down vulnerably with the blunt side of the Ka-Bar in his mouth and both hands occupied raising the handlebars out of the dirt. Then he's got it. He stops to sheathe the knife and look eastward; his enemy now is the violet-pink border edging the night clouds to the east. Once again he's balancing on two wheels and he whirls around out of the dog's property and onto Dyer Lane with the animal maybe barking inside or chained up and not able to reach him now he's on the road. He's not heading back down to Route 1 but straight up this very road that rises fast, turns to gravel and crosses the Ledgeport Hills to intersect Route 13 on the high ridge, right where he needs to be. By feel he figures out the handlebar twist grips and gears down but then the chain slips off the smallest ring and he's got to dismount and press it back on, then wipe the grease and yard dust on his wet pants cuff. The voice is now quieter and accented like Omar their translator who had lived in Amsterdam. They all use the same language like the tower before He struck it, with superhuman organization and command. The voice demands cleanliness but that is impossible now. Hands, pants, camo jacket soaked with salt water and smeared with grease; he doesn't know why cleanliness would have anything to do with his objective or any significance at all in the dark of night. Unless there's a cleanliness that can't be seen.

He passes the shapes of trailers and double-wides with a light on in one of them and then another. After a lifetime of rising at this hour these crabbers and lobstermen couldn't sleep late if they tried. The summits of the Ledgeport hills can already be distinguished against the sky. His arms and back ache from the row and his legs have not cranked a bike since September, but he shifts to the middle chainring and pumps harder, pushing through pain to the place where he's just counting rotations and the machine under him is climbing on its own. It's growing light now and he's entered the state park, which means no more residences and no chance of dogs, though the ascent angle gets even steeper. He has to slow and gear down so his veins and arteries don't explode, while behind and beneath him the predawn is lighting a cloud ridge directly above the islands. Pedaling with his eyes squinted and head down and now on the largest ring he feels the gravel under his tires become black pavement and he can see for the first time the stolen green bicycle beneath him, derailleurs front and rear on their highest settings as the road levels and approaches the intersection with Route 13.

Not even stopping or changing gears but grateful to the kid that kept this bike in decent shape, he heads west on high level ground with the sun leaching its blood color on the horizon clouds. A Muscongus Seafood truck passes him, then a lobsterman's pickup with L. LUNT lettered on the door. The rotting contents of its bait pails stream a visible odor into the air. As the road takes a slight downhill turn he tries to keep up with the slow-moving seafood van but can't, even on the blacktop bike lane. Route 13 is the road to the VA hospital that sent him home with his ears dead and his insides gutted not only by loss and grief but medication till he didn't know what they had given him or who he was. His mother's voice is upon him saying it's not too late—even now you can still go back there and take something that will help you and get your name on the cochlear implant list.

This road also leads to the little airstrip they flew from almost a year ago, and here are the buildings they took off over, the white farmhouse already sporting the Stars and Stripes from a tall pole, the Lanier construction company with its gravel pit, the blank unlabeled warehouse whose white roof reddens from the refracted dawn. Then the big hangar and outside a handful of small planes with wings tied down against the wind.

He's acting as if everything will be as it was, the Cessna between two others in the hangar with the open door, though it's been almost a year, anything could have happened. Mr. F may have already taken off for an early flight or gone for the holiday to some other airport or even sold his plane or acquired another which Nick would not recognize. You move in a fixed direction but all around are others with their own calling and determinations that can further or obstruct your own. He passes an antique biplane with a machine gun mounted behind the propeller arc. Planes make their random commercial errands but from the beginning their inner and highest function has been for war. The Pilot knew that when he diverted United 291 from its meaningless transport of civilians to the tower revealed as its destination.

Among the four planes of the first row inside the hangar there are two green-and-white Cessnas, one of them with a varnished wood propeller exactly like Mr. F's. As he walks close it has Brenda's birthday number, N1002: pale body straddled above him with her hair brushing the blue nylon, screams of a lynx or bobcat in the tent's blue light. The plane looks just washed or even freshly painted as the sunrise strikes it like a bright plaything whose true purpose is hidden even from itself. His whole life was training and preparation for an hour unknown till it arrived; now this too is a preparation for something still latent below the horizon, like the sun. The Pilot took step after step without ever knowing, and then he knew.

The wind sock is rising from its total slack and he feels a dawn breeze in his hair and blowing across the dead eardrums, trying to wake them for another day. Now with the sea-rim the color of an acetylene torch he knows what Henry D meant on the last page—*The sun is but a morning star.* He's still the only person around, but it's a cloudless Fourth of July morning and before long some owner will arrive, so he must hurry. He approaches his teacher's Cessna from the front and rubs his fingertips on the varnished wood prop, slick with dew, then kicks the chocks out and loosens the tie-downs that restrained it from solo adventures in the night. The pilot's door has a lock he didn't notice before and he panics for a moment, thinking he'll have to break a window. But it's Maine where nobody locks anything and it swings open and he steps up on the wheel strut to grope through the papers and random cloths under the seat and there's the key.

He hauls himself up from the strut step to the pilot's seat and shuts the door. He has brought with him the folded start-up sequence Mr. F gave him back in September; but as he surveys the levers and instruments their flight returns to him as if it was the day before. The plane is already aligned with the wind sock so he won't have to turn, the misted grass runway directly pointed at the fire-veined eastern sky. Mr. F's own aviator sunglasses appear on the dashboard like a deliberate gift which he puts on as the sun's upper limb spills over the runway like molten steel.

It is not like the Pilot taking control of the 737 in midflight with garrote and box cutter slitting the crews' throats like cattle. He must get the aircraft into the air himself from its dead stop. Among the babel of voices around him in the cockpit one sounds like Mr. Fischer in English class; speaking aloud he asks his old teacher for understanding and forgiveness and also to help him as he makes his way. As on their first flight together he places his hands under Mr. F's control and they find the battery switch first, alternator and fuel. He skips the compass because it's a clear morning with the sun almost a full circle and his flight plan exactly follows its blinding path. His hand slides the mixture knob to the rich setting as he memorized it, pumps the priming lever three times, then turns the key in the starter switch like any vehicle, though the last thing he remembers driving was an M1025 Armament Carrier with Dupuy Williams on the gun.

The prop spins and stops and he twists the key again, wishing for just a moment of hearing so he can start the engine, but he must do it by the tach alone. He twists the key as far as it will go and the prop spins on the starter but the tach flicks only to 700 and back to zero; again the tach rises and dies, then he leans the mixture and it suddenly catches and it's spinning at a silent 1,700 rpm, too fast, and the plane tries to nose forward against the wheel brake. He's in Mr. F's seat now and there's no one beside him, but the voice of his old teacher comes strongly through. First lower the rpm. Next to the mixture control he finds the throttle and pulls it out so the tach drops to 900 and the plane relaxes against the parking brake. Push on the toe lever and release the black handle on the left, his voice says, and as he does so the plane moves forward as it's been straining and wanting to, though the rpm's still only 1,000, out of the hangar's shadow to point east over the dark islands as if the Cessna had been pre-aimed toward an Assyrian desert halfway around the world.

He hits the toe brake again and the plane stops. Move pitch to T/O. Flaps to zero. He finds and adjusts these levers while his peripheral vision watches the traffic on Route 13, hoping no one turns into the airport drive, not for a minute yet, then let them come. Ease off the brake, press the throttle lever a bit forward so the plane moves slow and silent at a walking pace from paved apron to grass runway, then more throttle till the speed is a runner's, then a bicycle's, then fast as a noiseless hybrid as he turns slightly with his left foot to stay on the grassway and faster, throttle almost all the way in to 1,900, and then, under Mr. F's calm but strict guidance, he pulls back on the control yoke, slightly at first, and the tail drops, his own body slants upward, and pulling just a hair more it stops shaking with ground motion and enters the sea-like wave patterns of the air.

He's still too low and the plane's tipped to the left but as if governed by the controls in the copilot's empty seat, the yoke turns clockwise—too far at first so it tips southward, then it swings over and finds its level and he's well above the first farmhouse past the runway and still climbing, with the throttle maxed but completely inaudible as if exceeding the speed of sound. From the right-hand seat Mr. F speaks in the same voice that read from *The Red Badge of Courage* in English class: *The flap control next to the mixture, move it from T/O to zero.* As soon as he does this, it's easy to press the yoke forward and bring the nose parallel with the ground.

At 2,000 rpm he's flying level with the summit of Mount Amatuck, serene as a hang glider with the pinkening houses like a model town far below. Briefly over his own rooftop with his room again empty now that Angela's back in New Mexico, he crosses the airspace of his sleeping family like a dream. They are the two children in their beds and he's the parent above them looking down, more deeply experienced and closer to death, inhabiting a future they couldn't have conceived of when they blindly engraved it in the dark. Down past the nosewheel which still dangles beneath the engine, small uniformed figures hang the American flag from lampposts and utility poles, to honor the sacrifice that carries a free nation through the night of war. Then he's over a Nimitz-class destroyer decorated fore and aft with cruise missile launchers and an alphabet of colorful signal flags hoisted for the Fourth.

His level and steady course into the sunrise will carry him well below Amber toward the fishing port at the southern tip of the Fox Islands. Just past the breakwater lighthouse, the plane strikes a shock wave of air that yaws it sharply to the right and down. Turning the yoke counterclockwise corrects the angle but he needs practice if he's ever going to make a controlled descent. With the gentlest rudder and yoke pressure he starts a tranquil and steady climb past the long shore of the Fox Islands up to 1,800 feet, then gently declines, testing the precision of his hands on yoke and throttle, to 1,750, 1,700, 1,650, then push in and nose up to 1,700 again, as the cockpit fills with the sun's warmth and light. The slightest foot pressure and tilt of the yoke start a slow clockwise rotation for a few minutes of free circling flight as his body adapts to its new wings. It would have been like this to look on Babylon: artisans of all nations speaking the same language in the complete symmetry of human labor, constructing a skyscraper so high it had to be taken down.

Air movements on every surface force him to keep adjusting in three dimensions. Beneath him the open Atlantic wheels in its blue silence, broken only by the outpost of Matinicus, its fishing fleet asleep on their moorings, the stark stone lighthouse on the lonely rock. He holds the long right turn at a constant altitude that would have satisfied

Mr. F if he had done it himself, then straightens the rudder as the bay before him narrows and snakes through wilderness toward the blue summit of Katahdin. His father stands watching as he kneels at the small swift-running brook by their campsite, trying to scrub with his bare hand an aluminum skillet crusted with burned butter and fish scales. Three trout swim motionless nearby, heads facing the current.

"Get a handful of sand, from the streambed."

He scoops it and scours the pan clean and passes it to his dad to rinse and dry. Raw syllables of Arabic pour through the plane's radio. *The time for play is over and the serious time is upon us.*

Slowly he throttles back to 1,500 and eases the yoke forward; the plane, gradually descending, tracks the route of Archaic hunters returning from the swordfish grounds. The nose attitude reads negative five degrees, then ten. A huge familiar shadow comes out of nowhere into the copilot's space. *Yo, check out the tanker bringing us oil on Independence Day. Chill and slow, jes' follow that mo'fo up.*

He can only stay with the ship's track for a minute or two, then he's beyond it and headed toward Amber as the sun catches the glass tower with an outburst of sheer faceted light. From the moment the ground thawed he dedicated himself to its construction. Though unable to hear orders he followed the foreman's gestures as they lowered and fastened each wall segment into place, anchoring it to the iron staircase by the radial floor joists. His only communications were through the Blackberry, which he now takes from his pocket and switches on, his last view of Julia Fletcher leaving the island with her daypack and the sniper's tripod strapped to its side. They then assigned him the granite facing for the foundation, the stone hearth and the tongue-and-groove birch over the subfloors. He worked to his highest personal standard in memory of the stoneworkers Peter and Guido Colonna, and the architect, her father, whose hand shaped every element of the design, including this.

Julia's voice that guided his row over the night channel is absent,

Dupuy Williams has vanished and Mr. F has gone mute. The hands on the yoke beside him belong to the Pilot, whose speech like the Babylonian masons is both English and Arabic at the same time. *You should feel complete tranquility, because the time between you and your marriage is very short.*

With mild steady forward pressure on the yoke and one backward notch of the throttle he's lost 600 more feet, so it's at 650 and he can home in like a ship on the line of red and green navigational buoys that lead to Mark Island's day beacon, then Bridle and Amber beyond that, where the tower now like a raw diamond gathers and reflects the sun. On this day Henry took possession of a cabin self-built and roofed like his own from recycled discards and refuse of the earth. A nation born from battlefield chaos and blood sacrifice of revolution, followed by the war that freed Dupuy's ancestors from their chains. The last image of him was from the left side so he could see the American flag proudly on the shoulder of his uniform, up there above him in the Deuce turret of the Humvee, throwing Mr. Goodbars to the Arab street kids for no reason but his generous heart.

He has the yoke and throttle set now for a constant descent and passes the triangular green beacon on Mark Island at an altitude of 300 feet. His throttle is most of the way back with the prop idling so slow he can see the wood grain of the individual blades. The tallest spruces are just a few yards beneath him as he overflies the estate on Bridle Island with the green mist steaming from its lawns. Mr. F says *Pull up* so he draws the yoke back and with his left hand pushes the throttle because he's so close to the treetops he can see ravens' nests crowded with red open beaks.

He slows the Humvee for the intersection so Ramos can look one way and the other for trouble on the cross streets, then he slows further for this old Samarran female in a black burqa who walks slowly from a stand selling piled cabbages to someplace on the other side. Dupuy starts throwing the candy again though there are no children in sight. Ramos unplugs his earbuds so the salsa gets deafening and now a white dog limps out after the old woman, going for the Mr. Goodbars, blind probably and deaf, because when he blasts the horn at it, it keeps coming. It's been in a fight or some hadji abused it because its hind leg is hiked up as if broken and a gash girdles its stomach like an appendectomy seamed with the coarse red stitches of a baseball. As it gets closer the scar is still oozing and the belly distended with a tumor, or pregnancy. The dog bleeds from its mouth. He stops dead in the road and even Ramos turns down the salsa so they can hear the agony in the dog's whine. In this pitiful country the best gift they can give it is to free it from misery. He doesn't have to say it, just lifts his hand as vehicle commander, and Moby pops a single round from his M4, then the street dog explodes through the right windshield and rips Ramos's face off and high in the gun turret nothing protects Dupuy Williams from the shrapnel so the whole upper half of his body is torn away.

He flies straight and level in motionless air altitude 150 above the north tip of Bridle with the voice of the Pilot in his ear. *Give us victory and make the ground shake under their feet.*

He's over the unnavigable rock-strewn shallows between islands at treetop level, then the south cove, and though the air's banging the wings around, he forces the throttle to airspeed 120 and fights the lift down with his whole weight on the control yoke as he crosses the fresh-shingled bunkhouse where everyone's still in their beds after last night. Her father's tower of glass and redwood, much of it the craft and labor of his own hands. He drops the nose slightly to engage the third story as the same plane comes forth to meet him out of the mirrored glass. His own face is behind the windshield and next to him is the Pilot with his hands on the dual yoke, though the voice is a young woman saying in Arabic, *Did you think we created you without purpose?*

Now it is time.

17

The phone by her sleeping ear vibrates with an incoming text at 8:38 a.m. It's Nicole's number. *FIRE ON AMBER. CHAD IN LEDGEPORT HOSPITAL. NO CELL USE. IF STILL IN USA PLEASE COME.*

She's wearing only a T-shirt but she starts to sweat from every point of her body as if in a sudden sauna. She tugs Vira's shoulder to show her the text with her hand trembling so Vira has to hold the cell herself.

"Vira, do you think this is real or are they just raising the pressure?"

"It is a true thing. I had a dream of it."

She texts both Nicole and Will, waits for an answer, tries calling one sibling after the other and gets only their voicemail. At last night's farewell party they gave away all their possessions but backpacks and their double sleeping bag and two one-way tickets to Helsinki. She's not going to see the island again nor any part of the nation this day birthed in violence with its blood-striped flag.

Vira can't really drive a shift but Julia puts her behind the wheel anyway cause she's too shaky to drive, trying to visualize a fire on Amber that could put someone in the hospital. But where? Trucks with full fuel tanks could have touched off the trees, as if the island weren't damaged enough already; then there's the caretaker's woodstove with its rusted-out chimney, but that wouldn't explain Chad. There must have been an accident at the resort, with all that electrical stuff, plus the propane supply for the twins' six-burner range.

The plan was to drive straight to Boston on I-95, donate the Sidekick to NPR, and catch the night flight from Logan, in two days to be free of a country that began in radical insurrection but now follows a path of hegemony and greed. But everything's changed. They're creeping down Route 1 in summertime traffic through a tunnel of red-white-and-blue flags and banners, now brought to a dead stop while the Volunteer Fire Department passes by, then a float bearing the Seafood Queen in a jeweled tiara. Her iridescent blue gown tapers fishlike to her silver heels.

"Your country had a Declaration of Autonomy," Vira says. "Now you crush revolutions around the world. You showed the way but did not follow it."

"What do you expect?" Julia says. "It was founded by slaveholders. They had the Liberty Bell in one hand and a bullwhip in the other. We're out of here on the fifth."

"Out, maybe. You don't know what this is today."

In the mirror a car behind them breaks from the stopped line, then disappears down a side street.

"They know a detour, Vira, follow them!"

The back road snakes them behind the quaint little Potemkin village of Coveside, and suddenly trailers appear with their snowmobiles squatting in yard puddles, mailboxes and Yield signs riddled with bullet holes, old men and women drinking beer in aluminum lawn chairs with little flags planted all around them, overturned rusted cars in the driveway, their four tireless wheels in the air like fossilized iron dogs.

"Vira, can you go a little faster? Push the shift up and to the right, that's fifth."

"You should be driving yourself."

"I need the time to think. Mom was to go out there today for the big opening, that's what Will told me. Now some kind of fire, and Chad hurt. I want to let go of that place but it won't let me."

"Do you think certain people are doomed, Julia? I do. It is retribution for something in the past."

"I don't. There's no doom, outside of ourselves. If you mean Chad, yes, he has a doom, which is to want and want, no matter what you have, to need more. And Nicole's an enabler. You should have seen the palace they had in the Virgin Islands. It's not his fault. He's like the whole country. That's why I'm getting out."

Once past the mobile-home parks, their backroad detour takes them through upland farm country with sheep pastures and a llama ranch, then climbs steadily to rejoin Route 1 on a coastal hill. It always takes her breath away to reach the top of this ridge and suddenly, dramatically, behold all of shimmering Penobscot Bay maplike beneath her, crisscrossed by ferry wakes and punctuated by white sails. From one of the islands there's a distinct blackish smoke plume rising vertically in the windless air.

"Vira, pull over, there it is!" She grabs the binoculars. "Smoke. Like a fire is burning on the southern end, near where we camped. So much smoke you can't even see the building. Look! There's a helicopter right over it, looks like it's going to land. Okay, we've seen it—it's true. Now drive!"

At the hospital Vira parks across two spaces with the line running down the middle of the car, which must be how it's done in Finland and Julia will have to learn. They go through the main entrance past a greenish-brown Marine Patrol SUV with emergency strobes on top. Beside it a plain blue sedan with State Police license plates and concealed blue lights. There's some kind of deputy in uniform with a newspaper in his lap but he's not reading it, he's looking over toward the receptionist as they go up to her and say, "Chad Dormant's room, please."

The lady looks up with slow curious eyes behind her large circular glasses, then asks in a voice loud enough for the policeman to hear,

"Your relation to the patient?"

"Family."

"Both of you?"

"Yes."

"Room three-oh-two. Take this elevator and go right down the long corridor. It's almost at the end."

On the way up, Vira supplies a quick emergency kiss and nuzzle between levels, which she needs, then the door opens directly into the third-floor waiting room, with Nicole, Will, and their mom under a rippling American flag that occupies the whole screen of the wall-mounted TV. Her mom wears the stolid expression she gets in crises but she must be in deep shock underneath. Will's talking to a heavy-set stranger in a coat and necktie who looks like another policeman, with a dark mustache and a lump under his too-small suit that could definitely be a gun.

Nicole instantly runs forward and wraps her arms around her, her hair smelling of charcoal and gasoline.

"Julia, I'm so glad you came. I was afraid you'd left the country."

"Nicole, were you out there? How is Chad? Are you all right yourself?"

"Yes, yes, I'm okay. I mean, physically. But Chad's still unconscious. The girls are in there by his side."

"Nicole, this is Vira. She drove me here. Vira, this is my mom, my brother Will, my sister Nicole."

"These are not the best circumstances to meet," Nicole says. "But bless you for coming. Nobody should be alone."

"I feel like I know you already," Vira says. "I am so sorry to hear this. What a terrible thing."

"Nicole, we saw the island from Route One. I looked with bin-oculars. There was no structure, just a smoke column beside the wind turbine."

The man in the suit talking to Will starts to come over; he wants to hear.

"Let's find a place where we can talk for a moment. Vira, will you excuse us?"

Nicole leads her out past the elevators, and Julia looks back to see Vira and her mom already in conversation like old friends, in the instant intimacy of disaster. Just off the corridor they find a laundry room smelling of ether and iodine, overstocked on every shelf with bleached sheets and towels and medicinal-green hospital wear.

Nicole hugs her again, this time letting herself cry silently for a few moments before pulling away, the younger comforting the old. "Forgive me, it's been a nightmare."

"Nicole, what caused the fire? Was it the propane supply?"

"It was an *airplane*. And the fuel tank exploded. We didn't know it till we were on the helicopter that took us out of there, then they pointed and you could see the plane's tail through the fire and smoke. I have no idea who was in it. That's why the police are here."

"An airplane? Were they were trying to land on the island? You do have an airstrip."

"No, it's just a helipad. It's the size of a tennis court. A plane couldn't use it."

"Where were you? Did you see it happen?"

"I *felt* it. I was asleep in the bunkhouse and I woke to this tremendous roar and vibration shaking the whole place, then an explosion and shock wave like a bomb. The girls jumped out of bed. I reached over for Chad but he wasn't there."

"Where was he?"

"I remembered he was getting up early to install the flag. We had to find him. We went out the rear exit and circled way around the fire to the other side. We couldn't get near it. We couldn't even see the building 'cause it burned our eyes—it was a fireball of orange flame. I was afraid he was in there, then we saw him on the other side. He had crawled away from it and he was just lying there in the grass. Lanie had us get down under the heat and crawl and we crept toward him, then she felt his wrist and he had a pulse. The three of us dragged him away from the heat and flames. Then the Coast Guard helicopter arrived with a stretcher and landed us all on the roof of the hospital."

"Was anyone else hurt besides Chad? How about your workmen, and the caretaker?"

"The workers had the day off. They were up till midnight, including Nick. Mom was in Ledgeport. He must have been down in his cabin. It's bizarre, with that forest between them, he could have slept through the whole thing. They had us out of there before anyone could look for him."

The tap on the doorframe is Brit accompanied by a doctor, who says, "If I could interrupt to talk with you about your husband, Mrs. Dormant."

"Dr. Goldman, this is my sister Julia. I'd like her to listen too. Julia, is that okay with you?"

Julia nodded.

"Of course. Your husband is stabilized, but we're keeping him under sedation. He received a concussion and he has a pretty severe leg fracture that suggests he might have fallen from a height—your daughter said he'd been working on a ladder? He received cuts on the legs and torso. He has second-degree burns on his hands and wrists, consistent with raising them to protect his face or contact with hot debris. He's a survivor. Not everyone would have made it."

"What about the airplane?" Julia asks. "And who was in it? Do you know anything?"

"Nothing whatsoever. That's outside my specialty. You can come into your husband's room now."

❖

Chad looks like a demonstration of every kind of injury known to medicine. A half sheet holds his right leg down but his left is swaddled and raised in traction. Both hands are bandaged, as well as his upper skull, diagonally across his forehead, and his hair on one side's all shaved off. A tube, taped to his cheek, goes into one nostril and another into his forearm above the bandaging. The unbandaged portion of his face looks as handsome and suave as ever, despite the tube, impeccably composed like a professional actor portraying an injured man. With Brittany on one side of him and Elaine on the other, Nicole bends down to kiss his forehead, everyone hushed so they don't disturb him even though he seems completely out.

Julia tiptoes away and returns to the waiting room, where her mom's still in animated conversation with Vira. Her heart brightens for a moment at seeing those two together, talking like that, framed by the window which looks out on the ocean and the distant island marked by a wisp of smoke. Without this collision of one world with another, they would never have met.

Will's still talking to the man with the suit and tie, who introduces himself as Detective Nagel of the Maine State Police.

"You've had a hell of an accident out there this morning, Miss Fletcher. If it *was* one. We'd all watched that building go up, we were proud of it, and it was everyone's loss. Mr. Dormant got the worst of it, but it looks like he'll pull through. We're working with the Coast Guard and Homeland Security, trying to sort this out. Your brother tells me you're the one that's spent the most time on the island."

Will answers for her. "She's spent a lot of time there recently, as a photographer. She knows Amber as well as anyone."

"There's a lot of people that would like to know who was inside that cockpit. We know who the owner is, and he's on his way over here now, so we may learn something. Whoever it was borrowed the plane without permission, or stole it. So if you can think of anyone, Miss Fletcher, who might possibly have taken a joyride out there, it would help us out."

Julia says, "I don't even know anyone who can fly a plane. And I haven't set foot on Amber since April."

"I understand there's a caretaker out there," the detective says.

"He lives at the far end," Will says. "He's severely hearing-impaired, so chances are he wasn't aware of what was happening."

"Well, you'd think he could see the smoke, or smell it. Anyone contact him?"

"His phone's for work only," Will says, "so he can text the crew. He leaves it up at the house at night. I don't think he'll be using it."

The elevator rings and a younger guy steps out, wearing a kelp-colored uniform with his pistol visible in its oiled holster.

The detective says, "Officer Steve Doucette, Marine Patrol, these are two members of the Fletcher family that owns the property out there. Will and Julie, or is it Julia?"

"It's Julia," says Will.

"Julia. A pleasure to meet you, and a lot of sympathy for your family," Doucette says. "It's a beautiful island, but right now it's a crash site. I've just come back from there. Coast Guard boat's going to be out there twenty-four/seven, with a no-go perimeter around the island."

"Can they get into the wreckage?" Nagel asks.

"They can't. It's too hot and smoky, and the place is a minefield of glass shards. The plane's buried in debris. Anyone in that aircraft would have been incinerated. The Coast Guard intends to foam it down when it cools and clear a path to the cockpit by nightfall, so the FAA team can get in there in the morning. They have the technology."

"We'll have an idea who's in there tomorrow," the detective says.

"One of the older guys said the antique planes from Owls Head used to land out there, back in the days it was a sheep pasture."

"They did," Will said. "There's a picture of a barnstormer with an open cockpit, right above where we camped."

Steve Doucette says, "Well, if that was a landing, their aim was a little off."

"Or it wasn't," the detective says. "Depends if they were trying to land an airplane, or something else."

Then a third man comes up, looking around at the Fletchers and the investigators to see if he might be in the wrong room. He's a serious-looking, graying old guy with a black T-shirt under his denim jacket, mustache and hair too woolly to be any kind of policeman. He's something else.

Detective Nagel puts a consoling arm around his shoulders as if he somehow shared in the family's loss. "This is Mr. Stan Fischer. Stan was my English teacher. Now he's teaching my kids. Stan, these are the island owners and it was their building that got hit. I understand you've been out to see your aircraft. That's a hell of a way to spend the Fourth."

"They needed me out there to confirm it because the numbers had burned off. I picked up Peter Colonna—that's the caretaker's father—and we took the Whaler 'cause they'd seen the fire and hadn't heard from Nick. I didn't have to land. I took one look at the tail shape and I knew."

"Sorry about your plane," Will says. "That's quite a loss."

"It's nothing compared to yours. Such an achievement for all of you, then it hardly stood for a day."

"Did you see any signs of the caretaker?" the detective asks. "He's the last person unaccounted for. Apparently he lost his phone in the fire."

"That was our first thought. What if he'd been working in there when the plane hit? He wouldn't even have heard it. His father was frantic. We headed right for his cabin and his dory was gone. That meant he was not on the island—a huge relief, especially to Peter. Nick had the day off, so maybe he went up to Lime Key for stripers, or he's gone ashore."

"Nick's more than a caretaker," Will says. "A lot of that building's the work of his own hands."

"It's been a healing environment for him," Stan Fischer says. "Fixing up that cabin, living off the land all winter, then throwing himself into the construction. It's been more than a job to him—it's his life."

Julia is sensing a dark possibility that she's not voicing even to herself. No one else seems to be thinking it, but who knows? You don't know what's in people's heads, but it sometimes turns out to be what's in your own.

"I want you to think, Stan, if you know any pilots that might have borrowed that plane this morning or thought they had a right to use it? Any co-owners, time shares? Any students? Are you a flight instructor? It's not like auto theft. Anybody can drive a car. This one knew how to fly."

"Well, they didn't know how to land," Steve Doucette says. Then his belt radio squawks and he excuses himself, returning a few moments later.

"Another piece of the puzzle. Coast Guard found your caretaker's skiff adrift off of Wolf Neck. That's five miles north of Ledgeport. They're searching the area."

"Okay," the detective says. "We have a missing person and an unidentified person. Are we dealing with two incidents that just happened to occur on the same morning, or are we dealing with one?"

"I see where you're taking this," Stan Fischer says, "but it's impossible to believe. Will's right—a good part of that place exists because of his own labor. He'd put his life on the line to protect it. And he doesn't have the skills to have made that flight."

"What makes you so sure of that? He's ex-military. A lot of them get trained. And he's seen combat."

"I took him up once last September, after he got home. He was an absolute beginner. He could take the stick for a few minutes in midair with me beside him, but he couldn't have gotten her off the ground. You can't get a plane into the air if you don't know how."

"He didn't take lessons over the year?" Officer Doucette asks.

"No way," says Stan Fischer. "That flight was the first and last. He never once left the island with the exception of Christmas Eve."

"It's all hypothetical till someone gets into that wreckage," the detective says. "We'll know tomorrow when the Feds arrive."

At that moment Nicole and her mom appear in the waiting room with smiles of relief. Even before they say anything it's clear there's positive news about Chad.

"He opened his eyes," Nicole says. "Just for an instant, but he looked around. He recognized Lanie, who was right beside him, and I think he recognized me, before he closed them again." She gives her sister a big squeeze as if she were the cause of it, then hugs Will too, and even Vira gets an embrace and a cheek kiss. Then she ducks back into 302, leaving Julia with a feeling of the inevitable that's been occluding her brain like a thunderhead.

He seemed determined to live forever to protect his discovery but he may have found a better way. His old teacher seems to be reaching the same conclusion, despite his denials. She'd like to speak with him alone, but now he's saying good-bye.

She takes his arm as he's leaving, detains him a moment, looks briefly and directly into his eyes as if a thought which is not yet on the verbal level could be established and communicated without words. It's good that Chad's going to recover. The only death Nick might possibly have wanted would be his own.

She last laid eyes on him at a prehistoric site she'd passed a thousand times without ever suspecting. In less than a year he had come to know the island better than she did. Maybe his lack of hearing let him sense their presence under the soil like a diviner. He wanted a burial in the same place, but she was the wrong person. She already held a one-way ticket to Finland and another life. He was in a state of mind she understood because it comes after grief and loss and she'd been there too, maybe still was, and is.

There was the other thing too—a kiss, no other word for it, unforced and unconfessed, almost submerged now under floods of them shared with Vira, but that one remains, like the island, quarantined in her heart, in the one chamber sealed even from the eyes of love.

She agreed to his burial arrangement because it had seemed impossible. He barred the door to her the night of the rainstorm and brandished his gun. Like her own brother Will he sold out his skill and labor to Amber Retreats LLC. He killed human beings in pointless genocidal conflict, serving an aggressor nation which she is about to renounce and leave.

But this other event, this morning of incendiary demolition and leveling, of something so reckless and violent that it stopped time and turned it back—could that have been in his mind as they huddled together at the Archaic site? In accepting his idea, and confirming it with physical contact, was she somehow complicit in this day? The thin tongue of smoke over the flat stone-colored water of the bay this morning: If it could speak and ask whether this is an outcome she might have desired, what would her answer be?

Will has already followed the family into Chad's room. The detective looks at his watch again and turns to Officer Doucette.

"Come on, Bud, it's almost three. This going to be a late lunch or an early supper?"

The Marine Patrol officer walks with him down the hall.

Julia is finally alone with Vira, who says, "You'll want to go in."

She doesn't, though. She needs respite from this hospital where the air itself is anesthetized and inert.

"There won't be room. I'll visit later. For now let's get out of here."

Outside, it's a serious heat wave in Maine terms; it must be almost eighty in the hospital parking lot. Faint strains of patriotic music come from the village bandstand across the harbor. They cross to a shaded picnic bench with a view of the riprap breakwater and its red-roofed lighthouse, the sail-spangled harbor opening to the southeast. At their feet a couple of herring gulls struggle over an empty hot-dog roll.

The reddening late-afternoon light turns Vira's hair the color of an October leaf fire. Their twin shadows are already elongated on the grass.

Julia puts a hand over hers, quietly says, "Vira, did you understand at all where that conversation was going?"

"The burning tower. You know it came up in my tarot. Alexa would not interpret. She said we must remove that card out of the deck."

"It's not just the tower, Vira. It's the pilot. They didn't exactly say it, but I know they're thinking it's the caretaker, Nick. That he deliberately flew the plane into the building."

"I'm not surprised, Julia. He comes back wounded from a war fought in a desert of burning hell. Like Nietzche, he believes he can erase history by recurrence."

"He erased himself in the process."

"And created himself in the same moment. The bone hook he gave you—it was a promise."

"He knew he'd do this beforehand, then? All this time he worked on the building?"

"He did not. He didn't know it until it happened, and then he knew."

"Vira, *I* should have been the one, not Nick. If someone had to sacrifice everything, no cowardice or holding back, that should have been me, but I was too small and fearful. I had this big cause but I had no idea how much you have to give."

"Perhaps that is learned only in combat." Then, with no one visibly around, she leans close, allows a little fox-nip of Julia's ear. "He also had the same the feeling I have for you. And for your island. You shared it with him."

"He held a gun pointed right at my heart."

"It was himself that he was aiming at. It is all mirror image in this thing."

"Vira, would you have gone this far in this?"

"For you? I would go anywhere you asked me—maybe not quite all the way as he did."

"I don't know where this is going to end. First we have to check in with my family. They'll try to get us to stay, but we can't. We'll tell them we're going home tonight, that we have to pack."

"But we are already packed. So we're going to Bar Harbor, or Boston, or someplace else?"

"We're going to Amber."

"No. You heard them say, trespassing not allowed."

"Vira, it's my island. My family's. We own it."

"How will we go to it? Everyone knows the blockade. And for what to do?"

"Trust me. I can get us there. But you shouldn't feel obliged. You can take the car and go back—just keep in touch by cell and meet me tomorrow."

"No cell. Keep in touch by touch. I'm going with."

In two hours it's getting toward dusk and they're carrying their double sleeping bag, a six-pack of Poland Spring, and four bagels from the bakery by the hospital. There are so many people in the waterfront park it seems that the land will subside into the harbor under their weight. Sailors in bleached-white uniforms stream out of navy launches at the town dock, descending on the local girls as soon as they step ashore. The martial band of the morning has been replaced by the local heavy metal riffing and tuning, big amps piled one on the other to shake the ground. Kid groups of different ages emanate the rich agricultural smell of marijuana. Out on the water the sinister gray navy warship dominates the Ledgeport fishing fleet and the slender masts of the yacht club. Its rows of guns and missiles point upward in all directions in impotent defense against what has already happened.

"The military sent that because of you?" Vira asks. "We will have to pass beneath all those guns?"

"No, the navy comes every summer, for the festivities. There's a helicopter, too."

The chopper circles low overhead, WLBZ CHANNEL 5 ACTION TEAM on its side, the crowd now waving their red-white-and-blue hats, their oversize lobster-claw gloves, their US flags mixed with yellow-ribboned Support the Troops banners. Then it takes off, skirting the warship, heading northeast over the lighthouse breakwater in the direction of Amber Island.

"You will be on the news," Vira says.

"The crash will be on the news. The pilot will be on tomorrow, when they confirm who it is."

"You know."

"I don't know anything. I have a speculation."

She heads for the boat rental concession beside the Public Landing, SUNSET KAYAK TRIPS, decked with a big patriotic swag, VIEW THE FIREWORKS underneath. They pay the deposit for an overnight rental and choose a blue two-person Old Town Voyager that looks like the same one they rented the summer before, when the tower was still a concept and Nick Colonna was on the far side of the world and nothing had yet been constructed or destroyed.

Vira is a much stronger paddler who has kayaked the coast of Greenland alongside belugas with the Inuit. They shove their belongings one by one into the waterproof compartments and screw them shut. The rental people hand them each a flashlight to clip to their safety vests and wish them a Happy Fourth.

"Fireworks in forty-five minutes. Gonna be beautiful from the water. Stay a hundred yards from the explosives raft."

Julia insisted her lover take the bow so she could watch her. When they push away from the float, her strong Sámi shoulders flex and pull from the sleeves of her life jacket like the wings of a pelagic bird. Their blue kayak threads through the anchored fleet, low and purposeful as a submarine, its intentionality hidden below the visible surface, just two random young women seeking a fireworks view. All around them are summer's yachts with evening cocktails aboard, barbecue grills hanging over the sterns, fat sizzle and thick steaky smoke. Towering cruise schooners loom over them bedecked with tourists and musicians, accordions, fiddles, baritones incanting sea shanties and occasionally "The Battle Hymn of the Republic" or "The Star-Spangled Banner" as if it were a typical Independence Day. In the morning, rumors of chaos may have swept through the transient population—a plane crashed on an island, a visible plume of smoke, occupants presumed dead, absorbed by these travelers as part of the festivities. She remembers a poem Will sent her at Hampshire, which stayed on the suite refrigerator for a while: *Insignificantly off the coast, the splash went unnoticed.* Someone who'd failed to give his life in a far kingdom had succeeded at home.

In the flat evening calm the water has taken the sanguinary color of the sunset over the Ledgeport hills. Beyond the breakwater she can see Amber with its dying smoke plume that by now could come from a campfire or charcoal grill, vertical as a flagpole in the windless air. She stops paddling for a moment in the stillness, just touching the water to steer while Vira's strokes propel them like a diamond blade through red glass. She has the courage to approach musk oxen and narwhals, but deep inside she's as delicate and complex as a swamp orchid.

The entire native and tourist community are gathering with their blankets for the evening of fireworks. Boats all around them passively await the spectacle, sails furled, motors shut down. The blue kayak is the one craft with purpose and destination, angling across flood current past the lighthouse toward the green "PB" mid-channel marker, whose color deepens toward black in the fading light. The huge buoy towers above them, rises and tips and falls with the sea's restless insomnia. The clangor is deafening as they get close. When they actually come alongside to rest from paddling, its bronze gong sounds through the blue hull like a kettle drum.

Just as they turn to face back toward Ledgeport the first rocket goes up, higher than Mount Amatuck as it climaxes in a shower of descending sparks like parachutes on fire. They push off into the helpful strength of the flood tide and quietly sneak by the Coast Guard boat guarding her island, glowing with work lights as if part of the celebration. Nonmetallic, undetectable by radar, they cut northeast and race each other over the last mile as if they could tear the hull apart into two half-kayaks, striving and competitive to the end.

Amber's a silhouette of itself in diminishing light, with a reddish glow from the last burning embers exaggerated by the charcoal sky. Tendrils of smoke sear the nostrils with molecules of charred redwood and aviation fuel. They paddle the whole length of the island and slip around the northwest point into Nick's cove. No gray dory, no visible life but a tall ink-blue heron that twists its neck toward them for a moment, then glides to a safer position on heavy wings.

They ground out on the small sand spit and drag the kayak above the high-tide line, then turn it over to sit on its cool damp hull. Through the scrim of foliage they can see back to the lights of Ledgeport beneath the looming silhouette of Mount Amatuck. Then high in the air a skyrocket bursts like a spore pod scattering seeds of red and blue light into the atmosphere. There is a pause without time as the sound crosses the ship channel and just as it reaches them another instantaneously goes up, so they are hearing the sound of one as they watch the next one ascend and bloom, creating a multicolored daylight as their flashes illuminate the little cove and in it the blue heron stabbing at minnows in the tide pool, freezing its instantaneous poses like a strobe.

"We have nothing like this," Vira says. "We have midsummer night marking the solstice which is from the Sámi, before King Eric subdued them. But it is peaceful and everyone just parties under the midnight sun. No bombs or rockets red glaring."

"Our identity is in war," Julia says. "Otherwise we wouldn't know who we are."

"Your caretaker was a soldier. He knew exactly who he was."

Finally in utter silence the grand climax exfoliates over the town and hills; not till a half-minute later does the sound ripple the lit water surface with thunderous shock and awe that resonates in the kayak hull and spooks the heron into the unlit woods.

They detach the flashlights from their life vests but before switching them on and going up the path to Nick's cabin, they stop for a moment of true night. Sunset and fireworks are over and the late moon is not yet up. The kayak shape and the low breakwater ledge have vanished into the equality of the dark. As their eyes adjust, though, Vira suddenly whispers, "Look, someone is in there."

From the cabin's one window a rectangle of yellow light extends like a hologram into the misted air. She's wrong, and the detective was wrong; he wasn't the pilot after all. It's someone else buried beneath the wreckage, and he's there inside, having heard nothing, with one of his foraging seafood recipes or his Thoreau book or staring at some artifact pulled from its subterranean dream.

"Vira," she whispers. "Do you think he even knows what happened?"

She approaches the window till she can see almost the whole interior illuminated by the lantern high on one of the stove shelves.

Vira, having crept up behind her, whispers, "Do we know it is him?"

"I'm going to look inside." Julia presses her face against the smoke-crusted pane. She can make out the stove and the bed under the window where she once stripped her clothes off as he stood outside in a deluge of hail and rain. No one is in there, though there's the one corner with his chair and work table that she can't quite see. Someone could be sitting there, or not.

"You could knock first."

"I tried that the last time. Remember, he doesn't hear. Stand back away from the light, so it looks like I'm here alone. I'm trying the door."

It's not locked.

She slowly swings it open and peers around it, half expecting to see him—or someone, anyway—but the chair is empty. The walls are papered with what look like book pages or printouts and the work table has a knife stuck into it by the point.

She calls Vira in from the darkness.

"Look. The lamp has a huge bowl and it's turned down low. He must have gone out and left it."

Vira draws up warmly against her back, arms around Julia's waist like a biker chick, standing on tiptoe to look over her shoulder as the flashlight beam double-checks every possible hiding place. The thin mantle of red flame over the lantern wick flickers and declines to an ember line in a plume of acrid smoke. It must be either filled or put outside.

She flashes around, spotlights a spouted can beside the woodpile.

"Is that the lamp oil?" Vira asks.

"Must be."

Vira refills the lantern and screws the top back while Julia gets the matchbox from the upper stove shelf. Soon as it's relit the smell dies and a well-trimmed yellow flame mounts up so they can douse the flashlights. The jackknife stabbed into the wood tabletop is not the military bayonet strapped to his leg but a regular folding one with a bone-textured handle and a single blade. The knife is pinned into one of the book pages, and they both walk around the table to read it right side up. It's torn from *Walden* with the knife point through *the real possessor*.

"This is a private message to you," Vira says. "He knew you would find it. He knew you would be the first one here. It would not have meaning for any other. You are the real possessor."

"Not me," Julia says. "He means the old Archaics that made the bone hook and the harpoon. He had this impossible idea."

The heron croaks from the cove ledge, then the ululation of a saltwater loon. They step outside, stand close beside each other but not touching.

"The nights look dead here but they're always so full of noises," Julia says. "He never knew them."

A single skyrocket rises and arcs over the hills. A damp southerly gust brings a smell like a drowned campfire; she remembers all of them in their tents and cots ready for sleep, her father a male silhouette with his small personal firehose watering the embers, their steamy hiss always the last sound of the day.

Then a soft pelting begins as of sand or small stones striking the tarpaper roof. Vira holds up her open palm. "Rain."

"Let's get the sleeping bag inside. We'll set our phones to three a.m. and walk through the dark so they don't see us from the ship. There'll be just enough light when we arrive. Pray this stuff stops by then. But it might be a blessing, cooling off the site."

The rain brings with it a dank chill and a draft shudders the lamp flame even though the door and window are closed. They unroll the double bag and shake it upside down for spiders, then Julia spreads it over Nick's plank bed, which now sports a thin striped cot mattress, a gift maybe from his poor mom. Vira puts her side of the bag down and accuses, "You slept with him here. Or he would not have done this."

"I didn't. He cooked me a meal entirely from the island: shellfish and beach peas, except for the canned milk. Then I walked back to the kayak."

"You had his clothing on when you came home."

"Fantasize all you want." She takes her shoes and hoodie off and slips into the satiny nylon shell. The cot mattress feels like it's stuffed with pinecones that twist and crunch under every bone, as if he abstained from comfort even in his sleep.

Vira zips in beside her and they hold fast and listen as the rain intensifies to an unbroken cataract then subsides, followed by complete silence as if his deafness has possessed the land. Vira shivers the length of her body. "I have slept in a skin tent in the territory of wolves, but it was not like this."

"I am a young she-wolf," Julia growls, biting her softly on the nape, where the canines would snap her prey's spinal cord. "You're my first victim."

"I do not feel dead," Vira says. "Quite the opposite." She turns with a wet kiss that means everything's wet, the rain too where she once waited for the door to open, this place where a living person arose and set his lamp burning and pinned one page to the table with his knife.

She keeps her teeth's pressure on the soft lightly downed skin over the bumps of the upper spine while her hand finds the full breasts always a surprise on such a compact figure and Vira convulses as if by electrocution, saying something in Finnish that sounds like *too soon, too soon.* She lets her mouth relax and the prey falls by gravity into the moment after.

18

The sun is a black circle and even though it's summer the island is knee-deep in drifted snow. Nicole is cooking on a green Coleman stove while her father and mother dance some kind of lindy hop from the Depression era. She opens Will's tent flap and sees that his penis is missing, then the tent fills with overpowering light and her eyes open.

Her phone says four a.m. She leaps up and wakes Vira. They wash down a few mouthfuls of cold bagel with the Poland Spring water and dress by darkness, thankful to hear no rain.

They grab two pairs of Nick's oversize work gloves from the cabin and tie their sweatshirt hoods against the predawn chill and fog. Her right glove is missing the index finger so she has to fold her own up inside. Her feet find the pathway up over the open field and through the spruce grove with the high grass and wet sodden branches soaking their clothes. By the time they reach the high meadow, the whole atmosphere is a broth of burned charcoal particles and petroleum fumes. Absolute silence is necessary in case the Coast Guard or some other watchdogs have left sentries ashore. The ground throbs gently from the slow thudding vibration of a supertanker out in the ship channel. The shadow and shocked wing flap of a night bird come over them, making a sudden course change. The grass path becomes hard asphalt as they stumble on the helipad, then the chuff of the turbine invisibly rotating in the night wind. They touch glove tips briefly, let go, then touch again, Vira a dark silent shape beside her like a shadow.

The crash site is a low smoldering boneyard of ash and glass that they find by its burned smell in the granular fog, sniffing like animals dropped on an ember planet, then picking their way over soil corrugated by bulldozers and skidders and soaked by the night's rain. Burned teak and redwood and the book-burning smell of the island library that Will assembled, the pigment fume of some irreplaceable painting, the char of summer clothing and raingear and varnished birch, the gasoline smoke pervasive through everything along with the odor of grilled meat left in its heat source carelessly and too long.

No entering this place blindly; they have to risk flashlights. The two beams irradiate the fog like divers' torches searching for something in a sunken liner. Now they are stepping on warm wet glass shards layered one on another and slippery with sprayed chemicals that make footing difficult and cause them to touch hands almost constantly, trying for the stability of a quadruped. A sharp spear point punctures the side of her left sneaker and she can feel blood ooze into the Wigwam sock. They trace the access path half-swept by the Coast Guard, till they become part of the wreckage as if their own bodies had been immolated then slaked with detergent foam.

They put the lights in their mouths to free both hands and grope their way forward toward the cockpit door, Julia in the lead, crouched like gloved primates feeling and touching the ground ahead. The sheared-off nosewheel blocks their way like a huge prosthetic leg. She heaves it aside so Vira can pass. Broken glass mounded as high as the plane's body is topped with a smashed skylight and twisted metallic squares that look like solar panels from the roof. The wings must have been ripped away and buried on impact as they are missing; a wing stub extends over the glass shards like a shoulder with its arm torn off.

The plane's door is also absent and the door opening on the left side is crushed down to a diagonal slit, which explains why they had to wait for the special equipment to get in. The fuselage is slanted nose downward under the debris pile as if trying to bore through the building into the earth. She shines her light up into the windshield but it's squeezed shut like a crushed eye and completely crammed with glass tarred from charcoal and petroleum soot with the lighter-fluid aroma of a barbecue.

Julia has the light in her hand now and just inside the pilot's door slit it shines on a folded burned crust pinned between a broken control wheel and the metal seat frame. It is deformed and carbonized beyond all identification, yet in the depth of her spine her body recognizes a thing of its own kind and shivers like a convulsion.

Vira's light is more concentrated and she runs it down the slit's length and stops on a metallic glint jammed between the seat and the folded one-dimensional shape that was a human being.

"What is it?" she whispers, breaking the silence with her flashlight focused on a gray corrugated grip.

Julia's seen it before, maybe not from this angle but she knows immediately what it is.

"His knife. He wore it strapped to his lower leg. He opened an oyster with it. Can you stand to bring it back with us? I have to carry something else."

"Yes. I will take the knife."

Julia grabs a door hinge for support and slides the steel blade from the remains of its leather sheath, the handle still warm from the memory of fire. He must be terribly alone wherever he is now, though the whole island's transfigured by the courage and gravity of what he did.

"Look," Vira whispers. "I wipe off the knife, there's engraving."

Julia turns away from the wreck to read the initials NMC just below the knife hilt where Vira has rubbed off the creosote with her glove. Out in the fog, a diesel coughs and turns over, which could be an early lobsterboat but could also be the Coast Guard minders, and they have to retreat. Vira raises her head to the engine noise, turns back to wrap the bayonet with her violet scarf. It must be now.

Julia removes her right glove to reach between the torso and the warped metal seat, its upholstery shriveled from the heat. She makes contact with what she can hardly see but there is a cluster of small charcoal objects that once must have been the individual fingers of his hand. Gingerly she touches the smallest and nearest of these for a moment as she had in life but she can't bear to move it. Then she considers the huge scale and totality of his offering, and on her part only a fraction of what he wanted, partial and incomplete like everything she does: this small human fragment to be joined with the others in the gravel bank. She thinks of cutting it free with the bayonet but they'd find the severance and know. It must look as if the finger was torn off on impact; and amazingly, with minimal resistance it flakes away from the hand as a blackened twig would bend off after a forest fire. The bones in that burial have lasted six thousand years; these will lie among them and their hooks and tools. He's just starting the journey but he will catch up with them in time. She wraps it in a pale yellow head scarf her boyfriend Russell gave her a million years ago, then turns to follow Vira, picking their way back through the glass shards toward the turbine becoming visible in the fog.

"You found something else," Vira says. "Is it what you came for?"

"Partly. We'll bury it with the knife and leave. Our asses have to be out of here before the investigators come."

They're able to see now at least in their small radius of brightening fog. She glances back to the rubble now looking like firebombed Dresden on the cover of *Slaughterhouse-Five*. With the night wind subsided, the soot-coated turbine blades stand cool and detached as witnesses from a galaxy not our own. Next must come the long-term and utter cleansing which this tragedy has begun. All will be bulldozed and removed by the same green-and-yellow machinery that constructed it and must still be somewhere hidden in the dark and fog. She wishes her mother were here on this spot where they camped out and cooked on the Coleman stove, so she could see the outcome of a decision counter to nature even if inspired by her compassionate heart.

Instead of the straight path back to the north cove and their kayak, she leads the way over the new walkways, then through the low sheep tunnel directly to the Archaic site. She crouches down with one hand cradling the object in Russell's scarf and the other pushing aside thick summer foliage with Vira close behind. In the shadowy yellow fog light she locates the gravel embankment where they sat with their heads touching and spelled out a pact on his Blackberry that has now almost reached its end.

Vira catches up and joins her at the low slanting bank which is now covered and camouflaged by wood ferns where it was bare before.

"You'd never think anything was in there, let alone a whole culture. He must have planted it over so it would never be found."

"But it was found by you."

She scuffs the lowest level of ferns with her foot till it finds the oval blue stone beneath the entry point.

"This is his landmark. They're in there at eye level. My eye, not his. That's where he put our hook. But if they find us the whole place will be dug up and confiscated by the State. So quick, give me his combat knife. We're going to bury it in this bank so it will be among their tools."

"It's black with gasoline smoke," Vira says. "Can we clean it off?"

"Look at the sky, Vira. We don't have time. If they find us digging around in here, they'll know."

Julia scoops a handful of red pigment from a spot where it's leaching out of the streambed, smears it on the knife blade, then reaches it to her arm's length in the sand. She leaves the knife deep in the cavity, then pulls the last object out of the yellow scarf.

"The other thing," Vira says.

"It's just a fragment. I can't rub the color onto it. It's so fragile it would fall apart."

"I am a biologist. Let me."

She watches as Vira gently applies the pigment. A curl of irreducible black carbon that all life is and returns to, its knuckles clenched like the sharp curve of the bone hook. She wraps it again in the soft fabric, then inches it deep into the shaft till her own fingers contact a honed edge and it comes to rest beside his bayonet, then scoops up more russet clay with both bare hands and daubs it loosely till the filled shaft is flush with the surrounding bank. Later she'll inter her dad's ashes in the same spot, both of them cindered like planets drawn by gravity into the raw sun. She's carried her share of him for a year in the Keepsake urn and now finally has a place to lay it down.

The fog's scaling up as they hike back past the quarry pool: a white table and four Adirondack chairs where the rusted crane structure once stood and Vira swam with the granite block dangling perilously above. The water is clear as an aquarium. Half-concealed among the trees of the east shore they can see the fluorescent colors of the earth-moving machines whose fossil energy can reset the hands of time.

"What made you do it?" Vira asks.

"I had a commitment. I didn't think it would mean anything, but it did."

"You loved him."

"No, I don't think so. I hardly knew him. I never thought of him. Then this."

"It was a gift from someone who could not speak."

"I only heard him say one word. It was in his cabin, that second time."

"What was it?"

"*Yours.* I'll never forget it, it was such a shock."

"And he has said it again."

The ground under their feet starts shaking as if the bulldozers had started up, but it comes from above, and as they look up an orange-and-white Coast Guard helicopter descends out of the fog as if it had been waiting all night up there. They cut diagonally through the spruce grove toward his cabin hidden by the first row of trees.

"We have to leave," Julia says. "If they didn't see the kayak already, they will, as soon as the fog lifts."

They roll up the sleeping bag, then get their life vests on.

Julia stops for a last look. They haven't disturbed a thing. This is what they'll find when they search the cabin after learning who the pilot was, the most nonviolent book in the world nailed to the plank walls page by page so it surrounded him day and night. Outside, the blue heron twists its neck warily, then spreads its wide wings to cross the cove and land among the rocks of the breakwater ledge. They squeeze the bags into the waterproof compartments and then graze the kayak down the long sloping low-tide beach.

As they round the headland the heron looks up but does not scare. Boats come and go; the tide pool remains constant in its shifting light. Heading out to sea from the cove, the clearing air shows the helicopter at rest and now a large orange inflatable coming in from the Coast Guard boat. Deeper within the fog is some other official vessel, larger and more ponderous, black-hulled, with the angular USCG stripe on the bow.

Vira turns around to say, "They are all here now, the inspectors to inspect the crime scene."

"Don't worry, they won't inspect us. We're not persons of interest. We're just a couple of kayakers passing by."

They strike out northward against the current for a while to stay clear of the authorities, then in mid-channel they cut diagonally south-west toward Ledgeport harbor. It's still early and the water offers no resistance. A porpoise fin breaks the surface just ahead of them and

Vira gives a little shout of surprise and joy. Two more appear to their left and Vira cries out, "Speak, prisoners of the sea!" As if in answer, a porpoise rises and blows so close that the air's misted by its breath. They've been paddling hard in still water and they're already abreast of the crash site now, where there are official boats in the south cove, two helicopters on the landing strip, uniformed figures crawling into the wreckage with equipment to extract the occupant, not knowing he's already been set free.

19

They collect the kayak deposit and lug the bag to her orange car. Their sweatshirts are stiff from carbon and aviation fuel impregnated with ground glass; those go into a municipal dumpster, and then they hit the backseat to change out of their ripped and blackened jeans. The whole town's sleeping it off still on July fifth except municipal workers with green vests picking up trash and discarded flags and the men tying the spent fireworks barge to the marina dock.

"Let's go to Aaron's. He has sidewalk tables."

They walk diagonally across the long sloping park past the vacant bandstand and the Ledgeport pier, where a few small craft are already taking on fuel or hoisting sails in the slack air. In front of the marina office, a scarred-up gray rowing skiff sits on a trailer attached to an official-looking olive-drab SUV. A man in Marine Patrol uniform gets out of the truck to look it over, not Officer Steve from yesterday but a younger, burlier guy with a bigger holster and another one uniformed in multiple shades of blue.

"Vira, I think that's his boat. I remember it on the beach near his cabin. They said they'd found it. That was when I knew."

"Don't stop. On to Mr. Aaron's. You've done enough for today."

But then, as they're climbing the stone steps from the park up to Main Street, a helicopter comes chopping out of the offshore fog bank and dips down north of the marina, probably aiming for the hospital roof. She can't make out the writing on the side but this is blue-striped and smaller than the orange-and-white Coast Guard one.

"They may have come over from Amber. Maybe he's in there, but I'm trying not to visualize it. I want to remember him as he was in life, not as we saw him at the site."

"Or didn't see. It was dark as a dream, the whole time."

"It wasn't a dream, Vira. It was real. It was the only real thing I've ever done."

"And I?" Vira says.

"You're real. But I'm not done with you."

They approach the cluster of old-fashioned wire-legged round sidewalk tables outside of Aaron's.

"Choose the farthest away," Vira whispers. "We have not showered."

She sniffs Vira's clean tank top and bare arms. "Not a thing!"

"Skunks too have immunity to each other."

The nearest table's occupied by a young Asian couple with sunglasses and blinding white Red Sox caps. It's hard to believe the carefree happiness of the summer street. Flags angled out of every lamppost flirt with the early breeze. Next door, someone's passing out helium balloons in the doorway of Planet Toys, three at a time together, so the first kid that takes one looks like he's going to levitate and float away. A couple of others then tie a balloon to their dog's collar and the dog tries to jump up and catch it but the balloon only rises out of reach. A driver puts one on the antenna of an old squarish roadster so as he drives off, it hums and vibrates in the wind.

How can anything be remembered when time keeps moving like this? You ask it to stop, for just a moment, to study and understand, but it keeps driving into the future like a red convertible, no one turning to look back.

Vira leans forward across the miniature table discreetly but with sheer intent, one of those Sámi smiles that could get a whole tribe of foragers through an Ice Age winter, which makes her forget for a moment what's happened and what may be ahead. She dips a napkin

248

in her water glass and tries to wipe something off Julia's chin, dips
again and scrubs hard on the left cheek.

"You are disfigured from the underworld."

"I was abused there as a child. There was no refrigeration and all
I wanted was ice cream."

Aaron appears from the dark-wooded interior, more aged than ever
but with the young baseball-playing kid still visible underneath. He's
wearing his white open-collared shirt as always and his white papery
hat like an old soda-fountain barista from her father's day. He stops
to get their order, then double-takes and looks again.

"You're from the Fletcher family, aren't you? I remember when
your legs wouldn't reach the ground from that stool. That was a tragedy
out there yesterday, any way you look at it. All your people okay?"

"Well, not exactly. My brother-in-law was injured. But they think
he's going to recover."

"Thank God for that. That's what counts. All the love and work
you'd put into that place. And I'll tell you, you knew a great architect
was behind it. When Trudy and I drove up the mountain road, the
sunset reflected off those glass walls illuminated the whole bay. It's
always been a magnificent view, but your father gave it a spirit it never
had. What an insane act, some cuckoo joyriding with a stolen plane.
Build something and there's always someone to bring it down. Have
they determined who it was yet?"

"It's still under investigation," Julia says.

"Nothing much goes as intended in this world. Some other world
maybe, not this one."

"I'm learning that."

"I held the *Times* for your dad every week when he was out there.
He'd sit and read it while you ate your sundae. And now this. More
than one family should have to endure. He was a giant of his time.
And now we must have your order."

"Two of the glazed Danish, please, from your window display, and iced coffee with double sugar," Vira says. Against all nutritional principles, Julia orders the same.

The street's picking up to its full Ledgeport summer pace, traffic nearly stalled on the main street, sidewalk filled with vacationers on the day after a holiday, not just Americans either, travelers from India and Japan, the whole globalized vacationing world oblivious to each other in their different time zones. They were united for an hour or two yesterday when natives and tourists alike stared at a distant smoke column and plane-crash rumors rippled through the town. Then life went on, with toddlers lagging behind or in strollers and newborns in kangaroo pouches, leashed dogs and a man with a white macaw on his shoulder, his wife feeding it raisins from a red Sun-Maid box.

Vira dips her Danish in the coffee, takes one of her small chipmunk-like bites, touches Julia's arm to draw her close and whisper almost in her ear. "You did what he asked of you. You don't owe him anything more. You are free."

"I'm not. It was a failure, a broken-off fragment of what he wanted. And he gave everything. It would take a lifetime to answer what he did. I can't help envisioning the moment, when he saw himself reflected and did not stop."

"There was no stopping. You were behind the mirror and he flew through."

"No. Not me. It was the island. He knew there would have to be sacrifices to restore it and he knew I didn't have the courage. I believe he also knew if he ceased to be caretaker I would take his place." She grips Vira's hand and says, "You know what this means. Everything's changed now. I have to stay here and see this through." Eyes of an ice owl cloud over with tears that are rarely seen. "I wanted it more than anything, you know that."

"Not more than anything," Vira quietly says. "This other is more."

"For now. The future is something else."

Across the table, there's a small fear in Vira's look. "I don't want you to follow him into the mirror if I leave."

"I'm not going to follow him. He left me too much to do. But I can't follow you either. Not now. You have a life there and a future, your summer pre-med and med school and your Sámi clinic. I'll catch up. You'll have two seats, anyway. You'll be able to grab some sleep."

"How will I get there? Without you I cannot drive the manual shift."

"Oh, Vira, you don't have to drive. There's a noon bus to Boston from the ferry terminal. It stops at Logan. I've taken it a hundred times. But we'll have to get going. It's eleven-thirty and the flight's at six."

They work their way along the crowded holiday sidewalk to the Concord Trailways station adjoining the ferry terminal. The southbound bus has already arrived. It's discharging its passengers to their waiting families in a swirl of squeezes and backpacks. Her hand finds Vira's and all their fingers clasp but she can't suppress images of the crushed cockpit and the shape inside.

"I leave you among such sadness," Vira says. "Your family and your wounded island. I will take some with me if it would help."

"No, it's mine. I have to deal with it. Besides, it would weigh the plane down. You'd never get off the ground."

"They're all loading, Julia. I have to go. Text every midnight. I will wake up to it."

"Take your orgo class, dude. Get an A, if that's what they do over there. Don't ever not think of me, even for a minute, or I'll cease to exist."

Vira gets up and slings her pack over a sun-freckled shoulder, bared by the tank top. She's also wheeling her carry-on, but Julia grabs the handle and takes her other arm. They stop at the bus's rear wheel, drop everything on the asphalt, and smother themselves in a full kiss, tasting of every past physical moment and the future to come. The

growling impatient diesel spews blue-black smoke and shimmers the
air with waste heat.

Alone in the car with its empty passenger seat Julia climbs the
switchbacks of the Mount Amatuck road to the summit overlook.
Below her the bay sparkles with afternoon whitecaps and the triangles
of heeled sails. On the distant island she can make out the black shaft
of the wind turbine sending its renewable energy into the lifeless debris.
The alternative station's playing a sad Dar Williams song, but she can
supply her own melancholy, and she turns it down till she hears just
the faint chords without words. The breath of the air conditioner suddenly freezes her. Even when she turns it off and opens the windows to
the heat-wave day, she can't shake the chill that started when the bus
pulled out. The flight will take Vira to Scandinavia and med school
and her dream of the Sámi clinic, science and shamanism, reindeer
and permafrost: this stranger encountered at a contra dance who's
been her heart and timepiece for sixteen months.

Nick would have looked down from this perspective as he passed
over the town, the breakwater and its lighthouse to descend crossing
the ship channel toward the glass house like a bird seeking its image in
a windowpane. He built it with his own labor, day after day, in what
must have been growing awareness of annihilation, while she blindly
partied in Bar Harbor. Or did he live in the present, as Vira thinks,
and rise up out of a traumatized dream to carry it out unplanned? So
much of it was his own creation. The inspiration might have been her
father's, but the work was his: timeless materials and painstaking labor
for what would stand but a day or two then return to nature. There's
no defecting to Scandinavia, not even for love; she is embedded in
that island as if she were buried beside him in the sand.

❖

She drives to the old Excelsior Hotel where her mother has always stayed because you can see Amber from the upper floors. She hasn't washed her face or hair since she and Vira pawed like a pair of jackals through the crash site.

The concierge at the desk can't believe the apparition coming through the revolving door. "You looking for something, miss?"

"My mom. Camilla Fletcher. They have the suite on the sixth floor."

On the Fourth of July her mom and brother woke up expecting the sun glint off the tower's windows and instead saw the smoke column in the morning air. She's glad neither of them was there alone.

She taps on a paneled door where she once had to stand on tiptoe to reach its porcelain knob. It opens immediately and she accepts a doorway hug, then her mom draws back from the fumes and scent.

"Oh, Mom, I'm sorry. I know—yuck. We went to a bonfire last night, and the smoke was intense."

"So that's where you were. We couldn't find you. Let's sit down, you look exhausted." Her mom leads her to a white couch facing a floor to ceiling window with a view of the bay and islands. "I was afraid you'd flown already. Nicole just called from the hospital and Chad's awake, thank God. But do you know who they think might have been in the plane?"

"I've heard. That's why I want to talk to you. Is anyone else here?"

"No, they're at the hospital. But I wanted to take a moment for myself, trying to understand. He seemed so dedicated to the house, and to Marston's vision, almost like an apprentice. I just find it incomprehensible."

"It speaks for itself, Mom. Now we have to answer."

"How can we? It's a complete ruin, sweetheart; it would have to be rebuilt."

"No, Mom. Not rebuilt. Restored. It can be beautiful again. The Amber you originally saw, with Dad."

"Julia I understand. I've thought of nothing else since I heard the news this morning. But first I should talk to Nicole."

"You've already listened to Nicole. Talk to *me*. I'm not in The Hemlocks anymore. If you'll support me, I'm willing to give up my life and forget Europe and move out to Amber and live there, where he did, till it's brought back to what it was. For Dad, for all of us. If you'll support me."

"It may be months."

"Time is not an issue. There's no alternative, Mom. It's a gravesite now. They're not going to start that thing again. They can't. Who'd stay in a resort with that kind of history? Would you?"

"No, I don't think so. I have a memory of it. It was a gift from another time. It only existed for a brief moment, but that was enough. I can't imagine anyone choosing to live out there, but if you can manage the solitude, and if we could provide some creature comforts for that little place. I couldn't bear to think of you frozen and hungry."

"Mom, that doesn't matter. Nick gave up everything, his whole existence for Amber. A soldier, a man, a victim of his own country's twisted war. *Our* country. I have to honor him, and Dad at the same time."

There's a moment of absolute silence between them. Her mother squeezes her hand with gentle pressure.

"I understand, Julia. We will. This has changed everything. Here is my thought: we are amply insured. We'll use the settlement to restore Amber to what it was."

Mother and daughter draw closer together as the clouds darken over the horizon and their own faint reflection in the window superimposes on the sky and sea.

Despite her total unkemptness and disorder, Julia lets her head lean on her mom's shoulder. That hair, the color of a gray owl, softly brushing her face, she sinks into the familiar body where she started out.

20

In her dream they're both living at The Hemlocks and Vira has brought an old-fashioned musket into their bed which she's cleaning and loading under the duvet. The weapon's about to go off with a serious explosion but before it happens Julia wakes with wide-open staring eyes and a pounding heart. She doesn't know where she is. The new skylight overhead is the pale peach color of sunrise and only as it illuminates the new floorboards and crisp corners does she recognize this cabin where she lives. There's a gun leaning against the wall under the new double-paned east window, its stock glowing like heartwood in the light. It's not Vira's musket from the dream, it's the caretaker's .22 caliber rifle, and that difference allows her slowly to peel apart the Velcro layers of night and day.

Stan Fischer came out to gather up the guns with the rest of Nick's belongings to be returned to the Colonnas, but she stopped him when she came to the last one, the eight-clip .22 he kept for coons and squirrels to keep them away from the sheep grain. She knows what else he did with them from the book *Woodland Cuisine* on his stovetop, with grease stains and bloody fingerprints on the recipes in the "Varmints" chapter and Peter Colonna's signature on the flyleaf. *Season with rosemary and oregano, then roast at 350 degrees in its own fat.*

Will took riflery years ago at his boys' camp and he was able to show her how to use the .22. They set up some paint cans in front of a fallen spruce behind the cabin and she practiced till she could shoot out the letters of TRUE VALUE one after the other. The perforated cans now lie on their sides like colanders, except for the one Will bracketed to the woodshed roof for a cold shower when the rain collector fills. She'd grown up hating all guns on principle, so she was surprised at the camera-like concentration and focus of aiming, and the shock of accomplishment as it penetrates the target. All those holes in a paint can make it a more interesting object; but if a living creature were in the gunsight she wouldn't be able to pull the trigger. Yet he must have done it in that other landscape, when he could hear, careful sighting of a human being labeled as the enemy, the lead ripping through cloth and flesh in its envelope of explosive sound. Then, in the plane, he was both weapon and target as he centered his own reflection in the sight.

This was the cabin she came to in the hailstorm, and she's repaired it in recognition of Nick's courage and discipline and the life he created here. If he should return as a hungry spirit he can spend the night. With Will's help she's worked for two months to winterize and equip it for year-round living, while on the south end, George Plummer's backhoes and bucket loaders cleared the debris from the crash site, broke up the tarmac helipad, and dismantled the wind turbine. The machines that built it never left the island. All this waste and wreckage was returned by sea and she witnessed each barge load from when it left the dock in the south cove till it was out of sight.

George says the work crew for this autumn deconstruction were not the ones who assembled it in the spring. She doesn't blame them. Who'd want to handle the scraps and shards of what you raised story by story less than a year ago, and who'd want to work on the same site where they'd lost a friend? The last thing they did was to cover the graded remains of the crash site with rolls of landscaping sod that already contained the seeds of some artificial grass. It will look like a golf course for a while, but eventually the real ground cover will return, the ferns and bunchberry and coniferous seedlings of a time when the future has finally buried what took place. The guys wave but she doesn't talk to them. She watches, and though she vowed she wouldn't, she takes pictures—not of the wreckage and defoliation but of the young men, and a couple of women, who are correcting history where a mistake was made.

Will's been living with the whole household on Chestnut Street while Chad recovers, Saabing up to Amber every weekend to work on the cabin. They scavenged the cleanup operation for plywood and insulation and all-season double-glazed windows from the bunkhouse, along with two solar panels and an airtight Jøtul woodstove that will last all night. George lent them a gifted carpenter, Tom, to install and seal everything against what is to come. They fashioned a rain collector to store the runoff from the panels and plumbed a hand pump and filter for a water source. From the twins' kitchen they brought two stainless-steel cauldrons to melt snow and ice, bread pans for the wood oven, and a red whistling teapot, its handle a rooster comb.

There's no way to set up a darkroom, so she's reverted to digital and uses her D70 instead of the beloved F3. She'd left color for black and white after her father died, when it felt like the cones of her retina had been numbed. Somehow this second death has restored them. Olive-brown of the milkweed and blatant gold shanks of the migrating yellowlegs, pileated's firecrest hammering above the sheepfold, cold blue hearts of the small breakfast quahogs that slip raw and salty down her throat.

After Tom fitted the skylight in the south roof over the unwindowed wall, he rigged a solar panel on either side of it to charge her Nokia along with her camera and laptop so she can see her work. Will says it's the cabin Thoreau would have if he lived now, no carbon footprint, but she's thinking of their father and his devotion to Leave No Trace. No trace will be left from the cycle of violation and deliverance performed on this island like an amphitheater under the stars.

She'd duct-taped together Nick's copy of *Walden* that he had cut up and posted like artwork around the walls. Her dad had loved and quoted this book that she could never quite make herself sit down and read. Nick's copy is fingerprinted with soot, text highlighted all over in different colors as well as circled in pencil, so it looks like it's been read by a whole school. One of the circled sections is about deafness. *Speech is for the convenience of those who are hard of hearing.* Maybe it takes the complete loss of language to truly open our eyes. In the silence of his being he might have seen things that led him to what he did.

She texted one sentence to Finland as they head toward their twenty-four-hour night. *The Laplander in her skin dress, and in a skin bag which she puts over her head and shoulders, will sleep night after night on the snow.* Vira's absence is like missing the flesh of her own body, no longer knowing where she ends and the world begins, as naked of covering as a shorn lamb. But Nick gave up his life for this island; there's no possible repayment but replacing it with her own.

Will brought her a small Poulan chain saw which she could easily start and handle, and they put up another cord of blowdowns in the woodshed. Like the rifle, the chain saw was new to her—her first thought was of Leatherface—but she's getting to know and trust it and every day she adds to the woodpile that will see her through the winter if she has the courage to stay. *I love to be alone,* Thoreau says, highlighted by Mr. Stan Fischer and circled also by Nick's pencil point. He got through a hard winter with the wind blowing through floor cracks and unglazed windows, so with all these upgrades she should at least make it to New Year's. For now she'll stand with her chain saw and .22 over the contractors till they remove all traces of the resort.

It's a crisp northerly day whose unmisted sky blows in the direction of autumn and the future, the first fall in her memory that she's not going back to school. She steps out the new door with its beveled glass window, appropriated from the cookhouse, and heads for the sheepfold with a pail of organic feed. The blue heron, which used to startle and fly off when she first appeared, now barely looks up from its tide pool. The day before, when she came out after breakfast, it was standing tall on her overturned kayak. It's getting used to her presence, and she wonders if it perched on Nick's boat too, and if it can tell that there's been a change of residents, or if we appear the same, as all herons do to the human eye.

Then suddenly it startles and flaps off in a disorder of blue wings, and here comes Hallett Bunker in the *Alice B.* with her brother Will ready to drop anchor from the bow. Will has a new job at Macalester College in Minnesota and she knows he's coming to say good-bye. The two men cross the cove in Hallett's orange inflatable and beach up on the grassy spot where Nick kept his dory. In the strong sun Will has taken off his ever-present Red Sox cap and she realizes how sparse his hair is getting, like a November wheat field, and how he's gained weight from living on Chestnut Street. His movements have slowed since the days when he'd lead her leaping from boulder to boulder on their arrowhead hunts. Once Will was her superhero but now he's a human being and his body measures time like all living and perishing things.

Behind her the sheep bleat softly and hoof off into the woods at the approach of strangers. They're bringing bags of staples for the new caretaker and three forty-pound sacks of organic feed.

"I saw the wind turbine on its way out yesterday," Hallett says.

"That was the last load," Julia says. "It's gone. The whole island feels different."

"The sea breeze has stopped. Now it's blowing from the north woods and the mountains. Coming across today it felt like November. Think you can make it through the year out here? It's a long journey from now to summer."

"It's not impossible. He already showed the way."

"There'll be times you won't want to paddle that kayak across the channel. I'm on the water year-round and I pass this cove two or three times a day. You know my number. I can bring what you need, or drop you in town for a little R-and-R."

"Thanks, Hallett. You've been taking me out to Amber since I can remember. I wouldn't get on a boat with anyone else."

Hallett puts his arm around Will's shoulder. "You're going to have to survive without this guy. I hear he's going out west."

"My car's packed, leaving this afternoon. Classes start Monday morning."

"And did I hear you were working on another book out here, about the island?"

"Yeah, I was supposed to be writing a history. But Nick wrote it instead."

"That's the thing about history," Hallett says. "Ain't any end to it." His phone beeps. "Seems like I got another party from another island. Will, you catching this trip or you going to stay? I can get back to Amber after lunchtime, if you want."

"I have to drive a thousand miles this weekend. I'd better start."

Hallett steps over a couple of rocks to the inflatable and returns with a large cardboard box. "Julia, I almost forgot. This is from Martha Colonna. No idea what's inside."

It's a strawberry pie with an inch-thick layer of whipped cream and a folded card.

> *More where this came from. Please visit. Our home is yours.*
>
> *With all our love and support,*
> *Martha & Peter*

"She wants to see you," Hallett says. "When you're ready, I'll take you in."

Will says, "Jules, looks like we're deserting you. You have your rifle, you have your chain saw, your strawberry pie. You going to be okay?"

She looks over at the three bags of sheep feed they've left beside the cabin door.

"I'm in good company. And I have a lot to do before I go into hibernation. Don't worry."

Eyes closed, she wraps her arms around her brother for a final bear hug, imagining Will and Marston and perhaps another, as a single form. She rests the pie on her kayak hull and helps them ease the inflatable into the shallows, then they're aboard the *Alice B*. The big diesel kicks in as they accelerate past the western ledges and out of sight.

She sits at the small work table where Nick first showed her the fishhook and the barbed spear point. She has one more errand that must be done now that she's finally alone. Her fingers trace the contours of the small Keepsake urn that's been in the side pocket of her backpack since they left Bar Harbor. It carries the small physical presence of her father. She once thought she'd pack it around the globe forever, because it could not have found peace on Amber during the takeover. Now she's been given a way to release it, and a place.

She puts on the old camo shirt Nick left draped over his straight-back chair, then her backpack with the urn and a slate-colored stone knife they found under the cabin floor. She stops to empty a few scoops of fresh sheep feed in the trough, though they're nowhere in sight, then cuts across the open meadow to the old overgrown streambed that runs diagonally across the island like a scar. It never flows more than a rust-colored trickle but its depth speaks of some serious flooding or scouring in another time.

The thick grass of this field comes from Amber's agricultural days and probably maintained the feral sheep while they waited for the care-taker to show up. The wild asters growing everywhere appear like a living calendar on its September page. She bushwhacks directly through the underbrush toward the Archaic site, passing beneath the eagle nest where she remembers her dad guiding her gaze upward to their immense mass of tangled sticks. The eagles left during the spring construction and won't be back this year but she hopes in the spring they'll notice the gaping absence and reclaim their home. Already she hears the deep drumming that says the pileated woodpeckers have returned.

The Red Paint embankment is even more overgrown than when she came here with Vira in the night. She gets down on all fours to part the dense foliage of ferns and seedlings and finds Nick's stone, oval and sea-blue in the leafy light. She unseals the urn and sifts its contents into her open palm. The tiny bone fragments have the mass and weight of a child's finger, yet his hands could once play the Wald-stein sonata as well as create the DNA of a skyscraper. The gray dusty ashes feel as dry as a desert that has forgotten the taste of water. He made his choice to become smoke and just diffuse into the molecules of the air, but he loved one place in particular and he also belongs here in the solid earth.

Keeping the slate knife at eye level, she gently digs through the fern cover into the gravel bank. She doesn't want to damage the carefully sharpened point, but it seemed to be there deliberately for her to use. She works the blade in as far as she can; then, clutching the ashes in her hand, she reaches in to arm's length and lets them go. They'll mix with the soil of the island and with those that have lived and worked here from the start of time.

She'll never know how he found his way to this site. Her family and all their friends searched for artifacts on Amber for thirty years, let alone the stonecutters and farmers that came before. Maybe some heightening of senses after his hearing loss drew him through the foliage of the island to its archaic heart, where the Red Paints welcomed him to their buried village like a descendant. They sat here huddled around the tiny screen of his Blackberry with four thumbs stumbling into each other on the keys. At one time he wanted more than she could give him, but in the end she was able to bring him here.

She slides the slate knife into the opening and carefully repacks it with sand and soil without disturbing the surrounding ferns. In time the sea level will rise over the whole island and its complete silence will be his own.

ACKNOWLEDGMENTS

I am eternally grateful to those who helped oversee this book from start to finish. First always, my better half and life companion Donna Gold, who besides the sustenance of life provided a writer's insight and an editor's expertise; my colleague Blake Cass, MPhil graduate and now faculty member in the College of the Atlantic Writing Program; Staff Sergeant Thomas Winter, who added the viewpoint of an active service member; Christian Barter of the Acadia National Park trail crew who contributed a stoneworker's wisdom and a poet's eye; Dean Lunt of Islandport Press for believing in this book in the first place; my editor Genevieve Morgan, who recognized the book within a book and oversaw the labor of bringing it to light; my indefatigable agent Alison Bond; Emeric Spooner, for his eloquent representations of the Red Paint Culture; my former student Charles Bishop, who established the template for this narrative, and ultimately, the late Colonel Peter H. Liotta, USAF, pilot and poet, whose spirit was in the composition of every page.

ABOUT THE AUTHOR

William Carpenter grew up in Waterville, Maine, graduated from Dartmouth and got a PhD at the University of Minnesota, taught at the University of Chicago, then returned to Maine to help found the College of the Atlantic, where he was on the faculty for 48 years. His poems have been widely published and translated in the US and Europe, and have been set to music in performances at Carnegie Hall and the Boston Opera Company. He received the Pablo Neruda award, the Black Warrior award, the AWP award in poetry for The Hours of Morning and the Samuel French Morse award for Rain. He has been artist in residence at Haystack, the Maine Summer Arts Program, The Stonecoast Writers' Conference, and the Frost Place. He has had residencies at McDowell and Yaddo and an NEA fellowship in Venice. His previous novels are *A Keeper of Sheep*, set on Cape Cod in the 1980s, and *The Wooden Nickel*, set in a Maine Coast lobstering community, of which *The New York Times* said, "Melville would have approved." He and the writer Donna Gold live in an old coastal inn and spend summers exploring Maine islands in their family sloop, *Northern Light*.

PHOTO BY DAVE DOSTIE.